DYING WISH

Murder. Kidnap. Torture. Not words usually associated with Britain's beautiful New Forest National Park. But when local author Grant Mason has a heart attack, he makes a bizarre dying wish — for his loyal assistant Hilary to burn his house down. That request sets off a chain of events which leads to a massive police hunt for a missing couple and a deranged killer. DCI Jeff Temple and his Major Investigations Team must take on their toughest case yet — and in the process, uncover vicious depravities and horrors that were meant to lie buried forever . . .

JAMES RAVEN

DYING WISH

Complete and Unabridged

ULVERSCROFT
Leicester

First published in Great Britain in 2015 by
Robert Hale Limited
London

First Large Print Edition
published 2016
by arrangement with
Robert Hale Limited
London

A catalogue record for this book is available
from the British Library.

ISBN 978–1–4448–2870–2

Published by
F. A. Thorpe (Publishing)
Anstey, Leicestershire

Set by Words & Graphics Ltd.
Anstey, Leicestershire
Printed and bound in Great Britain by
T. J. International Ltd., Padstow, Cornwall

This book is printed on acid-free paper

This one is for Betty and Kenny,
with love

Preface

The New Forest National Park spreads across over 200 square miles of southern England. It was created in 1079 as a hunting ground for King William I. Now, it's one of the country's most popular areas for day-trippers, campers, hikers and cyclists.

The forest is a patchwork of open heath and dense woodland. The ubiquitous New Forest ponies are a major attraction. Hundreds of them roam freely alongside the various breeds of wild deer.

This is a dramatic landscape steeped in ancient history, where grim legends abound and sinister secrets lie buried.

Occasionally, those secrets are uncovered, and when that happens it leads to a new, and sometimes dark, chapter in the life of the forest.

1

The warning signs were there, but he failed to recognize them as such: the shortness of breath, the ache in his left arm, the slight pressure on his chest. They were subtle sensations that barely registered because too much was happening.

As the man of the moment, he was pumped up with self-importance and relishing all the attention. So it was easy to ignore a little discomfort, especially as two glasses of red wine had dulled his senses.

Usually his book signings attracted between fifteen and twenty of the same old faces. But this time, no less than forty people had come along to the store in Southampton for the launch of his latest work: *A Hiker's Guide to the New Forest*.

For a low-ranking author like himself, it was an excellent turnout. Only the big names attracted the big numbers. He would never be in that league, not by writing non-fiction books that appealed only to a small, niche audience.

But that didn't bother him. Five books over as many years about his beloved New Forest had provided him with a modest living, and given him the opportunity to indulge his passions for walking, taking photographs and, of course, those things he dared not talk about.

The name Grant Mason had become synonymous with the New Forest even though he hadn't been born there. He was a noted expert on the landscape and its legends. He was familiar with the people, the wildlife, the flora and fauna, the rich tapestry of life that made it such a special place.

His first two books had been walking guides, complete with maps and detailed descriptions of no less than thirty forest treks. The third book had been filled with coloured photographs that captured the majesty of the forest during the four seasons. The fourth book had been a history of the forest from the time of the Norman Conquest to the present day. And this latest work contained a bunch of new hiking trails, along with pages of useful information on the areas they passed through.

It looked set to be his most successful book so far, thanks largely to an article about him that had appeared in a Sunday supplement magazine. It had attracted a lot of attention in the run-up to the book's publication two weeks ago. No doubt that was why so many people had turned up to see him, despite the fact that it was a wet and miserable Wednesday evening in February.

'Are you all right, Grant? You look very pale suddenly.'

Hilary Dyer, his long-serving personal assistant, spoke as she stepped up to him. He'd only just got to his feet to stretch his legs between signing books. 'What's the matter?' she said. 'Has the wine gone to your head?'

He looked at her and felt a prickle of unease when he realized that her face was out of focus.

'I'm not sure,' he said. 'I was OK a moment ago.'

He blinked a couple of times until his vision cleared and he could make out her features. The thin lips and flared nostrils, the eyes that were set slightly too far apart, the heavy make-up that camouflaged the damage that fifty years on the planet had done to her skin.

'I think perhaps you should sit down again,' she told him.

But a wave of heat suddenly rose up his neck and he felt positively dizzy. He closed his eyes, hoping the sensation would pass.

'I'll fetch a chair,' Hilary said, a tremor of urgency in her voice. 'Lean against the table if you feel faint.'

His pulse quickened, and the rhythm of his

heart seemed to change.

He turned towards the table, which was piled high with his books, but at the same time he felt a knifing pain deep in his chest. It sent a spike of adrenaline rushing through the rest of his body.

'Oh God,' he gasped as he fell against the table, knocking the books over.

He heard Hilary cry out as the world tilted on its axis around him. He wasn't even aware he was falling until he hit the floor.

He didn't pass out, though. Instead, he lay on his back staring up at the high ceiling as figures closed in around him, their voices loud and anxious.

'I think he's having a heart attack,' someone shouted and he wasn't sure if it was Hilary.

Heart attack! Christ, no. Not now, not here.

The pain was spreading quickly from his chest along his arms and his mouth filled with bitter-tasting saliva.

As commotion raged around him, he realized that he was struggling to breathe, and he experienced a rush of despair and terror. There was nothing he could do but lie there and endure the pain. He bit down on his bottom lip, praying that he would not lose consciousness. If he did, he knew that there was only a slim chance that one of the onlookers would know how to administer CPR. And if someone did attempt it they would most likely do more harm than good.

'An ambulance is on its way, Grant,' Hilary said. 'Please try to stay awake.'

Her words offered no comfort. What was happening to him was obviously serious and he feared there was a very good chance he was going to die. He had never felt this bad in his entire life. Dread swelled up inside him like a huge, inflated balloon.

He'd always assumed that he had a healthy heart. No one had ever told him otherwise, not even the doctor who had prescribed him statins some years ago to control his high cholesterol. But then weren't most heart attacks sudden and unexpected? And hadn't he read somewhere that heart disease was the biggest cause of death on the planet?

Tears filled his eyes against the throbbing pain in his chest. He could feel his sweat glands open up and it was becoming even more difficult to breathe.

'I can hear the siren, Grant,' Hilary was saying. 'The paramedics are on their way. Just stay calm and hold on in there.'

He would miss Hilary. For five years she'd been his loyal assistant and one of few people he had allowed to get close to him. Not so close that she was privy to his dark secrets, of course, but close enough to qualify as a friend as well as an employee.

He wondered fleetingly if she would miss him — and not just because his death would deprive her of a cosy part-time job. He'd paid her a generous wage and had always shown her respect. And when her husband died of pancreatic cancer a year ago, he had even met the cost of the funeral. So would she say nice things about him when he was gone?

'The paramedics are here,' she told him after a few more seconds, or minutes, had elapsed. 'You'll be at the hospital in no time.'

But he wasn't convinced he'd make it. His throat was tight and he was struggling to get air into his lungs. The pain continued unabated, pulsing like fire through his body.

He was struck by the sudden thought that very few people would mourn his passing. He had never married nor had any children. His parents were both dead, and there were no siblings. But although his life had been a lonely one he'd been relatively content. He had his writing, his readers, his small circle of friends and his beautiful house in the forest.

He also had his reputation, which was suddenly very important to him. He did not want to be remembered as anything other than a decent, upstanding member of the community; a writer of note who had been appreciated over the years by thousands of people.

But if he died here and now, that reputation would be shattered when the world discovered the truth, as surely it would. Maybe not straightaway, but eventually. If only he had taken precautions, prepared for the worst. Instead, like most people, he had adopted the default position of believing he would live to a ripe old age.

What a bone-headed fool he'd been.

A man's face entered his field of vision suddenly. Square-jawed and black, his breath flavoured strongly with mint.

'Mr Mason. I'm a paramedic. Can you explain to me what's wrong?'

He scrunched up his eyes and managed to say through gritted teeth that he had a crushing pain in his chest.

As he spoke the man reached over to loosen his tie and unbutton his shirt collar. Then he placed an oxygen mask over his nose and mouth to help him breathe.

'I think you're having a heart attack, Mr Mason,' the paramedic said. 'But you're still conscious and that's a good sign. I'm going to give you an injection and then we'll get you to the hospital.'

He was in such a state of anxiety that he didn't even feel the needle go in. Seconds later, he was being lifted onto a stretcher. The relentless pain continued to contort his features, and tears began to gather in his eyes.

He felt himself being carried out of the book store. The ceiling quickly gave way to a dark sky from which a light rain fell on his face. He heard the hum of traffic and the clatter of pedestrians. And the air was thick with the stench of petrol fumes.

By the time they got him into the back of the ambulance, he was in even more pain and his head was spinning.

He heard the doors being pulled shut and then Hilary's voice close to his ear.

'I'm here with you, Grant. Try to stay calm. You're in good hands now.'

He realized she was holding his hand and sitting beside him while the paramedic fiddled with the equipment. He moved his head to look at her and saw the terror carved into her features.

He raised his free hand and gestured for her to move closer. Then with some difficulty, he pulled the oxygen mask down from his face and forced words out through gritted teeth.

'There's a chance I won't make it, Hilary,' he said. 'If I don't, th-then there's something you have to do for me.'

She leaned forwards so that her nose was

only about twelve inches from his own.

'Don't say that, Grant. You're not going to die. You'll be all right.'

He swallowed hard and focused his entire being on making himself understood.

'You c-can't be sure,' he said, his voice strained and barely audible. 'So promise me you'll do it.'

She glanced briefly at the paramedic, who was busy attaching leads to a monitor. When she turned back to Mason, her features were taut and he could see that she was struggling to hold in her emotions.

'Please, Hilary,' he said, his eyes pleading. 'Promise me.'

She heaved an anxious sigh and turned down the corners of her mouth. 'OK, I promise. What do you want me to do?'

He gripped her coat collar and pulled her so close there was barely a breath between them. This time, phlegm rattled in his throat as the words spluttered out.

'You have to b-burn down my house, Hilary — along with everything in it.'

She sat bolt upright and stared at him, mortified. Her face lost several shades of colour in an instant.

'That's absurd,' she said, keeping her voice low. 'Why would you ask me to do such a thing?'

He swallowed again to clear his throat. 'You don't need to know that. But . . . trust me that it has to be done.'

She narrowed her eyes at him. 'You're confused and in shock, Grant. You don't know what you're saying.'

'Just go to the house before anyone else does,' he said, the words now more breathed than spoken. 'No . . . no one has to know it was you.'

She shook her head. 'Stop it, Grant. You're not making any sense. And you shouldn't be talking of dying.'

'But . . . '

'No buts, Grant. Just try to relax and concentrate on your breathing.'

He held her stricken gaze for several long seconds and saw the blood retreat completely from her face. He didn't have the strength to argue with her and in any case, it was clear that if he died she wasn't going to do what he'd asked.

It made him all the more determined to fight to stay alive.

He squeezed his eyes shut and tried to ignore the pain and the rising panic inside him. With any luck he'd remain conscious until he was in the care of the trauma team. Hopefully they'd be able to pull him back from the brink.

Hilary slipped the oxygen mask back over his face and uttered something that he didn't catch. Then she took his hand again and held onto it all the way to the hospital.

2

Jeff Temple felt his eyes moisten as he stared down at the granite headstone. Reading the inscription never failed to charge him with emotion.

In memory of Erin Temple
Loving wife and devoted mother
She was taken from us far too soon

It was almost six years since she'd lost her fight against cancer and he still felt the pain, even though he had at last moved on with his life. Not a day passed when he didn't think about her and she still came to him frequently in his dreams.

He no longer visited the cemetery as often as he did during those first two years. Now it was only on special occasions such as Christmases, anniversaries and birthdays.

Today she would have been forty-six and no doubt they would have gone out to celebrate. Erin had always made a big thing of birthdays during their fifteen years together. When their only daughter Tanya became a teenager, Erin organized a surprise party at a local restaurant. And when he himself hit thirty she booked a weekend away in Paris. The memories were still vivid in his mind, especially when he came here and stood beside her grave.

He could barely believe that so much time had passed and so many things had happened. Their daughter was now in her twenties and living in London, and he'd been promoted to Detective Chief Inspector with Hampshire's Major Investigations Team.

There was also a new woman in his life, a woman who had helped him rediscover a degree of contentment. Her name was Angelica Metcalfe — Angel for short — and she was twelve years his junior. A month ago, eight months after their relationship began, she finally vacated her rented flat and moved in with him.

He'd come to the cemetery on that day too because he'd been plagued by guilt and had felt the need to explain himself. Talking to his dead wife had failed to assuage the guilt altogether, but it had to some extent been cathartic. He wanted so much to believe that Erin would be happy for him and that she wouldn't want him to wallow in grief and self-pity for the rest of his life.

He blinked back tears and shifted his gaze away from the headstone and the flowers he'd placed in front of it.

The cemetery was quiet at this time in the morning but the drone of rush hour traffic broke the sombre silence. The day was overcast with clouds that were fluffy and benign. It had been a wet start to the New Year, and the forecasters were predicting more rain and maybe even some snow.

He couldn't remember the last time it had snowed in Southampton. Last winter had been a cold one, but this winter the temperatures had rarely dropped below freezing.

He glanced at his watch and saw that it was ten past nine. He'd been here for three quarters of an hour already and yet it didn't feel like it.

'I have to go, sweetheart,' he said, as he reached out to touch the top of the headstone. 'Wherever you are I hope you have a great birthday.'

He pulled up the collar of his overcoat and shoved his hands into the pockets. A cold weight settled in his stomach as he headed back to his car. He walked past the little chapel where Erin's service had been held and then, through the cemetery's arched entrance, he could see across the road to the city's general hospital where she'd died. It was always an ordeal to come here and be reminded of that painful period in his life.

His eyes felt like they were burning at the edges as he approached his car, a battered 8-year-old Mazda. As soon as he was inside, he drew a tremulous breath and blinked rapidly as tears streamed down his cheeks.

As always, he was unable to contain his anguish. So he just sat behind the wheel until the wave of emotion had swept through him. Then he dabbed at his eyes with a tissue and checked himself in the mirror.

His fleshy, nondescript face was grey and pallid and he looked all of his forty-eight years. Red veins laced the whites of his eyes and perspiration had gathered around his receding hairline.

He took a few more deep breaths to compose himself and then switched on the ignition. But just as he was about to pull away from the kerb his mobile buzzed. He fished it from his pocket and noted the caller ID before thumbing the green key. It was Detective Constable Marsh, the youngest member of his team.

'Hello, Fiona,' he said. 'I'm on my way in. Ten minutes at the most.'

'That's not why I'm calling, guv,' she said. 'We got your message about being late so we've put off the morning briefing until ten.'

'What is it then?'

'It's about that missing couple, guv. There's

17

been a development.'

'What kind of development?'

'Their car has been found in Paget Street, down near the football stadium. Dave's already there with a forensic team.'

'Do we know who spotted it?'

'A guy who lives in the street apparently. He saw the appeal we put out on television yesterday, and realized the description of the car matched that of a car parked in front of his block of flats.'

'OK, I'd better swing by there and take a look. Delay the briefing until I get in. This will probably have to go to the top of the agenda.'

He ended the call and sat there for a couple of minutes while he got his mind in gear. It was time to stop thinking about the past and focus on the present.

Or more specifically, on the case of a missing couple that was giving him increasing cause for concern.

3

Bob and Rosemary Hamilton had disappeared five days ago and from the start, it hadn't appeared to be a run-of-the-mill missing persons case, which was why Temple and his team had become involved.

The couple were in their late twenties and lived in the centre of Southampton. They'd been married for five years and had a two-year-old son named Peter.

On Saturday they'd left the boy in the care of Mr Hamilton's mother, and had set off on a short journey along the south coast to the market town of Christchurch. Their destination had been a four star hotel where they'd been due to attend a dinner-dance with two of their closest friends. They'd booked a room at the hotel for the night and weren't planning to return home until the following afternoon.

But they didn't arrive at the hotel, and nobody had heard from them since they left home.

According to family and friends, they were a happily married couple who doted on their son. They had no financial worries and Mr

Hamilton had a well-paid job as an executive with a public relations company. There was no reason to believe that they had chosen to run off somewhere by themselves.

They both had mobile phones, but these had been switched off so there was no way to contact them. Their car had been picked up on traffic cameras as they drove out of the city at about eleven on Saturday morning. The couple had decided to take the scenic route to Christchurch through the New Forest. This had become evident when they were spotted on a traffic camera entering the main forest town of Lyndhurst.

But there were no more sightings after that. With so few traffic cameras in and around the forest that in itself wasn't really surprising.

Temple had spent much of yesterday looking into the case after being alerted by the uniform division. He and DC Marsh had interviewed Mr Hamilton's mother, who was extremely distraught and absolutely convinced that her son and daughter-in-law had not done a runner. Her grandson had sat on her lap the whole time and the boy was clearly well-nourished and content. Temple couldn't believe his parents would simply abandon him.

It was pretty rare for married couples to disappear and leave their child or children behind. When it did happen there was almost always a blatantly obvious reason for it. But that didn't seem to be the case with Bob and Rosemary Hamilton, so alarm bells were understandably ringing.

After visiting Mr Hamilton's mother, Temple and DC Marsh had gone on to the man's office. His work colleagues had described him as an upbeat guy who enjoyed his job and adored his family. He'd told them on Friday that he was looking forward to their night out in Christchurch with friends they hadn't seen in some time.

Another detective had interviewed the two friends who lived on the other side of Christchurch, and they weren't able to shed any light on what might have happened to Bob and Rosemary.

With the discovery of their car in Southampton, the mystery deepened. Temple wondered if the couple had driven back into the city instead of going to the hotel. And if so, why had they left the vehicle in Paget Street and where were they now?

As Temple drove across town, a number of wretched scenarios unfolded in his mind and the questions continued to mount.

Was there more to Bob and Rosemary Hamilton than he'd been led to believe? Had they been forced to flee because they'd done something unlawful? Were they on some drugs or drinks binge and holed up in a flat close to where they'd abandoned the car? Or had something seriously bad happened to them?

The circumstances surrounding their disappearance were indeed unusual, and it was beginning to make Temple feel distinctly uneasy.

4

There were two patrol cars in Paget Street along with a Scientific Services Department van.

A couple of white-suited forensic technicians were already examining the bright red Honda Civic belonging to the Hamiltons.

The street was a stone's throw from Southampton Football Club's ultra-modern stadium. It contained a mixture of flats and small industrial units. The Honda was parked at the roadside in front of a small, grey apartment block.

Temple spotted Detective Sergeant Vaughan standing next to it on the pavement. He was smoking a cigarette while talking to one of the uniformed officers.

Temple brought the Mazda to a stop behind the forensic van. Killed the engine and climbed out. The street was close to the Itchen River that flows inland from the Solent, so the air was damp and salty. Gulls wheeled above them, riding the wind.

Vaughan gave a wave and blew smoke in a long plume towards the sky as Temple approached him.

'Marsh called me,' Temple said. 'I thought I'd better take a look.'

DS Vaughan was forty and painfully thin, with hollow cheeks and dark pouches beneath his eyes. He wore black-rimmed glasses that seemed too big for his head and his shoulder-length hair always looked a mess. He used to take pride in his appearance and weighed in at a healthy twelve and a half stone. But that was before his wife left him for another man. Since then, he'd let himself go and sometimes it looked to Temple as though the man was fading away before their very eyes.

'The call came in early this morning from a Mr Albert Teale who lives in the block over there,' Vaughan said. 'He says the car has been parked here since Saturday, but he didn't think anything of it until we put out a description on the news.'

'Did he see who left it?'

'Negative. He went out about nine on Saturday evening and the car wasn't here then. But he noticed it when he came home around midnight.'

'Is he sure about that?'

'He's positive. He reckons it was the only car parked at the kerb.' Vaughan pointed to the block of flats. 'That's his place on the second floor. And the entrance to the block is

24

just below it, He walked past the car to go inside.'

'What about his neighbours? Did anyone else see anything?'

'Not sure. I've called for help so we can go door to door, but I'm guessing most people will be at work by now.'

Temple made a thoughtful noise in his throat and looked up and down the street.

'Any CCTV cameras around here?' he asked.

Vaughan shook his head and tossed the butt of a cigarette into the road with practiced nonchalance. 'Not in this street. I've asked Fiona to check out cameras on approach roads and see what footage we can collect from Saturday night.'

'The couple might have parked here for a reason,' Temple said. 'It could be they're in one of the flats.'

'I've thought of that, boss, but my gut tells me it's unlikely. They only live a few minutes away by car. So why would they shack up in this part of town?'

Temple turned his attention to the Honda. A technician was sifting through the boot while another examined the interior.

'What have they found so far?'

Vaughan set his gaze on the car. 'There are two overnight cases in the back. It looks as though everything they packed for their hotel stay is still inside. No sign of their mobile phones, though.'

'What about keys?'

'Nope. The doors were locked so we had to break in.'

Temple stepped forwards, peered into the car.

'Any personal effects?' he said. 'Handbag or wallet?'

'Nothing like that,' Vaughan said. 'There are some CDs in the glove compartment along with a packet of sweets. But that's about it.'

Temple was disappointed. He straightened up, blew out his cheeks.

'The techies will give it a thorough going-over when they get it back to the compound,' Vaughan said. 'I've asked them to check for anything suspicious, including specks of blood, but on the face of it the car looks as clean as a whistle.'

Temple chewed on the inside of his cheek as he walked around the Honda and looked in the boot. It contained two small flight cases. One was open and the forensics technician was carefully poking around inside. Temple spotted some black lace underwear.

'Looks like they were planning a fun weekend,' the technician said. 'There's a vibrator and some KY Jelly in the side pocket.'

26

'So what could have made them turn around and come back into the city?' Temple said.

The technician shrugged. 'Maybe they had an argument that got out of hand.'

He'd considered that, of course. Something could have sparked a bust-up as they drove through the forest. Perhaps things had got so nasty between them that they'd decided it wasn't worth going to the hotel. It was certainly a possibility since even the most loving couples often take things to extremes when the red mist comes down.

Had Bob Hamilton harmed his wife and fled in a panic? From what Temple had learned about the man he found it hard to believe, but then after so long on the force nothing really surprised him anymore.

His mind flashed on an image of their little son on his grandmother's lap and he hoped to God that there was a far more innocent explanation for their disappearance. But for the life of him he couldn't think what it might be.

'I'd better get to the office,' he said to Vaughan. 'You coordinate things here and make sure every flat and industrial unit in the street is checked out.'

★　★　★

It took Temple ten minutes to reach Southampton's central police station opposite the city's bustling port. As he approached the eight-storey building, his mobile buzzed and the hands-free console displayed his home number.

'Aren't you supposed to be seeing the doctor?' he said.

'I just got back,' Angel replied.

'Is everything OK?'

'It's fine and the good news is I'm still on course to return to work in a couple of weeks.'

'That's great. I'll tell the team. They'll be ecstatic.'

Angel was desperate to get back to her job as a DI on the MIT. She'd already spent almost two months recuperating from injuries sustained when her car was involved in a motorway pile-up. She'd suffered fractured ribs, a punctured lung and concussion. The crash had been one of several caused by a madman who fired on rush-hour traffic with a sniper rifle. Angel had been driving on the motorway when he struck and was among the dozens of drivers and passengers who were badly hurt. But luckily she was not one of those killed during the murderous rampage that paralysed the country's motorway network for several days.

'Are you still at the cemetery, Jeff?' she asked.

'No. I'm on my way to the office. I had to make a detour.'

'Well, something has happened and that's why I'm calling. I thought you ought to know about it.'

'That sounds ominous.'

She left it a beat and he heard her draw a breath. 'It's about your friend, Grant Mason.'

'He's not a friend exactly,' Temple said. 'I've only met him a couple of times. What about him?'

'I'm afraid he's dead.'

Temple was genuinely shocked. 'What happened to him?'

'He was taken ill yesterday evening at a book signing in town. He had a heart attack apparently and died later in hospital.'

'Bloody hell.'

Temple thought back to the last time he'd seen Mason. It had been at a drinks party in a city centre pub three months ago. The party had been held to celebrate the fiftieth birthday of the author's personal assistant, Hilary Dyer. Temple had known Hilary for years because she'd been Erin's best friend. She'd introduced him to Mason shortly after she started working for the guy.

Temple had found Mason to be pleasant enough, although he'd always come across as uptight and painfully shy. Plus, he'd been one of those annoying people who avoided making eye contact during a conversation.

'I'd better call Hilary,' Temple said. 'I'm sure she'll be taking it hard.'

'Did Mr Mason have a wife?' Angel asked and Temple realized that she'd never met him.

'No, he was single. No family as far as I know.'

'They said on the radio that he was in his forties.'

'That's right. About my age, I think.'

'Then let it be a lesson to you, Detective. You need to do more to look after yourself.'

He smiled at that because he was losing the battle against middle-age spread. She'd been nagging him to drink less and exercise more. And he'd been promising her that he would. But it was easier said than done. Drinking in the evenings and at weekends helped him to wind down, and there was never enough time in the day for walking or jogging.

'I hear what you say,' he said. 'In fact I was planning to spend Saturday morning at the gym.'

'Is that the same gym you joined months ago and have yet to visit?'

He laughed. 'That's not fair. I've been busy looking after you and keeping the streets safe.'

'I don't need looking after anymore and even Robocop can find time to work up a sweat.'

'OK, point taken. I'll sort it.'

'Make sure you do. And try to get home early tonight. I thought I'd prepare something special for dinner.'

'Then I'll do my best,' he promised.

They said their goodbyes and Temple drove into the police station car park. On the way upstairs he thumbed through the contacts on his phone and called Hilary. But it went to voice-mail, so he left a message telling her he'd heard the news and was really sorry.

'If you want to have a chat, then don't hesitate to call me,' he said. 'In the meantime, my thoughts are with you.'

5

The morning briefing got under way soon after Temple walked into the open-plan office of the Major Investigations Team.

DC Marsh had already prepared the paperwork and she handed him a print-out of the agenda. There were five items to be discussed, including two on-going murder investigations, a serious rape and a village post office robbery that had happened five days ago. But the first item on the agenda was the discovery of the car in Paget Street.

Temple took his usual place at one end of the room between two mounted whiteboards. Photographs of Bob and Rosemary Hamilton were pinned to one of the boards and beneath them, someone had scribbled details about the couple in bold, black letters.

They were both aged twenty-eight and were saving to buy their own home. In the meantime they were renting a two-bedroom flat in the Northam area of Southampton. Neither had a criminal record and their joint bank account contained over £4,000. In short, they seemed a perfectly ordinary young couple.

'OK, let's get started,' Temple said, after removing his jacket. 'I want this to be a short session so we can crack on with things.'

There were eight detectives in the room, plus a couple of uniforms. They were all seated facing him except DC Marsh, who was standing to his right with her spiral-bound notebook out. She was wearing a self-imposed uniform of black trousers and white blouse. Her flaming red hair was tied back in a bun and as always, it looked as though she was impatient to get on with the business of the day.

Marsh was without question one of his best officers. Not only was she young, keen and sitting her sergeant exams, she was also erudite and articulate, which was more than could be said for some members of the team.

It was Marsh who started the ball rolling in her broad south London accent. She had news of a possible sighting.

'We've had a call from the landlady of a pub just outside Lyndhurst,' she said. 'She saw the photos on the news and she's convinced that Bob and Rosemary Hamilton stopped there for a drink and light lunch on Saturday.'

'Where exactly is the pub?' Temple asked.

Marsh consulted her notes. 'Just west of the town on one of the main roads to Christchurch. It's called the King's Tavern.'

'I know it,' Temple said. 'It's a popular

place set back from the road. So did she talk to them?'

'Apparently so, but she was in her car when she phoned here so she couldn't go into detail. I've arranged to go and see her straight after this meeting.'

'I'll go with you,' Temple said. 'It sounds like it could be a lead.'

He then went on to brief the team about the abandoned car in Paget Street.

'It's a real puzzler,' he said. 'We know they got at least halfway to Christchurch, but we don't know why they came back into town instead of driving to the hotel. Perhaps they had a row or maybe they're on some kind of bender. The problem is we're talking about a respectable young couple with a small child. Not a pair of degenerates who don't care about the consequences of their actions. That's why I'm more than a little concerned about their disappearance.'

DC Marsh said she'd contacted the traffic division and they were going to trawl through camera footage from Saturday evening in the hope of spotting the Honda. The city centre location meant there would be quite a few cameras on roads in the area.

'Have we checked cameras at the end of the A35 and on roads in and out of Christchurch?'

Marsh nodded. 'We have and there was no sign of their car so it's probably safe to assume they didn't even get to the town.'

Marsh also confirmed that none of the credit and debit cards belonging to the couple had been used since they vanished and their mobile phones had not been switched on.

'I spoke to Mr Hamilton's mother a few minutes ago,' another officer said. 'She knows of no reason why her son and daughter-in-law would park on or near Paget Street. She doesn't think they know anyone there.'

'How did she take the news of the car?' Temple asked.

'It's made her even more upset and confused. She broke down on the phone so I've asked uniform to send someone round to make sure she and the kid are OK.'

Temple empathized with the woman. Over the years he'd seen the awful impact a person's disappearance can have on their family and friends. He could imagine the pain he'd have to endure if his own daughter became a missing person. Not knowing what might be happening to her would be sheer torture and no doubt his mind would conjure up all manner of gruesome images.

'Are you still watching their flat?' he asked, and this elicited a response from a junior detective named Derek Whelan.

'We've had a man parked in front of their block all night,' he said. 'I'll be relieving him shortly. If they show up there we'll know it.'

'Did you go inside?'

Whelan nodded. 'Hamilton's mother gave us a key last night and we let ourselves in. The place has been left tidy and the wardrobes are full of clothes. There's nothing to suggest that they didn't intend to return.'

'OK, I think it's time we sent in a forensic team to examine the flat.'

Whelan then said that many of the neighbours in the block had been spoken to and two detectives were working through the couple's address books and phone contacts. But so far, no one had been able to shed light on the mystery of their disappearance.

Temple was satisfied that all the angles were being covered.

'Look, it's been almost ninety-six hours since they were last seen,' DC Marsh said. 'So maybe it's time we seriously considered the possibility that they've been harmed in some way. Who's to say they were actually in the car when it came back into the city? For all we know, they might be out there in the forest having been beaten up or killed.'

'If that becomes the most likely scenario then we'll have to mount a search of the forest,' Temple said. 'But it's far too early for that. There's no way I'd get it sanctioned, at least not until we've checked out all the traffic camera footage.'

'Searching the forest will be a pointless exercise anyway,' Whelan said. 'We're talking over 200 square miles and we won't even know where to start looking.'

Temple knew that Whelan was right. The New Forest was a vast expanse of open heath and woodland. There were rivers, lakes, ponds and bogs. Searching it presented a logistical nightmare.

'This case is going to attract an increasing amount of attention,' Temple said. 'So we need to give it priority. Ease back for now on the rest of the workload unless there are any major developments in those investigations. At best, the Hamiltons will turn up soon, wondering what all the fuss is about. At worst we'll find that something unpleasant has happened to them. So as of this moment we're ramping things up a gear.'

Temple went on to assign tasks, one of which was to check back through missing person files to see if there had been any similar cases in the area.

They then hurriedly worked through the rest of the agenda. There were no significant updates, which was just as well.

After winding up the meeting, Temple told

Marsh to organize a pool car for their trip into the forest. He then went to his tiny office overlooking the docks to check his emails. Nothing had come in that required his immediate attention, except for a message from his boss asking him to pop up when he had a moment.

Chief Superintendent Mike Beresford was a burly Welshman with broad shoulders and a misshapen nose. His hair was short and silver, and the lines in his face were cut deep. His large, carpeted office smelled of wax polish and dried flowers.

'I heard about the car that's turned up in Paget Street,' he said. 'I don't like the sound of it, Jeff.'

Temple filled him in on what was happening and pointed out that the couple's disappearance was now the team's main focus of attention.

'I think we ought to schedule a press conference for this afternoon,' Beresford said. 'Are you up for that?'

Temple nodded. 'Of course. We need to generate as much publicity as possible.'

'I agree. I'll get the media people working on it. Meanwhile, keep me in the loop. I've got a bad feeling about this case so I want to stay on top of it.'

Temple returned to his office to get his

jacket and overcoat. Marsh had left a message that she was downstairs waiting in a pool car.

He was on his way down to meet her when his mobile went off, and he answered it without first checking the caller ID.

'Hello.'

'Hi, Jeff. It's Hilary. I got your message.'

He carried on descending the stairs as he spoke to her.

'I'm really sorry about Grant,' he said. 'I can imagine what a shock it must have been for you.'

'It was terrible, Jeff. I still can't believe he's dead. It was so sudden.' Her voice was so thin he could barely hear it.

'Were you with him when it happened?'

'I was. We were at a book signing in West Quay. He just suddenly came over really bad and then collapsed with a heart attack. An ambulance came and he stayed conscious until we got to the hospital. But then shortly after we arrived, he had another attack and they couldn't save him.'

'Jesus, that's awful.'

'It was so unexpected. One minute he was fine and enjoying all the attention, and the next he was as white as ivory and struggling to breathe.'

'What about you, Hilary? Are you OK?'

'I suppose so. I just got back from his

house, which felt strange. I had to pick up some paperwork. I'm afraid it falls on me to organize the funeral and such.'

'So is there anything I can do to help?'

After a long, stilted pause, she said, 'You can meet me today, Jeff. I know you're always very busy, but there's something I need to tell you.'

She spoke in a voice that sounded strangely conspiratorial and he felt his brow furrow.

'Oh? What is it?'

'I'd rather not talk about it over the phone. It has to do with what Grant told me in the ambulance just before he died. I can't get it out of my mind and I'm really concerned about it.'

'It sounds serious.'

'To be honest, I'm not really sure. But it is weird, and I think I should tell someone.'

'So why me, Hilary? Isn't there someone else you can speak to?'

'You're a policeman, Jeff,' she said, with heavy emphasis on the word *policeman*. 'You'll know what to do about it. Or at least I think you will.'

The tension in her voice was almost palpable and it immediately aroused his curiosity. He knew Hilary to be a sensible, level-headed person, not given to exaggeration or overreaction.

'I can meet up with you later today,' he said. 'Will you be at home?'

'Probably, but call me first to be on the safe side.'

'I'll do that and in the meantime, try to relax. You've had a terrible shock.'

'I will, Jeff,' she said. 'And thanks for agreeing to see me. I really need to get this thing off my chest.'

6

The New Forest National Park lies just a few miles west of Southampton. It had always been one of Temple's favourite places. He and Erin had spent countless weekends walking across the heaths and exploring the quaint little villages and towns. There were only a few areas in the country that he felt were as beautiful and unspoilt.

As he and DC Marsh drove along the A35 towards Lyndhurst, his spirits were lifted by the sight of the lush landscape on either side of the road. One minute they were hemmed in by dark, dense woods and the next the scene opened up to reveal expanses of moorland where cattle and ponies grazed.

His thoughts inevitably turned to Grant Mason and he asked Marsh if she'd heard of him.

'I know he writes books about the forest because you've mentioned his name a couple of times in the office,' she said.

'That's right. Well, I heard this morning that he died of a heart attack yesterday at a book signing in town.'

Marsh, who was driving, turned to him and arched her brow.

'My God — that's so sad.'

Temple told her that the author's personal assistant was an old friend.

'I have four of his books on a shelf at home,' he said. 'Erin and I were keen hikers and before she died, we followed some of the trails in Mason's first walking guide.'

Temple explained that the trails were never too long or difficult, and they were always interesting. Mason wrote about the wildlife, the flowers, the trees and the colourful history of the forest. It was no wonder he'd become something of a local celebrity.

'I actually read something about him a couple of weeks ago,' Marsh said. 'There was an article in one of the Sunday magazines.'

'I read it too,' Temple said, and he recalled how the feature writer had penned a short, glowing review of *A Hiker's Guide to the New Forest*. He'd described Mason as a talented author who'd done a great deal to promote the area.

'So what was he like?' Marsh asked.

Temple thought about it. 'I didn't really get to know him. We met at a couple of social functions and our conversations rarely lasted longer than a few minutes. But I sensed he was a bit shy and standoffish. Or maybe he was just uncomfortable talking to a copper. We both know that a lot of people are.'

'Have you spoken to your friend Hilary?'

'She returned my call just before I left the office. In fact, she wants to talk to me about something Mason told her just before he died. It's got her rattled.'

'Why?'

'I don't know. She didn't want to tell me about it over the phone.'

'Did she give a reason?'

'No, she didn't. But she's obviously worried about it.'

Marsh pursed her lips. 'Perhaps he revealed some deep, dark secret from his past.'

Temple shrugged. 'I'll find out soon enough. I said I'd go and see her later today.'

'Well don't keep it to yourself once she's told you,' Marsh said. 'You know how I like a good mystery.'

★　★　★

The sky was a grey blanket over the forest as they followed the road that Bob and Rosemary Hamilton had driven along on Saturday.

They reached Lyndhurst after twenty minutes. The town was often referred to as the capital of the New Forest and as such, it was a popular tourist destination. But at this time of the year it was fairly quiet.

The King's Tavern was about a mile the other side of the town. Turning off the main road, they passed over a cattle grid and drove across a narrow stone bridge.

The pub was typical of those found in the forest — small, quaint and with plenty of character. Temple had stopped off here once with Erin during a hike some years ago. The memory flashed in his mind as they came to a stop in the gravel car park.

He was surprised how much he suddenly remembered of the visit. It had been a warm day so they'd sat in the garden out back, enjoying pints of cold lager and a plough-man's lunch. About six months later, Erin suddenly got sick and they found the cancer.

The pub's interior hadn't changed at all since then. It was like stepping back in time. The public bar had a low ceiling and a huge inglenook fireplace. Dark wood furniture and panelled walls made it homely, if slightly claustrophobic.

The landlady introduced herself as Leticia Keenan. She was in her fifties with an oval face, framed by shapeless brown hair that was liberally streaked with grey.

The place had only just opened and there were no customers. Mrs Keenan asked them if they wanted something to drink from the bar and Temple declined politely for both of them.

'Well, at least let me get you some tea or coffee,' she said.

'Thanks but we've both consumed enough caffeine already today,' Temple said. 'Would you mind if we just had a chat about Saturday?'

They sat at a window table with a view of the car park. Temple produced a photograph of Bob and Rosemary Hamilton and showed it to Mrs Keenan.

'On the phone, you told DC Marsh that the couple stopped here for lunch,' Temple said. 'Are you absolutely sure it was them?'

Mrs Keenan's eyes crinkled a bit at the edges as she examined the photo.

'It was definitely them,' she said. 'I remember clearly.'

'So what time did they arrive?'

She replied without hesitation. 'Just before noon. They came up to the bar and ordered two lemonades.'

'How did they seem?'

'Like they were enjoying themselves. They asked if we did sandwiches so I showed them the snack menu and they both opted for cheese and ham, plus a bowl of fries. After I took the order, I asked them if they were local and they said they lived in Southampton. They told me they were going to a hotel in Christchurch and seemed quite excited about it.'

'And it was just the two of them,' Marsh said. 'There was nobody with them?'

'They were alone. I'm certain of that because they were my only customers. It was just like it is now. In fact, they sat at this very table.'

'So what happened next?' Temple asked.

Mrs Keenan shrugged. 'Nothing much. I saw them chatting while I waited for my husband to make the sandwiches.'

'Do you know what they were chatting about?'

'They had a map of the forest with them and they were both looking at it. When I brought their lunch over, they asked me if I could direct them to the Knightwood Oak.'

'The what?' Marsh said.

'The Knightwood Oak is one of the oldest trees in the forest,' Temple said. 'It's been there for over 500 years.'

'It's a popular tourist attraction in the summer months,' Mrs Keenan explained. 'Mr Hamilton told me they wanted to take some pictures of the tree and some of the other forest landmarks while they were passing through.'

'And you told them how to get there?'

'Of course. It's actually only a mile or so from here and easy to find.'

'Did they actually have a camera with them?'

She gnawed at her lip as she cast her mind back, then nodded. 'After they finished their lunch and went outside, I saw them taking pictures of each other with the pub in the background.'

After asking a few more questions, Temple thanked the landlady and they left the pub. In the car park he called DS Vaughan on his mobile.

'I've got a question for you, Dave,' he said. 'Was there a camera in the Honda? It might have been in the luggage.'

'Negative, guv. I've been through it all myself. Why'd you ask?'

'Because we've discovered that the pair stopped in the forest on their way to Christchurch to take some photos.'

'Well, then, they must have the camera with them,' Vaughan said.

Temple ended the call and told Marsh to hand him the keys to the pool car.

'I'll drive,' he said. 'I know how to get to the old tree.'

They drove further along the A35 and turned right onto a minor road that brought them to a small parking area. From there, they had a short walk along a narrow path to the huge tree known as the Knightwood Oak. It was behind a low wooden fence that was there to help protect its roots. It towered above a clump of smaller trees and bushes. There was no one else around, which was hardly surprising given that it was a dull wintry day.

'We can't even be sure they came here,' Marsh pointed out.

Temple pressed his lips together, igniting deep lines around his mouth. 'For now let's assume they did. It won't hurt to have a quick look around.'

'It's certainly an impressive tree,' Marsh said. 'I can see why they would have wanted to take a photo of it.'

They strolled around the outside of the fence, taking in the scene. A light breeze stirred the bare branches of the trees and lifted some of the dead leaves off the ground.

'Mrs Keenan basically backed up what Hamilton's mother told us,' Temple said. 'Her son and his wife were in good spirits when they set out from home and they were looking forward to the evening ahead. So what could have made them change their minds and go back to Southampton?'

'It would help if we were able to track their

journey from this point,' Marsh said. 'But that's near impossible since there are no traffic cameras for miles.'

They paused for a few moments to admire the huge tree and Temple could see why his distant ancestors had regarded it as the monarch of the forest. It was a truly awesome sight.

They then headed back along the path to the car park, their eyes scouring the ground for any clue that would prove the couple had come here on Saturday. But there was nothing to be found, not even a scrap of discarded litter.

7

Temple decided to drop in on Hilary Dyer on the way back to the station. He gave her a quick call first to make sure she'd be in. She lived in the north east corner of the city so it only entailed a short detour.

He wanted to see her as soon as he could because he didn't like to think of her worrying about what Grant Mason had said. She had enough on her plate, coping with the grief and trauma of his death.

Temple had always liked Hilary and he could well understand why Erin had been so fond of her. She was kind, intelligent, quick-witted. Since her husband died, Temple had made a point of staying in touch and had occasionally met her for coffee in town.

She lived in a pre-war terraced house at one end of a street that had seen better days. It happened to be close to where DC Marsh lived.

'My flat's just around the corner,' Marsh said. 'But I'll be moving out next month, thank God.'

'Does that mean you'll be moving in with your boyfriend?'

She grinned. 'At long last. Did I tell you that he proposed to me and I accepted?'

'You did,' Temple said. 'In fact, that's all you've spoken about for weeks.'

He was pleased for Marsh because he reckoned it was time she settled down. She was thirty-four and her last long-term relationship had ended badly, leaving her with serious self-esteem issues and a total lack of self-confidence.

'What about you, guv?' she said. 'How are things going now that you and Angel are living together?'

'Couldn't be better,' he said. 'And I meant to tell you that she should be back at work in a few weeks.'

Her face lit up. 'That's terrific. I'll pop over and see her at the weekend if that's OK.'

'Of course it is. We haven't got anything planned.'

★ ★ ★

Hilary looked awful, Temple thought when she opened the door to them. Her eyes were red and puffy from crying, and she wasn't wearing make-up. There were broken veins around her cheeks and a nervous sweat sparkled above her top lip.

She had on a yellow cardigan and black

corduroy skirt, and her greying hair was gathered up and pinned.

Temple hugged her on the doorstep before introducing her to DC Marsh. She managed a smile, one that flickered on her face and was gone in a flash.

'We're on our way back to the station,' he said. 'So I'm afraid we can't stay long.'

'That's all right,' Hilary said, ushering them inside. 'I really didn't expect to see you until much later.'

She took them into the living room and Temple was surprised to see that she wasn't alone in the house. A man in a crumpled grey suit was standing with his back to the open fireplace. He was of medium height, about forty, with dark brown hair that was spiky and quiffed. His shirt was unbuttoned and his tie hung loose at the collar. Temple assumed he'd come here from the office.

'This is Tom Fowler,' Hilary said. 'He was a friend of Grant's.'

Fowler shook their hands and when he smiled, Temple saw that he had small, sharp teeth.

'Had you known Mr Mason long?' Temple asked him.

'Couple of years,' he said. 'I live close to his house in the forest. We used to drink and hike together. He was a good guy.'

'His death must have come as a shock.'

'It did. As far as I know, he didn't have a history of heart trouble. All that walking seemed to keep him healthy.'

Hilary invited them to sit down and offered to make some tea. This time, Temple accepted and said he'd join her in the kitchen. He motioned with his eyes for Marsh to stay in the living room with Tom Fowler.

When he and Hilary were alone, he asked her if she was all right.

'Not really,' she said, as she put the kettle on. 'My phone hasn't stopped ringing and I feel a bit overwhelmed. Thankfully, Tom has offered to help out with the funeral arrangements.'

Her voice was dry and hoarse, and he sensed that she was struggling to keep the emotion at bay.

'Did he go with you to Mason's house this morning?' he asked.

'No. I went before I told anyone what had happened. Tom arrived here about an hour ago. He's not staying.'

Temple watched her take cups and saucers out of one of the cupboards. She looked weak and fragile, and he noticed that her hands were trembling slightly.

'So what is it you want to tell me, Hilary?' he said. 'You sounded really anxious about it on the phone.'

She turned to face him, leaning her back against the sink. Tears sprang into the corners of her eyes as she spoke.

'In the ambulance Grant told me that if he died there was something he wanted me to do for him,' she said. 'He made me promise that I'd do it, but when he told me what it was it freaked me out.'

'So what did he ask you to do?'

She stared at him, her gaze intent. After a few beats, she said, 'He told me he wanted me to burn down his house.'

For a split second Temple thought she was joking, but as she began to blink back tears he realized that she wasn't.

'Was he being serious?' he asked.

Hilary nodded. 'There's no question in my mind that he was. It was really strange — and unsettling.'

'I'm not surprised. Tell me exactly what he said.'

She rubbed her eyes with her fingers and gave a little cough to clear her throat.

'His actual words went something like — *you have to burn my house down* — *along with everything in it*. I asked him why he'd want me to do such a thing and he said that I didn't need to know, but that it had to be done. He then said I should go to his house before anyone else did, and that no one would have to know that I'd been there.'

Temple felt his chest expand as he took a breath. He had no idea what to make of it, but Hilary was right — it was a strange thing for Mason to say.

'And before you ask, I didn't go to his house this morning to do what he asked,' she said. 'I needed to pick up some documents, but I also wanted to see if everything was in order there.'

'And was it?'

'It seemed to be. I checked all the rooms and nothing was out of place. I even went through his drawers and filing cabinets, and I didn't come across anything even remotely suspicious. Grant was a very tidy person.'

'So can you think of any reason why he'd want you to burn the place down?'

Her eyebrows made a dart in the middle of her forehead. 'It makes no sense to me. Absolutely none.'

'Well, I suppose he could have been spouting rubbish because he was having a heart attack,' Temple said.

'That's what I thought, and I told him that he was confused and in shock. But the truth is he was fully conscious and seemed to know exactly what he was saying. And he sounded desperate, like he knew he wasn't going to make it and wanted to express his dying wish before it was too late.'

Temple twisted his lower jaw as he thought about it. He wasn't quite sure how to react.

'I was careful not to make a mess at the house,' Hilary said. 'I left everything as I found it just in case the police wanted to go out there and have a look.'

Temple knew that he couldn't simply ignore it. What if Mason had been desperate to cover something up — something that he feared would come to light in the event of his death? He might have realized that burning down the house was the only way to destroy whatever it was.

'Why don't you give me the key to his house and I'll pop over there after work?' Temple said.

Hilary was clearly relieved and grateful. She pinched her face into a tight smile. 'I knew I could count on you, Jeff. Thank you so much.'

8

'So what do you intend to do about it, guv?' Marsh said in the car after Temple had told her about his conversation with Hilary.

'I'll go out to Mason's house and have a look around,' he said. 'I don't imagine I'll find anything, but you never know.'

'I'll come with you if you like. I'm more than a little intrigued by all this.'

'I'm sure you are, but there's no need. I want you to concentrate on the Hamilton case. I don't want you distracted.'

But he was a fine one to talk. He couldn't get the Mason thing out of his mind. Why the hell would the man have pleaded with Hilary to burn down his house? It was a bizarre request, and if at the time he truly believed he might die, then it was unlikely to have been a frivolous remark.

'Has she told anyone else about it?' Marsh said.

Temple shrugged. 'I don't know. I should have asked her. Did Tom Fowler allude to it before he left?'

'No, but then talking to him was like getting blood out of a stone.'

'What do you mean?'

'Well, after you went into the kitchen he just stood there staring at me. I asked him a few questions, but it was as though he couldn't be bothered to answer them. Then he suddenly said he had to go and walked out.'

Temple had been surprised to find Fowler gone when he and Hilary emerged from the kitchen. He'd wanted to pick the guy's brain about Mason and to get the low-down on the author's personal life. Hilary's knowledge of what her boss had got up to when she wasn't around was pretty limited.

But to be fair to Fowler, he hadn't been asked to hang around and Hilary hadn't been fazed by his sudden departure, which suggested that it wasn't out of character for him to leave without saying goodbye.

'If it becomes necessary, I'll get his number from Hilary and give him a call,' Temple said.

Back at the station, they both grabbed sandwiches from the canteen before going up to the office. There was no time for a leisurely break so Temple ate his quickly as the team gathered for a meeting. He washed it down with stewed coffee from the machine as he relayed the information they'd gleaned from the pub landlady.

'There's no doubt the Hamiltons visited

59

the King's Tavern,' he said. 'Mrs Keenan gave a positive ID on the photo and the couple told her they were going to Christchurch for a dinner-dance. She gave them directions to the Knightwood Oak, which for those who don't know is one of the oldest trees in the forest and a popular spot with sightseers. It's worth noting that they took photos of each other outside the pub, and were presumably planning to take more. But there was no sign of a camera in their car.'

A detective who'd been liaising with DS Vaughan gave an update on the situation in Paget Street.

'There's nothing so far from the door-to-door interviews,' he said. 'Most of the residents in the flats are out and those we've spoken to had nothing to tell us. There are a few CCTV cameras on the industrial units around there, but none of them facing onto Paget Street. We're seizing all the footage anyway.'

'What about traffic cameras in the area?' Temple said.

'Tapes from Saturday night are being downloaded as we speak from a whole bunch of cameras. We've already started viewing them.'

Not for the first time, it occurred to Temple that the police had become over-reliant on surveillance cameras. He wondered how they'd ever managed to catch criminals before Big Brother took over the streets. There was no question, it made their job a lot easier, even though it had failed to reduce the number of crimes in towns and cities. He was therefore anxious to know what the traffic camera tapes would show in this case, so he assigned more officers to the task of going through them.

'Start with the cameras in the southern section of the city,' he said. 'There's a good chance the car emerged from the forest on the A35 and entered Southampton along the A33. It might have kept going in more or less a straight line to Paget Street.'

That would have taken them past the police station and the cruise line terminals, a route with plenty of traffic lights and road junctions. So with any luck . . .

After winding up the meeting, Temple got another coffee and went to his office. He spent a while on some general paperwork and returned a few calls. Then he opened the file on the Hamiltons and felt a clutch of apprehension. The longer they were missing, the more concerned he became. He stared at their photographs and wondered what could possibly have happened to them.

Why had they not gone to the dinner-dance in Christchurch?

Why had they abandoned their car in Paget Street?

Why had they not bothered to check up on their 2-year-old son?

He was still churning the questions over in his head half an hour later when he got a call from Beresford.

'You and me are fronting a press conference in half an hour,' the Chief Super said. 'So I need you to come up right away to give me an update.'

★　★　★

The press conference was a small affair attended by the local media. The national newspapers and broadcasters hadn't yet picked up the story, but Temple was sure that they soon would. It wasn't every day that a young married couple disappeared in mysterious circumstances, leaving behind a 2-year-old child.

Flashbulbs popped and stuttered as Beresford kicked off the meeting with a summary of the situation. As he spoke, one of the uniforms passed around photographs of the abandoned Honda in Paget Street. They wanted them printed in the papers and shown on television.

Then Temple went into more detail about where the car was found and when it was left there. He said officers were trawling through traffic camera footage from Saturday night in the hope of spotting the Hamiltons. Meanwhile, the last known sighting of the couple was at the King's Tavern near Lyndhurst in the New Forest. It was believed they went on to visit the Knightwood Oak before driving to other forest landmarks.

The questions that followed were all straightforward and easy to answer. Did the police believe the couple had run off? Did either of them have a criminal record? Had they ever gone missing before? What were the police doing to find them?

Finally Beresford made a direct appeal to Bob and Rosemary Hamilton.

'If you are in a position to contact us then I urge you to do so,' he said. 'Just let us know that you are both OK. Your family are desperate for news.'

Back in the office, Temple was told they'd had a result with the traffic cameras. He hurried over to the side-room where detectives were gathered around computer monitors.

It transpired that the couple's car had been picked up by several cameras on Saturday. The first had been at 10 p.m. where it could be seen entering the city along the A33 from the direction of the New Forest. Next it appeared on a camera as it drove past the waterfront cruise terminals before turning left into the city centre. It was captured on yet another camera on one of the roads close to Paget Street.

'This is helpful in that we now know what time the car was driven back into town,' Temple said. 'But we can't see the ruddy occupants.'

Even when they went through it frame by frame and enhanced the images, there wasn't much of an improvement. The lighting was poor and there was too much reflection on the windscreen. All they could determine was a blurred figure at the wheel and an empty passenger seat. It was impossible to tell if there was someone sitting in the back.

There was more disappointment after the surveillance tapes from the commercial properties around Paget Street were examined. A few people were seen walking around on Saturday evening, but none of them were Bob or Rosemary Hamilton.

'So who the bloody hell was driving the car?' Temple said when the team assembled again for the shift changeover. 'Was it Bob or Rosemary? Or was it someone else entirely? We need to find out.'

The detectives were given their assignments and Temple asked to be informed if there were any developments. Some of the team were going for a quick after-work drink and they asked him if he wanted to join them. He was up for it until he remembered that for him the day wasn't quite over.

He'd promised Hilary that he would go and check out Grant Mason's house.

9

Temple called Angel as he drove back into the forest. He said he'd be late home and told her why.

'That's strange, I agree,' she said. 'But what do you expect to find at the house?'

'I don't know, probably nothing. But what Mason said can't just be ignored.'

'I can see that, but I don't understand why you're going there. Why not pass it on to uniform?'

'Because I told Hilary I'd look into it and because it's not an official visit. No point making it official if Mason was talking complete bollocks because he was having a heart attack at the time.'

He heard Angel tut into the phone.

'Are you OK?' he said. 'You sound a bit off with me.'

She gave a sharp intake of breath. 'It's just that you said you'd try to be home early. I've made dinner and there's something I want to talk to you about.'

'Oh? What is it?'

She started to tell him, but changed her mind. 'Look, it's not urgent so it can wait.'

'Are you sure?'

'Of course. Just text me when you're on your way back.'

'Will do.'

After the call ended he started to wonder what Angel wanted to chat about. He felt slightly uneasy because it had been obvious to him for several days that she'd had something on her mind. She'd been moody and detached and that wasn't like her. When he'd asked her if there was anything wrong, she'd said she was just tired. But he suspected there was more to it than that.

Perhaps it had something to do with the prospect of returning to work in MIT. Before the crash she'd been planning a career change, and had started studying forensics with a view to moving to the Scientific Services Department. But that had been put on hold while she concentrated on getting better.

Now that she was looking to the future again, she probably wanted to talk to him about her options. After all, he was still her boss as well as her boyfriend. He couldn't think what else might be bothering her, and he knew that if he dwelt on it he'd start to worry.

So he made a conscious effort to push it from his mind as he drove through the forest towards Grant Mason's house.

★　★　★

The New Forest is a very dark place at night. Most of the roads are unlit and communities are few and far between. You can travel for miles without seeing a single light.

Eight o'clock and there was hardly any traffic. The moon was hiding behind a canopy of cloud and the darkness seemed impenetrable.

Temple kept well within the speed limit, wary of encountering one of the New Forest ponies that are a major hazard. Every year, more than a few are hit by cars because drivers see them too late to brake.

Hilary had given him Mason's address and he'd located it on the map before setting out. The house was just outside the tiny village of East Boldre, about nine miles south-east of Lyndhurst. It was detached, but not exactly remote. There were other properties close by.

Temple knew the forest well enough not to get lost, but even so he drove past the narrow track leading to the house and had to double back. Tyres crunched over gravel as he followed the track through a small wood. Through the trees on his right, he could see the lights from the village only a few hundred yards away.

The house stood at the end of the track,

surrounded by tall trees. The headlights revealed a two-storey brick building that was probably only about twenty or thirty years old. There was a detached garage and a paved area at the front.

He stopped the car and when the lights went out, it was almost as dark as the inside of an eyelid. He took a torch from the glove compartment, undid his seatbelt and got out.

There was an ominous stillness about the place and it was eerily quiet, save for the chatter of insects in the surrounding foliage. Above the house a slice of moon appeared, silent and pale in the sky.

Temple switched on the torch and walked up to the front door. But as soon as he reached it, he felt a flare of unease when he saw that it was ajar. Had Hilary forgotten to close it after her visit this morning? Or had someone been here since then, someone with a spare key?

He pushed at the door with his fingertips and it opened a few more inches.

'Hello,' he called out. 'Is anyone here?'

No response. No sound from within. He felt a knot tighten in his throat. Something wasn't right. He could feel it in his blood.

He stood on the threshold and shone the torch into the small, square hallway. Polished wood floor. Small occasional table with an empty vase on top. A flight of stairs.

In the silence he could hear his own breathing, shallow and quick. He felt his heart pounding beneath his shirt.

'Is anyone here?' he called again.

When he got no answer a cold chill slid over him. Did it mean the house was empty or was there someone inside lurking in the dark? It was all a bit odd. No vehicles outside. No lights on inside. And yet the door was open.

He stepped inside and called out again. He heard nothing back but the taut, static hum of silence.

He located the light switch and snapped it on. Waited a few seconds to see what would happen and nothing did.

There were three closed doors ahead of him and he went to the one on the far left. It gave access to the living room. As he stepped inside and switched on the overhead light, his whole body stiffened, as though he'd been nudged with a cattle prod.

The room had been ransacked. It was a total mess. The floor was littered with broken picture frames, books, plants and cushions from two small sofas. He spotted a smashed-up handset from a cordless phone and a large pot plant on its side, soil and water pooled on the carpet around it.

But not everything had been trashed. An expensive-looking flat-screen TV was still on its stand and below it a Sky digital box. There was also a cabinet against one wall and on top of it, a collection of bottles containing various spirits.

Temple stepped back into the hallway and tried another door. This one led to the kitchen and there was more carnage. Drawers and cupboards had been pulled open and their contents emptied on the floor.

As Temple surveyed the damage he took a long, deep breath and expelled it. Then he moved back into the hallway and opened the third door. A small study with a desk, a couple of tall metal filing cabinets and a floor to ceiling bookcase across one wall. Most of the books were on the floor along with the files from the cabinets. On the desk there were cables running from a wall socket and a printing machine. But the computer or laptop they'd been attached to was missing.

Temple shook his head and clenched his bottom lip between his teeth. He couldn't remember the last time he'd seen so much vandalism inflicted on a property. He would call it in and get a forensic team out here as quickly as possible. Hopefully the vandal or vandals had left behind a fingerprint or DNA trace.

But as he was reaching in his pocket for his phone he heard something. The sound had come from above. A creaking floorboard. Quite loud and quite distinctive.

He realized he wasn't alone in the house and froze.

There was someone upstairs.

10

Temple took out his phone, only to find that he didn't have a signal. It didn't surprise him. Large areas of the forest were in so-called mobile dark spots and out of range of the relay towers.

He cursed because it left him facing the dilemma of what to do now that he couldn't summon back-up. If he went outside, the chances were he still wouldn't receive a signal and if he went further afield, the intruder would make a run for it.

He decided to front it out in the hope that he was dealing with an opportunistic burglar who'd be too scared to resist when confronted by the police.

'I know you're up there,' Temple called out. 'I'm a detective with Hampshire police and I suggest you come down right now. More police officers will be here any minute.'

Nothing. The silence screamed in his ears, and he felt a flash of heat in his chest.

He decided he needed something he could use to defend himself, just in case the intruder was armed. He stepped back into the kitchen and eyed a selection of knives scattered across the floor. He was tempted, but he picked up a wooden rolling pin instead because he didn't want to risk inflicting a serious or fatal stab wound during a tussle.

Then he moved back into the hallway and cautiously ascended the stairs. Every nerve in his body was vibrating and he felt his chest contract like a fist.

Halfway up the stairs, he paused to call out again and this time he was sure he heard movement above him. But no one appeared and this only served to quicken his pulse.

At the top of the stairs he switched on the landing light. There were three doors, all half-open. It suddenly occurred to him that he was taking a huge risk. He had no idea who or what he was about to confront. He was strongly tempted to go back downstairs and out to his car. But the reckless streak that had all too often clouded his judgement urged him on.

He held the rolling pin in front of him as he moved towards the door to his left. It was a bathroom and as he peered inside, he saw that it was empty.

He backed up along the landing to another half-open doorway. Through it he could see the bottom end of a bed.

He placed a hand against the door and gently pushed at it as he stepped forwards.

But suddenly there was a heavy thud and the door swung back against him with tremendous force, hurling him face-down on to the landing carpet. He heard footfalls behind him, but before he could react he took a brutal kick to the ribs. As he cried out, a second blow struck him on the right side of his face. The pain was explosive and water filled his eyes. But he managed to roll up against the wall and brace himself for another blow.

And that's when he saw his attacker, staring down at him through the slits of a black balaclava. The build and posture told him it was a man, an impression reinforced by the tight polo sweater and jeans. But that was about all Temple could take in before the guy let loose another vicious kick.

This time he was ready and raised both arms to protect his face. The guy's shoe struck the open palm of his right hand and he was able to push against it, causing the guy to lose his balance. Temple scrambled to his feet and hurled himself at the guy. He pushed him across the landing and they both went crashing down the stairs like a pair of grappling stuntmen.

They got separated halfway down, but it was Temple who came off worse, landing on his back with one leg twisted painfully beneath him. The other guy recovered more quickly and kicked out frantically before Temple could right himself.

The heel of the man's shoe slammed against the detective's crotch with what felt like the force of a jack-hammer. Temple was battered and bruised and his senses were on fire. He tried desperately to haul himself up, but a gloved hand grabbed the back of his neck and rammed his head against the wall.

The blow rendered him helpless and his body went limp. As he hit the floor again, his vision grew dark and he felt himself slipping towards unconsciousness.

But he clung on long enough to hear his attacker walk up the stairs and come back down again seconds later. Then he managed to force his eyes open as the guy walked past him to the front door. He was still wearing the balaclava, but now he was carrying a black rucksack over one shoulder. He paused at the door to look back and Temple tried to say something, but couldn't form the words. The man then walked out and Temple groaned as the darkness consumed him.

11

Temple knew he was awake because of the pain. It throbbed with a savage intensity, and not just inside his head. He could feel it in his chest, his shoulders, his stomach, his limbs. Even his face hurt as he struggled to open his eyes.

He was still lying on the floor in Grant Mason's hallway. His attacker had left the front door open and the cold air was creeping in.

As Temple heaved himself up to a sitting position, he was struck by a wave of dizziness, the likes of which he had never experienced. His heart was hammering, blood pumping round his body. For a moment he thought he was going to pass out again. He squeezed his eyes shut and pinched the bridge of his nose. Thankfully, the feeling passed after a few seconds.

Then he cursed himself for having been so stupid. He should never have ventured up the stairs knowing there was someone up there. It had been impulsive and unprofessional. He'd walked into a trap and he was lucky not to be more seriously injured.

Not that he could be sure what damage had been done. He might well have concussion and a couple of broken ribs.

Jesus.

He checked his watch. Eight thirty. He'd only been unconscious for a few minutes. He checked his phone. Still no bars showing.

He pulled himself up from the floor and shuffled across the hallway and out the front door. The frigid air helped to clear his head and he drew it deep into his lungs.

He was relieved to see that his car was still there. No sign of the man in the balaclava, though. He was long gone.

Temple tried his mobile again, but he was still out of range. He got in the car, started the engine, did a U-turn in front of the house. Then he drove back along the track while holding his phone in front of him.

At the end of the track he finally got a signal. He stopped the car and called 999. Told the operator who he was and what had happened.

'And make sure you alert my team,' he said before hanging up.

★ ★ ★

Thirty minutes later, the cavalry started to converge on Grant Mason's house. Three patrol cars, an ambulance and a fast-response vehicle with armed officers. The night was suddenly a riot of flashing lights and police radio chatter.

Temple was checked by a paramedic as officers swarmed over the property and ventured into the surrounding woodland with torches.

He had a lump the size of a walnut on his head and a nasty bruise on his right cheek just below the eye. Nothing appeared to be broken, but he was advised to go to hospital just to be sure. He said he would, but not right away, so he was given painkillers and a cold compress for his head.

DS Vaughan was the first of his team to arrive on the scene. He looked tired and dishevelled, and explained that he'd only just got home when he received the call. DC Marsh drew up in her car a few minutes later, looking more worried than tired.

Rather than repeat himself, Temple got everyone together in front of the house to tell them what had happened and why he was here. Vaughan's reaction was typically blunt. He called his boss a bloody idiot for confronting the intruder by himself.

'You don't have to tell me that,' Temple said. 'I should have known better.'

Temple was told that patrols were driving

around the area stopping cars, and teams on foot were searching the nearby village of East Boldre. A helicopter had been summoned and would soon be doing a night-vision sweep of the surrounding countryside.

'There were no cars here when I arrived,' Temple said. 'So the intruder must have fled through the woods or along the track. He either had a vehicle parked nearby or he lives in the village.'

He described the guy as best he could and said they were unlikely to find his prints because he'd been wearing gloves.

'I was still conscious when he walked out,' he said. 'He was carrying a rucksack. My guess is it contained Grant Mason's laptop which is missing from his office desk. I have no idea what else might have been in there.'

'So on the face of it, we're dealing with a straightforward burglary that went wrong,' Vaughan said. 'The perp got disturbed and panicked. He resorted to violence in his bid to get away, even though you identified yourself as a police officer.'

Temple bit his lip. 'Either that or he was looking for something specific. And we have to consider the possibility that the break-in is connected in some way to what Mason said to his PA.'

'Does she really have no clue as to why he

80

wanted her to burn this place down?'
Vaughan said.

'None whatsoever. She was shocked. And
she didn't get a chance to ask him about it
when they got to the hospital.'

'So how do you want us to play it, guv,
assuming we don't catch the guy tonight?'

'We start by sealing the property off until
morning,' Temple said. 'At first light I want
a forensic team brought in to carry out a
thorough search. Once the place is tidied up
I'll get Hilary Dyer to come over. Hopefully,
she can help us determine what's missing.
Meanwhile, the office can check out Mason's
email and bank accounts. See if anything
interesting comes up. And we need to canvas
everyone in the village to see if anyone saw a
guy with a rucksack.'

'So is this officially our case, boss?' Marsh
asked.

'It is for now, but we'll see how it pans out.'

Temple suddenly felt dizzy and a wave of
nausea washed over him. It was time he went
to the hospital. But he had to be persuaded
not to drive himself there. The paramedic
insisted he went by ambulance so Marsh said
she'd arrange for his car to be taken to his
house.

On the way to the hospital he called Angel.
She was understandably shocked to hear

about the attack. He assured her that it was nothing serious and that he'd be home as soon as he'd been checked over.

He spent two hours at the hospital. They ran a bunch of checks and did x-rays and a CT scan. It turned out his ribs were still intact and the blows to his head had not caused any serious damage.

He got home at almost one in the morning and Angel was waiting up for him. She fell into his arms as soon as he walked through the door and he could feel her shaking beneath her dressing gown.

'Are you all right?' she said. 'God, I've been worried sick.'

He put her mind at ease regarding his condition. Then he poured himself a much needed whisky and closed his eyes as it burned a track down the back of his throat.

Angel sat next to him on the sofa and he told her everything that had happened in more detail. She looked tired and anxious. Her short brown hair was still wet from a shower and the whites of her eyes were shiny and moist in the lamplight.

'I can't believe you didn't call for back-up,' she said. 'What you did was crazy.'

He was taken aback by the harsh tone of her voice.

'There was no mobile signal. I couldn't . . .'

'Then you should have left the house,' she cut in. 'What if the guy had been armed with a knife or a gun? You might have been killed.'

'OK, I'm sorry,' he said. 'I made the wrong call. We've all done it.'

A brief flash of anger in her eyes and the muscles in her neck tightened.

'You just don't get it do you, Jeff?' she said, her voice becoming high-pitched. 'You're no longer by yourself. You're with me and that means what you do and say will impact on my life. You can't take unnecessary risks anymore.'

Tears filled her eyes and she started to blink rapidly.

'Calm down, sweetheart,' he said. 'It was a mistake. I get that. But there's no need to go overboard. I'm going to be fine.'

She clenched her jaw and her spine went rigid.

'You were just lucky,' she shouted at him. 'Don't you see that? You might not be here now if the blows to your head had been any harder.'

She started to cry and when he reached out to her, she brushed his hand away.

He didn't know what to say. He was confused because Angel didn't usually allow herself to be overcome by emotion. Maybe she'd had a bad day and what had happened had been the last straw.

'Listen, sweetheart,' he said. 'I do understand where you're coming from and in future I promise to be more careful and more responsible. But be honest with me now. Is something else bothering you? You said earlier that you wanted to talk to me. Has it got anything to do with that?'

She took her hands away from her face and regained control of her sobbing. Then she lifted her head and stared at him, her swollen eyes shining with unshed tears.

'I didn't mean for it to happen, Jeff,' she said. 'It's just that — I slipped up.'

His jaw dropped and he felt a flare of unease.

'What are you talking about?' he said.

She took a deep, shaky breath and let the air hiss out between her teeth.

'I'm nine weeks pregnant, Jeff,' she said. 'The doctor confirmed it today.'

★ ★ ★

Neither of them went to bed. They stayed awake talking as the new day broke over Southampton.

Temple was reeling from the shock of what he'd been told, which compounded the relentless pain in his head. A baby had never

84

been part of the plan. Angel had always maintained that she didn't want children, preferring instead to concentrate on her career. It was a decision that Temple had been happy to go along with. He had a daughter and at forty-eight he wasn't keen to embark on another stint of fatherhood.

In hindsight, he should have had a vasectomy and not relied on Angel to always remember to take the pill. She said there'd been a couple of times just before the crash when she forgot. And now she was pregnant and telling him that she was sorry.

He told her not to be and that if she wanted to keep the baby then that was fine with him. But of course it wasn't really. The future they'd mapped out for themselves did not include children. They were going to have fun, be selfish, spoil each other rotten. But a baby would change things and have a profound impact on their relationship. He was almost fifty and he just couldn't imagine being a father at an age when most men are grandfathers.

Angel was just as worried and confused. She said as much. But he could tell from the look in her eyes that she was also excited at the prospect. And that was only natural, despite what she'd said about her career coming first.

Temple struggled to process the news. His head was muddy, as though he was trying to think through treacle.

'Look, I'll take the day off,' he said. 'We can both get some sleep and then we can talk about it some more when we're not so tired.'

'You shouldn't be going to work anyway in your condition,' Angel said. 'You need to rest.'

'Well, let me call the office and then we can go back to bed for a while. How does that sound?'

She smiled at him. 'Very sensible.'

But Temple's phone buzzed just as he got up to make the call. It was DS Vaughan who had been at Grant Mason's house with the forensic team since the crack of dawn.

'You need to get down here right away, sir,' the DS said. 'We've found out why Mason wanted someone to burn his house down in the event of his death. And trust me, you're not going to like it.'

12

Temple didn't ask the detective to elaborate over the phone. Instead he told him he'd get to the house as quickly as he could.

Angel was disappointed that he had to go out, but she said she understood and that they could talk again later.

Temple had a quick shower and shave, and put on a clean suit and shirt. Angel made him coffee and toast and before leaving, he gave her a long kiss on the mouth and told her that he loved her.

As he drove towards the forest his head was all over the place, but at least the tablets the hospital had given him were controlling the pain.

He wasn't able to control his thoughts, though. They rushed through his mind at a rate of knots. The baby. The burglar. The missing couple. Grant Mason's bizarre dying wish. He was struggling to make sense of any of it.

Fatigue was making it difficult for him to concentrate. At the same time, nervous energy was running through him and something cold and heavy had settled in his stomach.

He guessed he was still in a state of shock. But then that was to be expected. He'd been beaten unconscious by a burglar in a balaclava and then he'd been knocked for six by Angel's bombshell revelation.

Pregnant. Jesus. He hadn't seen that one coming. He wondered what he'd have said to his dead wife if he'd known about it yesterday morning. He and Erin had tried for another baby when Tanya was two. But she'd failed to conceive and it turned out she had a problem with her ovaries. They were both devastated to begin with, but resolved not to let it became an issue. They'd considered themselves lucky because they had a healthy, beautiful, mischievous daughter.

But deep down, Temple had always yearned for another child and he'd felt sorry for Erin because she thought she'd somehow let him down. The yearning had dissipated over the years, however, and now the thought of starting over again with another baby filled him with dread.

Angel's whole attitude to motherhood was bound to change, if it hadn't already. Her career would be pushed into second place and their life-plan would have to be re-written. She'd be desperate for his approval, his commitment to both her and the baby. She'd try to get inside his head to find out how he really felt. She'd tell him he wasn't too old to change nappies and push a pram. And he'd have to be careful how he responded. Every view he expressed would have huge significance.

He'd have to quickly come to terms with the situation; suppress all doubts and fears and act like they'd been blessed.

He knew that if he didn't there'd be a very real risk of losing her.

* * *

It was a dry, cold morning in the forest. A grey mist climbed off the fields and the moorland bracken was tinged with a delicate frost. Thin clouds hung like webbing in the sky and a weak sun was threatening to make its presence felt.

Temple reached East Boldre just before nine. There were three patrol cars on the road and a WPC was standing at the entrance to the track to prevent unauthorized access.

She waved Temple through and when he got to the house, he was surprised at the level of activity. Scene of Crime Officers (SOCOs) were there in force, along with a dozen or so uniforms. He also spotted DS Vaughan leaning against his battered SUV, wearing a white forensic containment suit.

Temple parked between the SUV and a

forensic van. He switched off the engine and took a moment to close his eyes and blink away thoughts of a future that was going to be very different to the one he had envisaged. It was time to focus on the present and find out what the hell Grant Mason had been up to.

'So what's this all about?' he said to DS Vaughan when he got out of the car.

Vaughan looked rougher than usual. He hadn't shaved and his eyes were dark and rimmed with shadow.

'They found stuff in the loft,' Vaughan said. 'It looks like Mason was using it as an office.'

'But there's an office downstairs.'

'This one's different, guv. You'll see. And it's all intact so we're assuming that last night's intruder didn't go up there.'

'Do we need to alert Beresford?'

'I've already called him. He's on his way here.'

Temple followed Vaughan into the house after putting on a forensic suit and shoe covers. Downstairs, it was very much how it had been hours before except that it was crawling with SOCOs.

Lee Finch, the senior SOCO, was well-known to Temple. Tall and sinewy with a stooped posture and a solid reputation. He wore small rimless glasses that gave him an air of studious charm.

'I wasn't sure you'd be able to get here, Jeff,' he said. 'I heard what happened to you last night.'

Temple shrugged. 'It could have been worse.'

'Well, I'm glad you're here. What we've found is more than a little disturbing.'

'Then lead the way,' Temple said.

They climbed the stairs to the landing. The loft hatch in the ceiling was open and an aluminium step-ladder had been lowered to the floor.

'We went up there to check it out as a matter of routine as soon as we got here,' Finch said. 'It took me a couple of minutes to realize what we were looking at.'

A few seconds later, Finch and the two detectives were in the loft, which had been converted into a large office with a desk, a free-standing wardrobe and a cabinet. The roof sloped steeply on both sides and was lined with thick layers of insulation.

There were no windows, but plenty of light came from two lamps fixed to the overhead rafters. In front of the desk was a leather swivel chair. On the brick wall to the right of it a large map of the New Forest. On the wall to the left, a montage of colour photographs in various sizes. Temple was too far away to see what was in them.

'Check out the stuff on the desk first,' Finch said.

Temple stepped up to the desk. On top was a large computer monitor with keyboard and tower. The screen was on, and showing a photograph of a naked woman tied to a chair with a ball gag in her mouth and small metal clamps on her nipples. She looked terrified.

'Jesus,' Temple said.

'Believe it or not, that's just Mason's screen saver image,' Finch said. 'We haven't looked beyond that yet.'

'Each to his own, I suppose.'

'Take a look in the top drawer,' Finch said.

Temple eased open the drawer. Inside was a collection of objects including a large hunting knife with a bone handle, a compact Sony camcorder, a stun gun that was capable of delivering 300,000 volts and a box of blue latex gloves, of the kind he and the SOCOs were wearing.

'Interesting, eh?' Finch said. 'Especially the stun gun. I know those things are widely available on the internet, but you don't often come across them in people's homes.'

'It's a strange thing for Mason to have,' Temple said.

'I know. Now look at the photos on the wall there.'

Temple moved over to the wall and

squinted up at the photos. At once the urge to vomit rolled through his stomach.

There were perhaps fifty photos and they were all explicit and repulsive. They showed a number of men and women being restrained by ropes and straps and chains. Some were close-ups of male and female genitals. A bruised and swollen penis. A blood soaked vagina. A woman's breast covered with severe bite marks.

Another photo showed a young girl tied face down across a table with her legs apart. A large black dildo had been inserted deep into her rectum.

In another photo a middle-aged man was hanging by a chain from the ceiling, his pale, naked body covered with whip marks.

'These must have been downloaded from the internet,' Temple said, knowing that there were hundreds of websites specialising in photos and videos of bondage and sado-masochism.

'That's what I thought,' Finch said. 'Until I checked out the camcorder in the drawer. The latest recording shows a young lad seemingly being raped by whoever is holding the camera.'

Temple snapped his head round and stared at Finch.

'Are you kidding me?' he said.

'I'm afraid not, Jeff. The lad — who looks to be in his late teens — is bent over the same table as the one in several of those photos and his hands are cuffed to the legs.'

'My God.'

'The guy with the camcorder is taping his own dick entering the lad from behind. The lad is begging him to stop so I don't think he's a willing participant in some sado sex game.'

Temple's heart was pounding now, booming in his ears. He shook his head as he struggled to take it in.

'There's something else that's even more disturbing than those images,' Finch said.

Temple looked at him and felt a tightening in his gut.

Finch stepped up to the map on the other wall and beckoned Temple over. It was a large ordnance survey map, showing everything from main roads to cattle grids.

'Look at it closely,' Finch said.

Temple saw that names and dates had been written with a ballpoint pen at various locations across the map. At each location, someone had also scrawled a small religious cross.

'There are ten crosses and fifteen names,' Finch said. 'Against five of the crosses there are two names.' He pointed to a cross next to the names Michael and Fiona Maitlin. 'The dates span two years, the most recent being that one — 28th December. Just two months ago.'

Temple pushed out his bottom lip and studied the map. His eyes homed in on the name and date Finch was pointing to.

'Paul Kellerman,' he said. 'That name rings a bell.'

'It did with me too,' Vaughan said. 'So just before you arrived I got the office to run a check. A twenty-year-old student named Paul Kellerman disappeared just over two months ago on 24th December. His car was found close to his home in Bournemouth, which as you know is only a few miles west of the New Forest. He was last seen earlier that day by friends he was visiting in Winchester.'

Temple nodded. 'That's it. I remember the case. The Dorset Constabulary were handling it.'

'It could just be coincidence,' Vaughan said. 'The name's not that unusual.'

Temple thought about it. 'But if it's not a coincidence, then why did Mason write his name on this map? And what's the significance of the date — just four days after the lad vanished?'

'The answer to that could lie with those religious crosses,' Finch said.

Temple turned to him. 'What do you mean?'

Finch paused for several beats. 'Well, a religious cross usually marks the location of a church or a cemetery — or even a grave. And I know for a fact that there are no churches or cemeteries at the locations pinpointed on this map.'

Temple arched his brow in disbelief. 'So what exactly are you saying, Lee?'

Finch sucked in a breath. 'I'm saying we need to consider the possibility that this map is telling us where fifteen people are buried in the forest. Among them a young student who disappeared two months ago.'

13

It was a shocking thought and one that brought Temple out in a cold sweat.

Was it really conceivable that those crosses on the map denoted clandestine graves? And that there were ten of them spread across the New Forest? Surely Finch was jumping to a macabre conclusion.

'I know what you're thinking, Jeff,' Finch said. 'That it's a wild conjecture. Well, that's exactly how people reacted when it was first revealed that Myra Hindley and Ian Brady had buried the bodies of their child victims on Saddleworth Moor.'

'But those two were complete psychos,' Temple pointed out.

'Sure they were, but isn't there compelling evidence here to suggest that Grant Mason might have been just as sick in the head as they were?'

Temple knew that Finch had a point and it sent a shiver up his spine. He paused to compose his thoughts and look around the loft. It was stark and sterile. Not the sort of place where an author would find peace and inspiration. But then Grant Mason obviously hadn't come up here to write his books. Instead he'd come to indulge his horrific fantasies and perhaps to gloat over the evidence of his own debauchery.

Temple went back to the photographs on the wall and felt a coldness grip his mind. He counted at least seven different people, all adults. Four men and three women. If it hadn't been for the blood smeared on their bodies and their terrified expressions, he would have assumed that they were sado-masochists indulging in their own peculiar idea of fun. But it looked to him as though they were being restrained against their will while being tortured.

'So let me get this straight,' Temple said. 'You're saying that these could be the same people whose names have been scrawled on the map?'

Finch nodded. 'It's certainly possible, given what we've got here.'

'As crazy as it sounds I have to agree,' Vaughan said. 'Mason might have abducted them. Then after he finished playing with them, he buried their bodies in shallow graves in the forest.'

'So why did he highlight the locations on a map?' Temple said.

'Same reason he put those photos on the wall, I reckon. To provide a constant reminder of what he'd done. It gave him pleasure and was all part of his sick thrill ride.'

Temple had to admit that as a theory it was frighteningly plausible. And it would explain why Grant Mason had desperately wanted his house to be destroyed by fire. He'd feared his sick little hideaway would be discovered.

Temple saw Mason in his mind's eye. The man had always looked so ordinary. Quietly spoken and seemingly respectable. A local author and pillar of the community. He certainly hadn't struck Temple as a sexual sadist. But that was the thing about such people — they were always so good at covering their tracks.

The evidence they'd stumbled upon did suggest that Mason had led a secret life. There was the camcorder, the stun gun, the photos, the video footage . . . it was pretty incriminating stuff and there was unlikely to be an innocent explanation for it all.

'So how do you want to play this, guv?' Vaughan said.

Temple turned away from the wall and pressed his fingers into his eye sockets, as if he could erase the images from the photos.

He took a deep breath and held it for a while before speaking.

'For starters, we keep a lid on this until we know for certain what we're dealing with. If our suspicions are made public it'll lead to a media firestorm. So we need to move quickly to see if the theory stacks up. That means carrying out a thorough search of the house and finding out what's on the computer and camcorder.

'We also need the data from Mason's phone and online activity. Plus, I want all the names on the map put into the system. Are they also people who are missing and if so, do the dates tally with when they disappeared?'

'I'll get right on it,' Vaughan said.

'And we need pictures. Start with Paul Kellerman. If we're right about this, then he might well be the poor sod who's being raped on the camcorder.'

Vaughan finished scribbling his notes and quickly descended the step-ladder.

'So what parts of the loft haven't yet been searched?' Temple asked Finch.

The SOCO gestured with his head. 'The computer, the wardrobe and the cabinet. As soon as I saw what was on the wall and inside the desk drawer, I called a halt because I thought you should see it first.'

'That was the right call, Lee. But now, let's go through the rest of it.'

Finch went to work on the computer and expressed his astonishment when he discovered that it wasn't password-protected.

Within minutes he was inside Mason's files and sifting through scores of pornographic images and videos. It was all violent material and some of it involved children and even animals. It made Temple's flesh crawl.

'We'll need to get this analyzed by the experts,' Finch said. 'Most of it has clearly been downloaded from the internet, but I'm not sure what Mason uploaded himself.'

'Check his browser history,' Temple said.

It turned out that Mason had been a frequent visitor to websites showing and selling all manner of violent porn.

'I'm guessing he spent a lot of time up here wanking himself dry,' Finch said.

Temple's body was rigid, his jaw clenched. He was finding it hard to believe the evidence of his own eyes. Mason's computer was full of the vilest forms of pornography. Simulated rape, incest, extreme bondage where women were cruelly beaten and sexually abused.

It made Temple feel sick so he turned away and decided to check the wardrobe and cabinet.

In the wardrobe there were three items of clothing — a green parka, a pair of denim jeans and a dark blue woollen sweater. Plus a pair of muddied Wellington boots.

Why the hell was he keeping them up here? Temple asked himself. Was it because he used to wear them when he went on the prowl?

Temple went to the cabinet. It was waist high and had two doors. Inside was a single shelf on which rested a number of objects and below it several stacks of hardcore porn DVDs. The objects on the shelf included an expensive looking man's watch, a woman's gold bracelet, three gold rings, two digital cameras and a Zippo lighter.

Temple felt his stomach flip when it struck him that these could be callous souvenirs from Mason's victims.

He reached in and picked up one of the cameras. A Nikon Coolpix L29. But the battery power had been spent. He replaced it and picked up the other one — a Canon IXUS.

It came on when he pressed the power button and seconds later, he was flipping through the photos stored on it. The first was a close-up picture of a squirrel eating a nut. The second, a wide-angle shot of dense woodland.

But the third picture caused every nerve in his body to slam to a stop. It was a shot of Rosemary Hamilton posing in front of the Knightwood Oak.

Taken no doubt by her husband Bob, just before the couple went missing.

14

Teams of officers — some with sniffer dogs — were drafted in to search the land around Grant Mason's house.

They swarmed through the woods and over the heathland in the hope of finding Bob and Rosemary Hamilton. It was pretty clear now that Mason had had something to do with their disappearance. Why else would their camera be hidden in his loft?

The photo of Rosemary Hamilton posing in front of the ancient tree was preceded by photos of both of them in front of the King's Tavern pub.

The discovery of the camera not only heightened fears for the missing couple — it also gave credence to the theory that Grant Mason had claimed at least fifteen other victims. But the Hamiltons' names did not appear on Mason's map. Did that mean they were still alive? And if so, where were they now? A thorough search of the house and detached garage had revealed no further trace of them or anyone else.

Temple viewed for himself the footage on Mason's camcorder to see if they were on it, but it showed only the young man being physically and sexually abused. There was even a sequence where the camcorder was placed on a tripod and the operator — a fully-clothed Grant Mason — walked into shot, carrying a leather paddle whip with metal studs. He then filmed himself beating the young man's bare buttocks until the young man passed out.

Revulsion pooled in Temple's eyes as he watched the footage and he had to suppress the urge to be sick when he was shown a photograph of Paul Kellerman. It confirmed that the lad on the video and the missing student were one and the same.

'That's not all, guv,' DS Vaughan said. 'The office just got back to me on those other names. There's a misper file on all of them. And the dates on the map more or less coincide with when they disappeared.'

'Shit. Are most of them local?'

'Not at all. A few are from London, a couple from Dorset and two are tourists from abroad.'

Temple's voice cracked with emotion as he shared this information with the rest of the team when they gathered inside the mobile incident room for the first on-site briefing.

The sheer magnitude of what they were dealing with had now sunk in. Even

Beresford, a detective with a wealth of experience, was visibly shaken. And he wasn't the only one. Fiona Marsh kept shaking her head and silently mouthing 'Oh my God' as Temple ran through the facts.

He said there was no correlation in age, status or gender between the people who had disappeared or been kidnapped.

'We have to work on the assumption that the Hamiltons were abducted, probably while visiting the Knightwood Oak,' he said. 'The stun gun we found in Mason's desk may have been used to bring them down before they were restrained.'

Temple went on to list what else was in the loft for the benefit of those who had not been up there. He described the photos on the wall and said that the desktop computer was being analyzed. He mentioned the clothes in the wardrobe and the personal belongings in the cabinet.

'The watches, the rings and the bracelet probably belonged to the victims,' he said. 'We need to talk to their relatives about that stuff.'

Temple then told them what little he knew about Grant Mason. He said he would talk to Hilary Dyer again, and wanted teams to visit the local village and all the pubs within a three-mile radius.

'I've met one of his friends,' Temple said. 'A guy named Tom Fowler. I'll get his contact details from Hilary. Meanwhile, someone should talk to his publisher. We need to build up a picture of Mason as quickly as possible.'

'What about the intruder you encountered last night, guv?' Marsh said. 'Could the break-in have had something to do with all this?'

'It's a good question, Fiona, but I really don't know. He may have been an opportunistic local thief who heard that Mason had died.'

'Do we know yet what he stole?'

'Not yet, but there's a laptop missing from the downstairs office.'

'So, what's the next step?' DS Vaughan said. 'With the map, I mean?'

Beresford answered this one. 'A specialist search team is already on its way to the location marked with Paul Kellerman's name and the most recent date. We don't know how accurate the map is or how big an area we'll have to check over, but if there is a grave there I'm confident we'll find it. Meanwhile, I just spoke to the Chief Constable about the other locations on the map. He's arranging for small teams to visit each one to see what the areas are like. But it'll be kept low profile and no digging will take place until I give the go-ahead.'

15

It was in a quiet part of the forest south of the A35 and about five miles from Mason's house. Open heathland dominated the area, but there were also woods and a small lake.

Paul Kellerman's name, along with the tiny cross, had been scrawled on Mason's map just above the lake and slightly to the left of a small parking area.

A couple of walking trails led away from the parking area. One went into a wood of silver birch and beech trees, and the other cut through a jungle of tall yellow-flowered gorse bushes.

By the time Temple arrived in the middle of the afternoon, the search was well underway. Strimmers had been used to clear some of the scrub and foliage. They were employing cadaver dogs and the latest ground-penetrating radar equipment to try to locate a grave. Success in finding a body would depend on how deep it was buried.

The parking area was crammed with vehicles and Temple knew the media would soon get wind of what was going on. Then the hordes of reporters, photographers and TV camera crews would descend.

The activity around Mason's house had already prompted a call from the local newspaper, which had been tipped off by someone in the village. If it turned out that Grant Mason had been a serial killer, then it would ignite interest around the world.

Temple was already feeling the pressure of an inquiry that was growing by the minute. His team were working flat-out. Fiona Marsh had gone back to the office to coordinate things from there and DC Derek Whelan had been left in charge at the house. Vaughan was with Temple as they waited to see if the search teams would make a grim discovery.

Fortunately for everyone, the day was mild and dry and the sun was making the occasional appearance through the cloud cover.

Temple called Hilary Dyer and told her about his encounter with the burglar, but not about what was found in Mason's house. She was shocked and said that she remembered locking the door after her visit to the house yesterday morning.

'Who else would have a key?' he asked her.

'I really wouldn't know,' she said. 'I didn't have one. In fact, yesterday was the first time I'd ever been in the house by myself. Tom Fowler might, I suppose, or Noah Cross perhaps.'

'Who's Noah Cross?'

'Another of Grant's friends. They played golf and drank together. He lives with his twin sister Amanda in East Boldre.'

'Do you have his number?'

'I've got his contact details on file, but it'll also be on Grant's phone.'

'Do you know where his phone is?'

'I have it here with me along with his wallet and personal stuff. The hospital put it all in a bag.'

'I'm going to arrange for someone to pick them up,' he said. 'Meanwhile I'd rather you didn't speak to anyone about any of this, especially the media.'

'What is it you're not telling me, Jeff?' she said. 'Did you find something at the house?'

'I'll come and see you a bit later, Hilary,' he said. 'We can talk then. And I'll want you to tell me everything you know about Grant Mason.'

'Of course, but it's really not much. We didn't socialize and only ever discussed his work.'

Temple asked her about Mason's laptop and she said it should have been on the desk in his office. He hadn't taken it with him to the book signing.

'Did you know he had an office in his loft?' he asked her.

'No, I didn't,' she replied. 'But then why would he? He worked in the study down-stairs.'

Temple told her to make a note of everything she knew about Mason, including a list of his friends and contacts.

'I'll drop by as soon as I can,' he said, before ending the call.

As Temple pocketed his phone, Vaughan handed him a steaming coffee in a Styrofoam cup.

'The van's just arrived with some sand-wiches, guv,' Vaughan said. 'D'you want me to get you one?'

Temple sipped his coffee and grimaced as it burned his tongue.

'I'm not hungry, thanks,' he said.

'Me neither. But then I don't suppose anyone here has got much of an appetite right now.'

'It's an unpleasant business,' Temple said.

Vaughan nodded. 'This Mason bloke must have been some piece of work. What he got up to was fucking sick.'

'And the scary thing is there are a lot more like him out there.'

'Too right there are,' Vaughan said. 'That's why I never want kids. I just don't think it's fair to bring a new life into this fucked up world.'

Temple immediately thought about Angel and the fact that she was pregnant with his child. In all the excitement he'd pushed it to the back of his mind. And he was too pre-occupied now to dwell on it. But Vaughan's comment caused a knot to form at the back of his throat because he found it hard not to agree with the sentiment.

The world was indeed fucked up. It was also cruel and corrupt and crowded. What sane person would want to throw another baby into the mix?

*   *   *

They had an unexpected result after only three hours. A GPR machine was sending short pulses of high-frequency radio waves into the ground close to the stump of a felled oak tree. Suddenly the receiver picked up returning pulses — an indication that there was an object below the surface.

The spot was in the woods about forty yards off the walking trail. The ground was covered with leaves and broken branches. When the cadaver dogs were called over they got excited, which was a cue to start digging.

Dusk was fast approaching by this time, so high-powered spotlights were set up and forensic technicians were summoned.

The GPR operator estimated that the object was about three feet beneath the ground, so it didn't take long for two men with shovels to reach it. A shout went up when one of the men spotted something in the soil. It was part of a black plastic bin bag.

Temple hunkered down next to the ditch as the earth was carefully removed and more of the bag was revealed. It was no longer intact and the body inside it was soon exposed.

The sick, rancid odour of decomposed flesh suddenly filled the air, and Temple found himself staring down at a face that had been half-eaten away by insects.

This was the third time in his many years on the force that he'd witnessed a clandestine grave being uncovered. But that didn't make it any easier to take in. He stood up and felt a rush of bile in his throat.

After two months in the ground the body was in a bad way, but it hadn't been completely reduced to a skeleton. It appeared it had been wrapped in several bin liners and bonded with tape. This had held back the rate of decomposition. There was still some decaying flesh on what they could see of the naked torso, and dark strands of hair clung to the skull.

'Looks like a young man to me,' Vaughan said.

Temple thought so too. 'We'd better get the pathologist here right away.'

He left it to the forensic team and walked away from the grave with the blood beating in his ears. He'd been hoping that they would be proved wrong about Mason's map. But now there was every reason to believe that another fourteen bodies were buried in the forest.

When he reached the parking area, Temple called Beresford and gave him the news. The Chief Super was in a meeting with the Chief Constable.

'Is it the body of the missing student?' Beresford asked.

'We won't know that for a while, but I'm pretty sure it is,' Temple said.

'Then we have no choice but to go public with this, Jeff. There's already a TV crew at Mason's house and the papers are pestering us for information.'

Beresford asked Temple to keep him informed, and said he would talk to the Chief Constable about cancelling all leave and assigning an army of officers to the case.

'I've got a feeling that Grant Mason is about to become as notorious as Fred West,' Beresford said. 'And that means the eyes of the world will be watching to see how we handle it.'

Temple knew what it was like to be at the

centre of a media storm. The last time he experienced it was when the sniper was shooting at motorway traffic. He feared that the pressure this time round would be even more intense. The nature of the crimes would have a chilling effect on the public. As did those murders committed by Fred West and his wife Rose between 1967 and 1987.

West was a sexually depraved killer who murdered at least eleven girls and women, including members of his own family. He, like Mason, filmed himself raping and torturing his victims. He then buried them in his garden and in fields around his homes in Gloucester.

Grant Mason might have murdered more people than West and if he hadn't suddenly died of a heart attack, God only knew how many victims he would have claimed.

'You want a ciggy, guv?' Vaughan said as he stepped up beside him.

Temple had officially given up the weed a year ago, but he occasionally had a smoke in stressful situations and Vaughan was well aware of that.

Temple was about to succumb again when his mobile buzzed. He took it from his pocket and saw the call was from DC Marsh.

'I was going to ring you,' he said. 'We just found a body. And it's probably that of the student Paul Kellerman.'

He heard Marsh mumble an expletive.

'I've got more bad news for you, boss,' she said. 'It's why I'm calling.'

'Then fire away.'

'We've been trawling through the stuff on Mason's computer,' she said. 'And we came across photos and some video clips that were a bit of a shock.'

'Why?'

Marsh cleared her throat. 'Well, they provide conclusive proof that Grant Mason wasn't doing what he did by himself — the bastard had an accomplice.'

16

As always, it came upon him suddenly, an animal lust that needed sating.

He had never been able to control it, except during those years in prison when he'd been forced to satisfy his cravings with memories and fantasies. But being free again meant that he could respond when the familiar desire stirred inside him. And that's exactly what he intended to do now.

All day he'd been in a state of high anxiety, wondering what, if anything, the police had found in Grant Mason's house. It had played on his mind to such an extent that he hadn't thought about anything else.

But now he could enjoy a brief respite thanks to those ever dependable demons in his head. It was as though they knew he needed a distraction, a release from the turmoil that was raging inside him.

His heart started to pound at the prospect of what he was going to do. And as he got up from the sofa and switched off the television, his excitement was already at fever pitch.

He bounded up the stairs to his bedroom and stripped off all his clothes. Then he studied his reflection in the mirrored door on the wardrobe.

He was pleased with what he saw. The narrow waist and hard, flat stomach. The sharp, delicate nose and full lips. The soft features and supple skin. The huge, pink-tipped penis that was already standing to attention.

Not bad, he thought, for a man in his mid-forties who ate all the wrong food and no longer worked out.

He went back downstairs, turned off all the lights in the house and then opened the concealed door in the hall that led to the basement. He stepped inside, pulling the door shut behind him.

The darkness enveloped him like a heavy cloak and a jolt of pure electricity pulsed through his veins. He held his breath and listened to the whispered voices below. The sound was something to savour and it suffused him with a giddy feeling of power and total control.

They knew he was back, and he was sure that he could smell their fear; it hung in the air like sweet perfume.

He waited thirty seconds before switching on the light. A single naked bulb on the ceiling filled the basement with a warm orange glow.

The temperature was the same as in the

rest of the house — a comfortable twenty-two degrees day and night. That was so his playthings wouldn't get cold. He didn't like it when their flesh was covered in goose bumps.

He reached the bottom of the short staircase and surveyed the scene before him. The basement was forty feet long by twenty feet wide. It was one of the features that had convinced him to buy the house. The other was the fact that the property had been considerably run-down and therefore dirt cheap.

There was a cement floor and blank walls on which were displayed all kinds of sexual paraphernalia. An array of whips, canes and riding crops hung from brass hooks. Chains with leather bracelets hung from the ceiling and walls. Shelves were filled with butt plugs, handcuffs, bondage tape, ball gags, coloured ropes and various other devices for inflicting both pleasure and pain. Grant, who had helped him to purchase and then set up all the equipment, had always referred to it as the dungeon.

The centre of the room was taken up by two single beds and a wooden dining table with three chairs. Next to the beds were two chemical toilets of the kind used by campers. In one corner, a tripod for use when taping the action.

His latest playthings occupied the beds and

had done so since being brought here six days ago. The beds were screwed to the floor so they couldn't be moved. His playthings were cuffed to the beds so they couldn't escape.

It was the perfect set-up. Clean, virtually soundproof, extremely intimidating. A great place for letting the imagination run riot.

'Please . . . let us go.'

It was the woman, whimpering as usual. Hadn't she realized by now that begging turned him on?

She was sitting up in the bed, clutching the blanket tightly around her shoulders. She stared at him pleadingly through one eye — the other was still bruised and swollen from the beating inflicted by Grant on Monday when he got carried away.

Her name was Rose Hamilton and she'd been a good catch. Just the right amount of flesh on her bones. A bubble-shaped butt and firm breasts with huge, round nipples. And when she cried she sounded like a child, which really got his juices flowing.

Her husband, Bob, was also sitting up with the blanket pulled around his shoulders. The beds were eight feet apart so he couldn't touch his wife. The studded leather straps attached to his left wrist and left ankle restricted his movements. When they first started bringing their playthings here, they secured all their limbs so they could barely move. But after a while they saw the sense in letting them feed themselves and turn on their sides to sleep. They made a lot less fuss that way.

He walked straight over to Rose's bed, grabbed the blanket and pulled it away from her.

'Oh, dear God, no,' she cried out.

He stared at her naked body and the many bruises. Then he smiled, his lips becoming thin and bloodless. She froze as he reached out and ran fingers through her thick, lustrous hair.

'Please leave her alone,' her husband said, his voice heavy and strained.

He turned to Bob Hamilton, whose eyes were glazed and haunted. It looked as though he was still in a state of shock from Tuesday night when he and Grant had taken turns to rape him. He'd cried like a baby and at one point had actually fainted.

'I want you to shut up and watch,' he told him. 'If you turn away or close your eyes I'll beat the crap out of her. You got that?'

Tears gleamed in Bob's eyes and he moved his head slightly.

'Just be grateful that I'm by myself and only in the mood for pussy,' he said.

The couple knew by now not to scream or

shout, that resistance was futile. Their spirits had been broken and the sedatives he'd been putting in their drinks and food ensured they remained subdued and compliant.

They were no longer the happy-go-lucky couple who had driven into the Knightwood Oak car park on Saturday. He recalled how they had been so busy chatting and laughing that they'd paid no attention to the white transit van that was already parked there. Or to him and Grant when they got out and followed them along the path to the tree. The couple hadn't felt threatened by another pair of sightseers and had even smiled a greeting as they took photographs around the tree. He and Grant had walked behind them back to the still-deserted car park and it was Grant who had nailed Bob with the stun gun. A second later he'd pounced on an unsuspecting Rose. Four minutes later the couple were bound and gagged in the back of the van.

Now the pair were shadows of their former selves, damaged beyond repair. He would no doubt be doing them a favour when he eventually killed them.

He returned his attention to Rose. She was shaking now and biting her bottom lip so hard it was bleeding.

'Just relax,' he said. 'You might even enjoy it this time. I know I will.'

17

Temple left the grave site at seven in the evening. He was tired and hungry and his headache had returned with a vengeance.

The news that Mason had worked with an accomplice had come as a shock to everyone. According to DC Marsh, a man wearing a sinister black leather head mask appeared in a video clip and several photographs on Mason's computer hard drive. In the clip, both the man and Mason were seen raping an unidentified woman on a single bed.

Temple wondered if he was the same man he had encountered at Mason's house the previous night. Maybe the man had gone there in search of the incriminating material in the loft. But if so, why hadn't he taken it? Could it be that he hadn't thought to check up there?

The existence of an accomplice ramped up the investigation — and the pressure. But the more Temple thought about it, the more sense it made. Abducting, imprisoning and then burying fifteen people in the forest would be an immense task for an individual. It'd be so much easier for two people working together. Two sexual predators on a mission to abuse and murder innocent people for their own gratification.

Mason and his accomplice had probably felt that they were bullet-proof — that no one was going to stop them doing what they wanted.

He wondered how long the pair had been partners-in-crime. Was it two years? Or did it go further back to before Mason started putting names and dates on a map?

Temple knew he couldn't go another night without sleep, despite the startling new developments. There was only so long he could keep going on coffee and adrenaline. When he was younger, he never had a problem staying awake while remaining alert. But these days he needed to re-charge his batteries to stop his mind and body from shutting down.

He dropped in on Hilary Dyer on his way home. She was expecting him and desperate to know what had been happening.

'I've been watching the news,' she said. 'They're saying there's a major search going on in and around Grant's house.'

It looked to Temple as though she hadn't slept either. Her bloodshot eyes nestled in tired grey folds of skin.

'Sit down, Hilary,' he said. 'I'll bring you up to date and then I need to ask you some questions.'

She listened in stunned silence as he told

her what they'd found in Mason's loft. He gave her all the details, leaving nothing out.

She broke down when he told her they had discovered a body in a shallow grave. The tears were pushed out by huge, racking sobs. She was so distraught that she couldn't speak for several minutes, so he made her a cup of tea and put his arm around her shoulders as she cupped it in her hands.

'I really had no idea,' she said between sobs. 'I can't believe it. Grant was always so nice to me. I didn't think he had a bad bone in his body. I feel awful because I didn't know what was going on for all those years.'

'You can't blame yourself,' Temple said. 'People like Grant Mason are experts when it comes to covering up their sordid secrets — even from the people who are closest to them. Besides, you didn't live with him or socialise with him. So I expect he never let his guard down when you were around.'

'Most of the contact between us was by email,' she said. 'I only went to his house about once every two weeks when he was writing or researching one of his books.'

She started to sob again, and her face seemed to fold in on itself.

Temple waited for her to calm down and said, 'Have you any idea where he might have taken his victims? We're pretty sure it wasn't to his house.'

She pressed her lips together and shook her head. When she spoke her voice was husky with emotion. 'I can't imagine. I'm certain he didn't have another property. Or if he did he never said.'

'Did he have any women friends?'

'Not that I know of. He knew Amanda Cross of course, Noah Cross's sister, but I've never known him to be in a relationship or even date.'

'So what about this accomplice?' Temple said. 'The man in the head mask.'

Hilary grimaced and her voice started to quiver. 'I don't know. I've met a few of his friends but I can't believe any of them would have been involved.'

'Tell me about the guy who was here yesterday. Tom Fowler.'

She covered her mouth with her hand and spoke through her fingers.

'Are you saying it could be Tom?'

'No, but he's a suspect like everyone else at this stage. How close was he to Mason?'

'It's hard to tell. I know they went drinking together, but I've only met him a couple of times. He seems decent enough.'

'So why did he come here yesterday?'

'He heard about Grant and decided to

drop in on his way home from work to see how I was.'

'Were you surprised?'

'A bit. I didn't expect to see him, but I was grateful nonetheless. I needed someone to talk to.'

'Did you tell him that Mason wanted you to burn down his house?'

'No. I didn't tell anyone before I told you.'

'So how did he and Mason meet?'

'At the pub, I think. The one just outside East Boldre.'

'You mean the Court Jester?'

'That's right. A few years ago, some of the regulars there formed a ramblers' group and Grant was made honorary chairman. He organized walks with them, mostly during the summer months.'

'And Fowler's a member of this group?'

'That's right. He was actually the one who got it started.'

'What does he do for a living?'

'He's an estate agent in Brockenhurst.'

'So he knows the area well then?'

'Like the back of his hand, I suppose.'

Temple started making notes on his pad. He decided that Tom Fowler would go to the top of the list of people he needed to interview.

'Do you know any other members of the group?' he asked.

'Only Noah Cross.'

'Does he know what's happened to Mason?'

'His sister called here yesterday to see how I was so I assume he does.'

'I'll need the phone numbers and addresses for all Mason's acquaintances.'

'Of course. But the numbers will be on Grant's phone which one of your officers picked up about an hour ago, along with his wallet.'

Temple glanced at his watch. 'Look, I'd better go. If you can think of anybody else I should talk to about Mason, then let me know.'

'I will. And will you please keep me informed of what progress you make?'

He said he would and then asked if there was anyone she could go and stay with while the media storm raged.

'The press will be clamouring for information on Mason,' he said. 'It won't be long before they're beating a path to your door.'

'I suppose I could stay with my sister in Portsmouth.'

'That's a good idea, Hilary. I suggest you go first thing in the morning before the vultures descend. In the meantime, if you're worried about anything, then don't hesitate to call me.'

'Thanks, Jeff. I appreciate it.'

'No problem. Are you going to be all right here tonight?'

She wiped her eyes and gave a small, tight smile. 'I'll be fine. Honest. I'll probably cry myself to sleep.'

Temple's heart went out to her and he felt guilty for leaving her by herself. But he was dog-tired and anxious to get home to Angel.

18

He spent forty-five minutes in the basement. When he left, Rose Hamilton was face-down, sobbing into the pillow.

There was blood on the white plastic sheet that covered the mattress. It was from all the probing he'd done with the various toys in the dungeon.

Her husband sat on the bed watching her, his face and body tense with impotent rage.

Back upstairs, he took a shower and put on his dressing gown. Then he went into the living room and poured himself a large brandy. He needed it now that he was forced to think again about Grant's death and the possible consequences.

It was bad enough that their highly successful partnership was over. They had made such a good team and had managed to remain undetected for over two years.

But without Grant it was going to be much harder to seize his victims. And harder still to dispose of them. They had talked about getting rid of the Hamiltons in a few days and had been planning to dig their grave on Saturday night. Now he would have to do it by himself and it wasn't going to be easy. In fact, it was going to be a real struggle hauling two dead weights in and out of the van and through the woods to the spot they had chosen as the couple's final resting place.

With Grant helping him, it had been no problem at all. They had got it down to a fine art and had never strayed from the well-established routine. First snatch the victims in a forest parking area when there was nobody else around. If they had a vehicle then Grant would drive it to another place — usually near their victims' homes — and he would follow in the van to pick Grant up. They had always been mindful of traffic and CCTV cameras and went to great lengths to avoid them.

They had then played with their victims until they grew bored with them, at which point they would take it in turns to strangle them with electrical cable before burying them.

But from now on, things would never be the same. Entrapping his playthings was going to be much more difficult in the future.

But right now that might well be the least of his worries.

He still hadn't figured out why the detective turned up at Grant's house last night. And why a police forensic team was there now in force.

What the hell were they looking for? Did Grant blab before he died? Or had someone discovered his collection of photographs and 'trophies'?

Before the cop arrived unexpectedly, he had searched most of the house thoroughly. But he hadn't found Grant's photos, or the camcorder, or the stun gun. Or even the stuff Grant had taken from their playthings. So where the fuck had he hidden them?

All Grant had ever said was that they were in a safe place. He had never been more forthcoming.

There were only two places he didn't get to search last night — the garage and the loft. In his panic to flee the scene he'd simply forgotten. And it was too late now. The police would have been through every inch of the house. But if they found Grant's stuff, then how much would it tell them?

The photos and videos and other objects would lead them to believe that Grant had been a sexual deviant and perhaps a murderer. But they wouldn't reveal the existence of all the bodies or where they were buried.

Still, he was going to have to be careful and alert because one thing was certain. It was only a matter of time before the police came knocking on his door.

19

By the time Temple got home he was groggy with fatigue. His eyes felt sore and heavy, and his stomach was growling from hunger.

Angel was waiting up for him with a plate of ham sandwiches and a glass of white wine. They sat at the breakfast bar and he told her about his day and how the shocking events had unfolded.

She listened patiently while sipping hot chocolate from her favourite mug. But it quickly became obvious to Temple that she wasn't hanging on to his every word, and he felt a frisson of guilt.

'I'm sorry for going on,' he said. 'You know what it's like. Difficult to switch off.'

Angel put down her mug and licked chocolate from her upper lip.

'It's OK,' she said. 'I want to hear about it. It's just that I'm surprised you didn't call me during the day to let me know what was happening. And to see how I was.'

She shifted her gaze away from him and stared off into the middle distance. He sensed straight off that something was wrong. She was pissed with him.

'I've been on the go all day,' he said lamely. 'I've had no time to stop and take a breath.'

She raised one shoulder in a shrug. 'So since leaving the house this morning you haven't given a single thought to me being pregnant.'

'Of course I have.'

'Then surely you could have found sixty seconds to ring me, if only for reassurance.'

He frowned. 'What do you mean by that?'

She looked at him squarely, a truculent gleam in her eyes.

'You still don't understand, do you, Jeff? What's happened to me — to us — constitutes a seismic shift in our relationship. I need to know that it's OK with you. That you want me to have this baby even though it wasn't planned and you always said you didn't want more children. Plus, didn't it occur to you that I might have been worried about you? Last night you took a beating and had to go to the hospital. You didn't sleep at all. And you weren't in a fit state to go to work. You should have let me know that you were all right.'

She was crushing tears with her eyelids and he thought she was going to lose it completely. But she held it in by taking some deep shuddering breaths that made her face go red.

He reached for her hand across the breakfast bar, but she pulled it away.

He started to fumble for words. 'I'm really sorry. It was insensitive of me. I should have called you.'

She wiped her runny nose with the back of her hand and shook her head again.

'Don't patronize me, Jeff. I can tell you don't really mean it. You think I'm overreacting because my hormones have gone berserk.'

He was suddenly beset by a stream of conflicting emotions. Of course he could see her point and he knew from bitter experience that raging hormones during pregnancy can make a woman behave out of character. But at the same time he felt that she was being a trifle unfair. What had happened today was not only unusual; it was bloody mind-blowing. So surely she should appreciate that he'd been fully focused on the horrific events. After all, she was still a police officer. And that didn't change just because she was pregnant.

He kept these thoughts to himself, though, and tried again to placate her.

'Look, this is really nothing more than bad timing,' he said. 'The news you gave me last night was a shock and I've not had time to digest it. And then this thing with Mason has totally thrown me. It's big, Angel, really big, and it's been hard for me to concentrate on anything else.'

She reached for the kitchen roll and tore off a sheet to dab at her eyes.

'I still think you should have called me, Jeff. I've been tearing my hair out wondering what you're thinking. I don't know if you're happy for me to have this baby or you want me to have an abortion.'

He tried again to take her hand and this time she let him. He gave it a gentle squeeze.

'But I told you this morning that if you want to keep it then that's fine with me.'

'And is that supposed to comfort me, Jeff? Christ, I need more than that. I need to know that you're not angry. That you really will embrace the idea of starting another family. Or if you think it's a bad idea and that I've let you down.'

Should he be honest with her? Totally honest? Tell her that despite what he said this morning he wasn't really sure?

'So come on, Jeff,' she said. 'How do you really feel about this?'

He swallowed hard and tried to think through what he was going to say before he said it. He didn't want to get it wrong and upset her even more.

'I think we should talk it through properly,' he said. 'I mean, I don't get the impression that you're absolutely sure what to do yourself. And that doesn't surprise me since you've always been adamant that you didn't want children.'

'But isn't that what we're doing now? Talking about it. This is the first chance we've had since this morning.'

'I know that. But we're both tired and you're upset. We're not in the right frame of mind to have a sensible and rational conversation about something so serious. Something that will have an impact on the rest of our lives.'

She started to speak but then stopped herself. Her eyes brimmed with tears again and her mouth twitched at the corners.

Temple got down off his stool and stepped around the breakfast bar so that he could give her a cuddle. He was relieved that she let him, and he held her close as she sobbed into his shoulder.

He was tempted to tell her that they should have the baby and that everything would be all right. But he resisted because he knew it wouldn't be fair — or honest. They needed to discuss it when emotions weren't running so high. And when he wasn't so tired that he couldn't think straight.

'Why don't we go to bed?' he said. 'We both need some rest and we can talk about this when I get home tomorrow night.'

She lifted her head to look up at him. Her eyes were red-rimmed, raw.

'I'm sorry, Jeff. You're right. It's just that I feel so . . . so confused and alone.'

'Well, you're not alone. I'm with you now and I'll always be with you. Please get that into your thick skull.'

A faint smile hovered on her lips.

'That's the kind of thing I need to hear from you, Jeff. And not just when you want to shut me up.'

He felt a wave of guilt flow through him and he realized that he was going to have to get his thoughts together on the issue of a baby — even as he struggled to oversee what was shaping up to be the biggest and most gruesome investigation of his life.

20

The following morning, Temple was up and dressed before Angel awoke. He took her in a cup of tea and said he'd get home as early as possible so that they could talk about the pregnancy.

She looked at him through half-open eyes and managed a small smile.

'We both know that's wishful thinking, Jeff.'

He sat on the edge of the bed and leaned over to kiss her on the forehead.

'I promise I'll try,' he said.

'I know you will, but don't panic if you can't make it. I'll understand. I just got myself all worked up yesterday. I feel less hormonal today.'

'Everything will be fine. We just need to get our heads around it.'

'Promise me one thing, though, Jeff. Promise me that you'll be totally honest with me. I really don't want you to tell me something just because you think it's what I want to hear.'

'I promise,' he said. 'It's still early so why don't you go back to sleep. And try not to worry.'

The new day was draped in billowy white clouds. According to the weather forecast, the sun was going to make an appearance during the afternoon.

As he drove across town, he had to make a conscious effort to push Angel's pregnancy from his mind. There would be time later to agonize over the implications. Besides, he didn't want to face up to the awful truth that if he was to be totally honest with her, it might well break her heart.

The radio news provided a distraction. The discovery of the body was the lead story on the BBC national bulletin. What's more, they were quoting an anonymous source as saying that as many as fourteen other bodies might be buried in the forest. They were even linking the investigation to Grant Mason and the disappearance of the Hamiltons.

Temple was angry that some twat had leaked the information, but he wasn't entirely surprised. The more people who knew about something the harder it was to keep a lid on it. And by now plenty of police officers and civilian support staff knew what was going on.

There was no way of avoiding a media circus. The search for graves was going to be headline news around the world, even if they didn't find any more bodies. But Temple was convinced that they would. Mason's map surely couldn't be anything other than a vile scoreboard; something for him to gloat over and feel proud of.

It wasn't unknown for serial killers to keep a record of their murderous rampages. Temple knew of at least two in the US who had kept scrapbooks filled with information on their victims, including newspaper cuttings and written descriptions of what they'd done to their victims and where they'd buried them.

One notorious killer in Germany had kept a detailed record of his eighteen kills in a two-year diary which police found when they raided his home. It led them to all of the bodies. In court, the man claimed that he got a thrill out of looking back over what he'd done because it brought back fond memories.

Temple wondered if Mason's accomplice had known about the map. He would certainly have known about the photos and video footage. But the map might well have been something that Mason kept to himself. His own sordid little secret. Perhaps he had just wanted to make sure that he didn't forget where his victims were buried, so that he could visit their graves during hikes.

Temple stopped off at a Tesco Express to buy a couple of newspapers. The tabloids were all leading with the story and the late editions were saying that the search for more bodies would begin today. The editors had had a field day with the headlines.

Horror in the Forest.
How many bodies are there?
Corpse found at forest beauty spot.

Gone were the days when news took time to filter through, Temple thought. Now the media got wind of things instantly via text, Twitter, mobile phone and email. And digital technology enabled papers and TV channels to process the stories in a fraction of the time it used to take.

It meant that for the police working a high-profile case, the pressure was relentless. Every development, every scrap of new information, was seized upon in order to satisfy the insatiable appetite of twenty-four hour news.

★   ★   ★

The MIT office was now a major incident room. When Temple arrived he was surprised to see how many people had beaten him in. They were bustling this way and that as phones rang and keyboards clattered.

141

There were half-empty coffee mugs every-where, overflowing wastepaper bins, tons of paper on the desks along with empty pizza boxes.

He hadn't seen the place so full and frenetic since the sniper attacks on the motorways, which had galvanized the whole force into action.

More whiteboards had been set up and Grant Mason's map had pride of place in the middle, between photos of the first uncovered grave and those of Bob and Rosemary Hamilton. Another whiteboard contained a list of the names from the map with photos and details of when those people went missing.

There was a bunch of post-it notes on his desk with various messages, but before he had time to go through them, Dave Vaughan came into his office. The DS had managed to shave but still looked rough. His tie hung loose and his shirt looked as though it hadn't been ironed.

'Have you seen the papers, boss?'

Temple nodded. 'Any idea who's been spouting off?'

'Negative, but it was bound to happen on a case this big.'

Temple looked at his watch. Seven thirty.

'Spread the word that there'll be a briefing

at nine,' he said. 'But first give me an update.'

Vaughan remained standing and read from his notes.

'Beresford gave the go-ahead last night for full-blown searches to start this morning at two more potential grave sites.'

'Were the locations picked at random?'

'No. We're going to base the search pattern on the dates Mason put against the names on his map so that we can uncover the most recent ones first. The pathologist is pretty certain that Paul Kellerman was buried two months ago in December. It tallies with the date next to his name. The date before that is 23rd September. The two names against it are Simon and Jane Cramer.'

'What do we know about them?'

'We're assuming they're a married couple from London who disappeared while on a touring holiday along the south coast. Their car was found in Winchester so no one suspected that they might have vanished in the forest.'

'Where's the location on the map?'

'Just outside the village of Burley. A pretty remote spot by all accounts.'

'What about the other location?'

'A patch of woodland to the west of Godshill. The date against it on the map is 1st August. The name is Angeline Bedel. It matches the name of a 22-year-old foreign exchange student from France. Angeline was staying with a family in Brighton and left there on 26th July to hitchhike around the country for the summer before returning home. When she failed to contact her parents in Lyon, the alarm was raised. Sussex police found that she stayed in a youth hostel in Chichester on the night of 29th July, but there was no sign of her after that.'

'So she might have been exploring the forest when Mason and his accomplice snatched her.'

'That's possible, boss.'

'OK. What else have we got?'

'The post-mortem on Paul Kellerman is scheduled for later this morning and the techies are still sifting through the spoil from his grave,' Vaughan said. 'But we'll be lucky if the body or the grave yield much forensic evidence after so long.'

'Anything more from Mason's house?'

'Recovered prints are still being processed and we'll get an update at the briefing. As you know, we picked up Mason's phone and wallet from your friend, Hilary. We'll soon have a typed-up list of all his contacts, calls and text messages sent and received. But I can tell you now that there are no suspicious texts.'

'What about his computer?'

'I'm told it's full of porno videos and images. Some of the stuff is clearly of his own making and there's a lot of extreme material from web sites and file-sharing networks.'

'I'd like to see the clips that include his accomplice.'

'I thought you might. I asked Fiona to have them cued up on her computer.'

'So Marsh is in as well, is she?'

'She was in before me,' Vaughan said. 'She couldn't sleep.'

Temple got up and followed Vaughan over to Marsh's workstation. She looked up at them, her mouth working hard at a piece of gum. Chewing was something she often did to stop herself going outside for a smoke.

'Morning, Fiona,' he said. 'Everything OK?'

'It would be if I didn't have to look at this filth,' she said.

'That bad, eh?'

'Worse than you can imagine.'

And she was right, Temple quickly discovered. There were three video sequences featuring a man who was naked except for a black head mask. In two of them, he and Grant Mason were taking turns to rape a young woman who was strapped to a bed. She'd been identified as a German tourist named Lena Klein who disappeared two years ago after holidaying alone in Southern England. In the third clip, the man in the mask was filmed whipping the backsides of a young couple who were hanging by chains from a ceiling. Mason could be heard out of shot egging him on and laughing. The couple screamed and cried for several minutes before they became too weak to even respond to the beating.

'We believe the couple are Sonia Jordan and Tim Leonard, from Dorchester,' Marsh explained. 'Boy and girlfriend. Disappeared seventeen months ago while visiting friends in Lyndhurst.'

Temple got Marsh to freeze-frame Mason's accomplice. The guy was of average height — maybe five foot eight — and looked fit. Lean body, narrow waist, a six or seven inch penis that was fully erect in every shot. But they couldn't see his face or his hair and there was no way of telling if he was the same man who had ransacked Mason's house.

'Any clues as to where this might be taking place?' Temple said.

Marsh shook her head. 'It could be anywhere. But I reckon it's a garage or a basement. We know this isn't Mason's garage because it's been checked and there's no basement in his house. On these shots the walls are grey and plain except for the stuff hanging from them. There's a table in a lot of the shots and two single beds. No windows or doors can be seen.'

'It looks like a purpose-built torture chamber to me,' Vaughan said. 'A regular chamber of horrors.'

These words made the hairs on Temple's neck quiver. It never ceased to amaze him what terrible things humans were prepared to do to each other.

'I can't help thinking that Bob and Rosemary Hamilton are there right now,' Marsh said. 'And Christ only knows what unspeakable things are being done to them.'

21

This morning it was a violent rage that drove him down to the basement even before he'd had breakfast.

The television news had caused his blood to boil and his heart to thud against his rib cage. He needed to vent his anger and there was no better way to do that than on his playthings.

As a child, he frequently unleashed his temper on the household pets. The dog and the cat that his parents had treated better than they'd treated him.

But with animals it was never enough, even when he broke their bones and drew blood. That was because he couldn't see the pain and humiliation in their pathetic faces. Their expressions never changed. But with humans it was different. Their suffering was reflected in their distorted features and the tears that spilled from their eyes.

And the tears were positively gushing from Rosemary Hamilton's eyes as she begged him not to touch her again. As he stared down at her, he was oblivious to her husband's desperate pleas. All he could think about was the agony he had just caused her. The pure, mouth-watering, beautiful agony.

It was just a shame that she wasn't Grant fucking Mason. That stupid moron had obviously given the game away. How else would the police have known where they had buried the student from Bournemouth? And according to the news, the cops believed there were up to nine other graves in the forest.

It was a catastrophe and one he should have seen coming. How many times had he warned Grant about the trophies he insisted on keeping? Plus all the photos and video clips.

Grant had always said it was all as safe as the Crown Jewels. But that would only have been true while he was alive. His sudden death had changed things by leaving all his worldly possessions unprotected.

He wondered if Hilary Dyer had stumbled on her boss's dark secrets and had alerted the police. Or perhaps Grant had told her something incriminating before he died.

But what did it matter now how the cops had found out? What mattered was whether they'd be able to establish a link between him and the victims. He had always been the most careful. He'd made sure he'd always worn the mask whenever his partner used the camcorder or took photos. And he had never touched the vehicles belonging to the victims without wearing gloves.

But he was bound to have made some mistakes during their two and a bit year reign. And he couldn't be sure that they wouldn't come back to haunt him.

'Dear God . . . please . . . no more.'

Rosemary Hamilton's voice seized his attention again. Her eyes were closed and she was gritting her teeth.

A memory flashed in his head of the first girl he had ever attacked. Her name was Shelley Prior and she'd been thirteen, just a year younger than he was.

They were in the park after school and she'd just given him a blowjob. But it hadn't been enough. He'd felt an uncontrollable urge to hurt her. And so he had slapped and punched her repeatedly before raping her.

After that he'd . . .

'Please . . . go away.'

Rosemary Hamilton's voice brought him back to the here and now. He re-focused on her face and drank in the sheer terror that was etched into her features.

Her eyes snapped open and she stared up at him through her tears. But then she turned her head and looked across the room at her husband who could no longer bear to watch. The man had covered his face with his hands and was sobbing pitifully.

He switched his gaze between husband and wife, and a wave of unbridled pleasure swept through him. He realized that he was really going to miss this couple. They ranked high among all the playthings who'd been brought to the dungeon. Their innocence and their vulnerability was as much a turn on as their pale, smooth bodies. And the love they clearly had for each other had served to fan the flames of desire.

But it was time for them to go. They'd served their purpose and keeping them any longer would be a risk and one he wasn't prepared to take.

So today he would turn his thoughts to how he was going to dispose of them without Grant's help and with the cops swarming all over the forest.

22

Chief Superintendent Beresford came down for the 9 a.m. briefing. He kick-started it with an ominous warning to whoever had leaked information to the press.

'On an investigation like this, I know it's going to be tempting,' he said. 'The press in particular will be throwing money around like confetti. But I swear that if I catch any member of this team feeding the vultures I'll come down on them hard. Is that understood?'

There was a lot of murmuring and nodding of heads. No one present doubted that Beresford meant what he said. The Chief Super had a strong physical presence in the room and a reputation for being fair but firm. That was partly why he had risen so quickly through the ranks.

'We haven't got time to dwell on this issue right now so let's get on with business,' he said. 'First, though, I want you to know that we need to pull together on this case. It's going to put an enormous strain on each and everyone of us. Not only do we face the awful prospect of uncovering more graves — but there's a serial killer out there who may be about to murder two more people if he hasn't done so already. All leave has therefore been cancelled and more officers are being assigned to MIT. I've also lifted restrictions on overtime, so be prepared to work long hours and don't expect this case to be over any time soon.'

Beresford went on to say that teams had been sent to two of the locations marked on Mason's map. Once again, cadaver dogs and ground penetrating radar would be used to search for corpses, and mechanical diggers would be brought in if required.

Beresford then handed over to Temple, who asked an officer named Porter from forensics to provide an update. Porter confirmed that the body in the grave had been identified from dental records as Paul Kellerman, the Bournemouth student. The post-mortem would soon be underway and hopefully that would establish how he'd died. Tests were still being carried out on the grave itself and the ground around it, but after so long the odds on find-ing any vital clues were slim.

'So what's the latest on forensics at Mason's house?' Temple asked.

'DC Whelan, as crime scene manager, has been liaising with Lee Finch,' Porter answered. 'I gather he'll be here shortly with a full report. There's been a delay because of queries in respect of fingerprints that were lifted from the property.'

'What kind of queries?'

The officer shrugged. 'I've not been told, sir.'

'Well, call DC Whelan now and tell him to hurry up,' Temple said. 'If they've come up with something odd, then I want to know what it is before the end of this meeting.'

Temple then relayed the conversation he'd had the previous night with Hilary Dyer.

'She told me she had no idea what Mason was up to,' he said. 'She didn't know about the hideaway in the loft or that he was into rough sex. And she hasn't a clue who his accomplice might be. But she did give me the names of two of Mason's male friends. There's Tom Fowler, a guy DC Marsh and I met. He started a ramblers' group at the local pub and Mason was made honorary chairman. The other guy is Noah Cross, who played golf and drank with Mason. He's also a member of the ramblers' group.

'I've got their contact details and I'll pay them a visit today. While I do that, DS Vaughan will distribute a list of the names from Mason's mobile phone contacts list. I want everyone of them spoken to. Plus, we need to check out all known sex offenders on the patch. Determine whether any of them are persons of interest to us.'

Temple then made it known that he'd asked two detectives to go along with uniform and break the news to Paul Kellerman's parents that their son's body had been found. They would also be on standby to make contact with other relatives if and when more bodies turned up.

'It's hard to imagine there could be so many more bodies out there,' Temple said. 'But we have to assume now that there are. Finding them is another matter and it's entirely dependent on how accurate Mason's map is. We can't be sure that all the crosses mark the exact spots.

'The evidence suggests that the victims were seized by Mason and his accomplice while they were visiting the forest. This happened on average every couple of months over the past two and a bit years. If the victims had cars, then it seems they were driven elsewhere so it wouldn't be obvious where they disappeared. That's why no connection emerged between those fifteen misper cases.

'The victims — and we're talking five couples and five individuals — were then taken to a place, probably in the forest, where they were systematically raped and tortured.

Some were kept for days and a few for weeks before they were killed and buried in shallow graves. We're onto them now simply because Mason died suddenly and was arrogant enough to have recorded the graves on a map, which was probably part of some sick desire to immortalize what he'd done.

'But the graves represent just one aspect of this investigation. Finding them is less important to us right now than finding the Hamiltons and Mason's accomplice. That's where we're going to focus our efforts.'

Temple then asked his officers to share the information they'd come up with yesterday. But to his disappointment there wasn't much to report. Nobody in East Boldre had seen a man with a rucksack the night before last. And no one had anything but kind words to say about Grant Mason. He'd been popular among drinkers in several local pubs, and had never given people the impression that he was anything other than a modest, quietly-spoken man who had devoted his life to writing about the New Forest.

'Most serial killers I've known come across as timid men who lead quiet lives,' Temple said. 'That's why no one ever suspects them and they get away with it for so long.'

'We have to dig deep into his background,' Beresford said. 'And we need to run down every single one of his friends and acquaintances. To that end we'll appeal for information at a press conference that's being arranged for this afternoon. The Chief Constable himself will be fronting it and it will be a good time to reveal that we know Mason had an accomplice.'

'Are we also going to release information about the map?' someone asked.

Beresford shook his head. 'Not at this stage.'

At that moment, DC Whelan arrived looking flushed and out of breath.

'Sorry I'm late,' he said. 'But we had to run some more checks on the fingerprints found at Mason's house. It was necessary to get the pathologist to send over more samples from Mason himself, just so that we could do some cross-referencing.'

'So is there a problem?' Temple asked.

Whelan raised his brow. 'Well, ninety per cent of the prints lifted from the house matched Mason's, which of course came as no surprise. But when we ran them through the database, they also showed up as a match with someone else.'

'How can that be?' Temple said.

'The prints on file belong to a man named Trevor Mason, who was jailed eleven years ago for a serious sexual offence in London.

No prize for guessing that his middle name was Grant.'

'Blimey,' Temple said. 'Trevor Grant Mason. The crafty sod.'

★ ★ ★

Having dropped his bombshell, DC Whelan revealed that Trevor Mason spent five years in prison.

'He was released just under six years ago,' he said. 'He then decided to drop his first name and use his middle name instead. That's about the time he started writing his hiking books. He also made some effort to change his appearance.' Whelan held up a computer memory stick. 'I've got Mason's file mugshot on here.'

Temple pursed his lips and let out a low, tuneless whistle.

Trevor Grant Mason.

Jesus.

It had been too bloody easy for the bastard to reinvent himself. No need to even change his name by deed poll. All he'd had to do was stop using his first name and have a makeover. That had enabled him to deceive his friends and his readers alike into believing he was someone he wasn't.

Whelan stepped up to the front of the

room, and plugged the device into the large flat screen smart TV monitor attached to the wall.

A few seconds later, a photo of a man appeared on the screen. He bore only a slight resemblance to the Grant Mason that Temple had known. In the photo he was much thinner and his hair was fair and shoulder length, instead of dark brown and short.

'So what can you tell us about him?' Temple asked.

Whelan consulted his notes. 'He was relatively new to this part of the world. He was born and raised in the Lake District, which was probably where he acquired his love for hiking. When he was fourteen, his father died. The family house burned down and the old man was in it. The boy moved to a new house with his mother but a year later, he was taken into care after attacking her with a hammer. She refused to press charges, but she wouldn't let him back into her home.'

'You can hardly blame her,' Vaughan quipped.

'He was convicted of his first offence at fifteen after he sexually assaulted a social worker,' Whelan went on. 'He spent a year in a young offenders' institution and then went off the radar after that for a number of years. He surfaced again while working as a tour guide for a hotel chain in Yorkshire. He organized walks across the Dales. But then he was accused of raping one of his clients. It went to court but he was cleared after saying the woman consented to sex. But he got the sack and moved to London.

'At the age of thirty-four, he was arrested again after a young male prostitute was badly beaten in a sleazy hotel where Mason took him to have sex. The boy was tortured and raped over a period of seven hours. DNA evidence led the Met right to Mason and he served five years of an eight year sentence.'

'What happened to him after that?' Temple asked.

'Well, according to his probation report, his mother died while he was in prison so he inherited her house,' Whelan said. 'On his release, he instructed lawyers to sell it and pocketed almost half a million quid. He used that to buy his place in the New Forest where he started writing books while preying on visitors to the area.'

'And he didn't mind if his victims were men or women,' Temple observed.

'That's because he was pan-sexual,' Whelan said. 'I got the Met to send me the file on him. It includes a short report from a forensic psychologist. Here's a quote.' Whelan opened his notebook and read from it. ''Mason acts on impulse and instant gratification. He's driven by his desires — be they emotional, physical or material. His sexual appetite is insatiable and voracious. Mason is pan-sexual — willing to have sex with any object, man, woman or child. He's not limited to gender-specific preferences, nor does he achieve long-term feelings of fulfilment. He enjoys inflicting pain and it's my considered opinion that he would achieve maximum pleasure from taking a life.''

It was a stark and accurate assessment of the man and it prompted a lot of excited chatter in the room.

Temple told the team he wanted them to talk to everyone who had known Mason — including officers who worked on his cases and those who got acquainted with him in prison.

Among other things he wanted to know was how Mason had managed to fit in with the normal flow of life, even though he was profoundly abnormal.

'I'm betting that along the way he met a like-minded soul who shared his passion for perversion,' Temple said. 'They decided to join forces and embarked on a two year reign of terror. And I very much doubt that the other guy plans to call a halt just because he no longer has a partner-in-crime.'

23

An hour after the morning briefing, Temple and Marsh were heading back into the forest. They were on their way to talk to Noah Cross's twin sister, Amanda.

Marsh had called ahead to arrange an interview with Cross himself. As one of Grant Mason's friends and hiking buddies, he was an obvious suspect. But his sister had said her twin brother was in London for a long stag weekend.

'We should talk to her anyway,' Temple had said. 'After that we'll go and see Tom Fowler.'

Before leaving the office, Temple had called Hilary to see what she could tell him about Noah Cross. He caught her just as she was leaving to go to her sister's place.

'I know very little about Noah,' she'd said. 'Other than that he lives with Amanda and works as a painter and decorator.'

'He's not married then?'

'No. And neither is Amanda. They moved in with each other after they both got divorced.'

Temple was convinced that Mason's deranged accomplice had to be someone he'd known long before they'd teamed up to embark on their wicked spree. Perhaps they'd struck up a friendship while in prison and had discovered that they shared the same compulsion to rape and murder people.

The annals of crime were packed with sexual predators who had worked in pairs. Ian Brady and Myra Hindley. Fred and Rose West. Angelo Buono and Kenneth Bianchi, the so-called Hillside Stranglers.

When two men joined forces it was often because they found it easier and safer to operate that way. And because they were turned on by the voyeurism. For them, watching another man have his way with a victim added to the thrill.

Temple had read various case studies on sexual sadists who were also serial killers. One notorious pair in the States brought terror to California in 1979. Lawrence Bittaker and Roy Norris teamed up to fulfil a prison-time fantasy — to kidnap, rape, torture and kill a girl for each teenage year. They hunted roads and beaches in a van and claimed five victims before they were caught.

The cops then discovered that the demented pair had recorded their victims screaming and crying for help on audio tape — in much the same way as Mason and his accomplice had recorded themselves on a camcorder.

One of the most disturbing case files he came across involved a man named Dean Corll who carried out what became known as 'the Houston Mass Murders.' He and two accomplices were responsible for kidnapping, torturing, raping and then killing at least twenty-seven people in the seventies. The victims were first abused in a bedroom at his home that had been converted into a fully-equipped torture chamber.

'Are you all right, guv?' Marsh said suddenly. 'Only you're way over the speed limit.'

Temple felt his heart vault in his chest.

'I was miles away. Sorry.'

He eased his foot off the accelerator, and the pool car went from sixty to forty.

'I was thinking about other cases involving serial killers and sexual sadists. It seems to me that when monsters get together they tend to plumb the depths of depravity.'

'That thought occurred to me when I was viewing the video tapes,' Marsh said. 'I found them exceptionally disturbing. In fact, I was physically sick when I got home last night and I just couldn't sleep.'

Temple knew exactly what she meant. The photos and video clips he'd seen wouldn't leave him, they were hovering on the edge of his consciousness, calling for attention.

'I fear it's something we're going to have to get used to,' he said. 'More and more pervs are recording the attacks they carry out on mobile phones and camcorders. It means they can relive them time and again. Some of them even swap footage with other pervs. There's a thriving black market on the internet.'

'I know. A couple of years ago, I arrested a guy who stabbed a young girl to death after having his way with her. He filmed her dying and then sold the footage on as a snuff movie.'

'I understand that none of the clips on Mason's computer shows any of the victims being murdered.'

'That's right. Why the hell they drew a line at that I've no idea. But I'm bloody glad they did. It was distressing enough watching them committing vile acts of rape and torture. Those images keep playing over and over in my mind.'

Temple gave a sardonic grin. 'One of the perks of being a police officer is that we get to see films that aren't censored.'

'Some perk,' Marsh said. 'You must be glad that Angel isn't working on this case. We both know that she's even more sensitive about that sort of thing than I am.'

Marsh was right. Angel took a hard line on

sex fiends. She wanted all convicted rapists and paedophiles castrated. This was partly because she'd been the victim of a nasty sex attack when she was a teenager in London. The event had profoundly affected her, and it was one of the reasons she'd become a police officer.

'I sent her a text message this morning,' Marsh said. 'I wanted her to know that we're all pleased that she'll soon be coming back to work and that I'll be popping over to see her as soon as I get the chance.'

'Did she respond?'

'Oh, yeah. In fact, she told me that she had something important to tell me. Any idea what it is, guv?'

Temple was taken aback. He could only assume that Angel planned to tell Marsh that she was pregnant and that would mean that she'd decided to have the baby, despite the fact that they hadn't had a proper discussion about it.

'I'm afraid I've no idea,' he said, but he was sure he didn't sound very convincing.

Truth was, he had no control over the situation. Angel was her own woman and at thirty-six, with her body clock ticking, she'd know that this might be her last chance to have a child.

He understood, of course, but that in itself

could not hold back the panic that was building up inside him. His head filled with negative thoughts whenever he turned his mind to becoming a father. The impact on his life, his work, was going to be tremendous. He didn't think he could be a good father and a good detective at the same time.

He remembered what it had been like to be tired all the time, the struggle to balance his life between home and work, the sheer, mind-numbing drudgery of caring for an infant.

Turning back the clock did not appeal to him. Not one bit. In fact, he wondered how the hell he would cope. He knew detectives who had started families late in life and he'd seen how hard it was for them. They missed out on promotion, were less willing to work overtime, became risk averse. He didn't want that to happen to him. He loved his job and he was still ambitious. But his whole approach to work would need to change.

He'd have to make sacrifices and be willing to focus less on his career. It was something that filled him with equal measures of dread and guilt.

24

Amanda Cross lived in a large detached property about two miles from Grant Mason's place. The house could be seen from the road but to get to it, you had to drive along a short asphalt lane.

There was a grass field in front of the house and behind it, a coppice of beech and ash, the trees tall and tightly spaced.

By now it was almost noon and the sun shone weakly through gossamer clouds, casting long shadows across the forest.

The two-storey, red-brick property was box-shaped with large sash windows and a porch over the front door. The setting was stunning, with beautiful views and no noisy neighbours.

Temple parked on a patch of gravel next to a blue Vauxhall Corsa and they got out. There was a slight chill in the air, but no wind to speak of; perfect conditions for the teams who were searching for graves in two other parts of the forest. Temple would be notified if they found something. There were detectives from his team at both locations, but he was hoping he wouldn't hear from them.

The front door was opened before they reached it by a tall and somewhat striking woman, wearing a long black skirt and chunky grey-knit sweater. She was slim, mid-forties, with fairly large breasts and shoulder-length hair the colour of burned wheat. Her face was narrow, with sharp features plastered with too much make-up. Her brown eyes were slightly magnified by thick-framed glasses.

'Can I help you?' she said in a thin, high-pitched voice that could have belonged to a man or a woman.

'Miss Cross?' Temple asked.

She gave a hesitant smile, revealing neat, white teeth. 'I am.'

'I'm Detective Chief Inspector Temple and this is my colleague, Detective Constable Marsh.'

'Oh, yes. I've been expecting you. Come in. And please call me Amanda.'

It was warm inside and there was a strong smell of polish and dried flowers. They followed her along a short, carpeted hall into a living room that contained an odd mix of inoffensive flat-pack furniture. Matching black leather sofa and armchair. Teak coffee table. White laminated sideboard. Glass TV stand. French windows gave access to a back garden and the sun was streaming through

169

narrow blinds, making Temple blink in the glare.

'Can I get you both something to drink?' Amanda said.

Temple shook his head. 'We're fine, thanks.'

'Then please take a seat.'

The two detectives sat on the sofa, and Amanda perched herself on the edge of the armchair facing them. Her posture was straight and assured but Temple sensed that she was uncomfortable. She didn't seem to know what to do with her hands and kept adjusting her glasses.

'I'd like to begin by asking you how much you know about what's happened over the past twenty-four hours or so,' Temple said.

She inhaled sharply. 'I know from the news and from speaking to Hilary Dyer that it's a ghastly business. You've found a body, and you suspect there could be more bodies buried out there in the forest. And I gather that you think Grant Mason was the person who kidnapped and killed those people.'

Temple raised an eyebrow. 'There's actually not much you don't know then.'

'It's what everyone is talking about,' she said. 'It's all over the internet and the papers are full of it. I really can't believe it, though. I met Grant a number of times and he's been a guest in this house. He always seemed so nice and gentle.'

'Well, appearances can be deceiving,' Temple said.

'I'm sure that's true, Inspector, but I tend to speak as I find.'

'So you never suspected him of being up to no good?'

'Of course not. As far as I was concerned, he was a mild-mannered man who spent most of his time hiking around the forest and writing about it.'

'But am I right in assuming that you didn't really know him that well? It was your twin brother, Noah, who was his friend and drinking buddy?'

'That's true. I did explain on the phone that Noah's not here and I'm not expecting him back until tomorrow.'

'I know, but we were coming to the forest anyway so I thought we should drop in to leave you one of my cards. And I was hoping you could contact your brother for us and tell him we need to talk to him about Mason as a matter of urgency.'

'I would if I could, Inspector, but his phone's switched off. I tried ringing him last night and this morning but got no response.'

'So when did he actually go?' Temple asked.

'On Thursday afternoon. He drove into Southampton and took the train.'

'Have you spoken to him since then?'

'Just the once. I rang him as soon as I heard Grant had died, but he'd already heard about it on the radio.'

'Do you know where this stag do is taking place?'

'Various venues across London. That's why he went up on Thursday. They're dragging it out over several days. He's staying with one of his old pals in Bermondsey.'

'Do you know who's getting married?'

'Someone named Dave. He's an old school friend. That's as much as I know. To tell you the truth, I wasn't very interested since it's just a glorified piss-up.'

'I've been on a few of those,' Temple said.

'And so has Noah. The last stag he went on was in Newcastle and he got so wasted I didn't hear from him for a week.'

Temple grinned. 'I understand your brother is a painter and decorator.'

'That's right. He works for himself and makes a reasonable living.'

'Do you work, Miss Cross?'

'I do now. After Noah moved in with me a few years ago, I started working with him as his secretary, bookkeeper and general dogs-body. Before that, I was living off the settlement I got from my ex as part of the divorce.'

'So how often did your brother and Mason get together?' Temple asked.

Amanda thought about it. 'Usually about two evenings a week at the pub. Sometimes they'd meet for a lunchtime drink. In summer, they occasionally played golf and went on hikes organized by the ramblers' group in the pub.'

'So that was about the extent of it?'

She cocked her head on one side. 'I don't understand why you're asking me all these questions. Do you actually suspect that Noah knew what Grant was doing?'

'Not at all,' Temple quickly pointed out. 'We intend to talk to all of Mason's friends and acquaintances and we'll be asking them the same questions. We know a bit about Grant Mason the author, but next to nothing about his personal life. And it's important that we find out as much as possible.'

'Well, I'm not sure how helpful Noah will be. They weren't really that close.'

'So who was close to him, Miss Cross? Do you know?'

Without hesitating, she said, 'The obvious person to talk to is Tom Fowler. He frequents the same pub and I know he spent a lot of time with Grant.'

'Doing what?'

'Drinking, socializing, hiking. Noah doesn't like him much. He thinks he's creepy, but that's mainly because Fowler is into kinky sex apparently and doesn't mind people knowing about it.'

Temple felt his pulse quicken. 'What exactly do you mean by that?'

She shrugged. 'He likes all that rough stuff. You know, where couples tie each other up and use whips and canes.'

'You mean bondage and sadomasochism?'

'That's it. Fowler is part of that scene. He goes to fetish clubs and S&M events around Hampshire. But then, so what? Each to his own I say. He's not married and if it's what turns him on, then it's his business.'

'So how do you know this?'

'He talks about it when he's drinking. Doesn't care who knows about it.'

Temple glanced at Marsh. She was busy scribbling notes on a pad.

'We intend to talk to Mr Fowler later,' Temple said. 'Can you tell me anything more about him?'

'Not really, except that he's an estate agent and he's not married. I've only met him once.'

Temple's phone vibrated in his pocket with an incoming text message. He didn't take it out immediately. Instead, he glanced at his watch, then asked Amanda if she had any questions for them.

'Well, I'd like to know what makes you so sure that Grant was a mass murderer. And why you believe that there are more bodies out there in the forest. It seems inconceivable and the television news isn't really clear on it.'

'We found a piece of evidence inside Mason's house,' Temple said. 'I can't give you the specific details but I can tell you that it pointed us in the direction of the graves.'

Amanda tugged at her bottom lip with her teeth and gave a nod.

'I can't imagine what you found,' she said. 'But whatever it was, I can assure you it had nothing to do with Noah. If he'd been involved in anything bad with Grant, then I would have known about it. My brother wouldn't hurt a fly, Inspector. And if he'd harboured any suspicions about Grant, he'd have told me.'

'I'm sure you're right, Miss Cross. And like I said before, we just need to talk to him. I can assure you he's not a suspect.'

'I'm glad to hear it,' she said. 'And when he gets back, I don't doubt he'll help you in any way he can.'

Temple got up and gave Amanda Cross one of his cards.

'When you hear from your brother, please get him to call me straightaway,' he said. 'Day or night. My mobile number is on the card.'

She said she would and showed them to the door. Temple thanked her for seeing them and said he'd be in touch.

As soon as they stepped outside, Temple took out his phone and read the message that was waiting for him. It was from the detective who had been sent to observe the search for a grave near the village of Burley.

The message was short and to the point and it turned Temple's gut to ice.

They've found two more bodies.

25

As they drove away from Amanda Cross's house, Temple asked Marsh to call the office and get them to check and see if Tom Fowler had form. Then he asked her to ring Fowler himself to arrange an interview. She got through to him at his estate agent's office in Brockenhurst. He said he'd be finishing work at lunch-time and agreed to meet them at his home.

'We could go straight to his office, guv,' Marsh said. 'It's not far from here.'

'First I want to see what they've found at Burley.'

'Well, I can't say I'm looking forward to that.'

And neither was Temple. He could feel his jaw tighten at the prospect. The discovery of another grave with two more bodies was a shock if not a total surprise. It was looking increasingly likely that Grant Mason and his accomplice had murdered fifteen people over the past two years, before burying their bodies at locations marked on the map.

'I reckon we've got a prime suspect in Tom Fowler, guv,' Marsh said, breaking into

Temple's thoughts. 'He sounds like a Grade-A pervert.'

'Just because he's into BDSM doesn't make him a perv,' Temple cautioned. 'You'd be surprised how many people are doing that stuff, especially in the wake of the *Fifty Shades* phenomenon. But you're right — he's an obvious candidate for Mason's partner-in-crime.'

'Maybe that's why he acted strangely when we turned up at Hilary Dyer's house. After you went into the kitchen with Hilary, he seemed awkward and wasn't keen to talk. Then he suddenly said he had to go.'

Temple conjured up an image of Tom Fowler standing in Hilary's lounge in his crumpled grey suit. He'd looked like a typical, hard-pressed office worker. Nothing about the man had struck Temple as odd, except perhaps his hasty departure from the house. Temple wondered why he'd left without bothering to say goodbye to Hilary. Did he panic when suddenly confronted by the police?

At that moment, Marsh took a call from the office, informing her that Tom Fowler did indeed appear on the Police National Computer.

'You're not going to believe this, guv,' she said. 'Fowler spent three years inside for manslaughter. This was twelve years ago. He killed his girlfriend during a kinky sex session.'

'You've got to be kidding.'

'He claimed it was a tragic accident, that they were playing a sexual bondage game that went wrong, but the jury found him culpable. He was lucky he wasn't charged with murder.'

'Have you got the details?'

She nodded excitedly and read from her notes. 'Her name was Jessica Cassidy. They'd been seeing each other for about six months, having met at some fetish club. Anyway, one night, he tied her up, put a ball gag in her mouth and covered her eyes with duct tape. He said it was with her full consent. But then he left her to go out for a drink and didn't get back for ten hours. While he was gone she died of asphyxiation.'

Temple shook his head. 'Christ, why was he away for so long?'

'According to the court reports, he got drunk and forgot about her. I've heard of that kind of thing happening before.'

So had Temple. In fact, he'd read a force briefing paper not long ago about that very subject. It was prompted by a series of bizarre deaths during bondage sex. It also reported that a growing number of people were putting their lives on the line by indulging in fetish activities with total strangers. One woman in Newcastle allowed some guy to tie her up the same night she met him in a pub. He then proceeded to rape her and slice up her face with a Stanley knife.

'Can you ring the office back and get them to check when and where he served his time?' Temple said. 'I want to know if he crossed paths with Mason while in prison.'

Marsh got straight on with it while Temple reflected on what he'd just been told. It was a significant development. Tom Fowler, Grant Mason's closest friend by all accounts, was a killer as well as a fetish freak. It was hard not to jump to the obvious conclusion that he was the man wearing the mask in the videos. And also the man in the balaclava who had ransacked Mason's house.

Temple wondered if it was just coincidence that two such unsavoury characters were living close to each other in a tiny rural community. Had they met by chance in the local pub? Or had they become acquainted before moving to the forest?

He added these to the list of questions in his head. The list was growing by the minute, but at the top were two questions that needed to be answered as a matter of urgency.

Were Bob and Rosemary Hamilton still

alive? And if so, then where the hell were they?

★　★　★

The second grave had been discovered just outside Burley, a quaint village surrounded by open forest and barren heathlands.

The exact spot was to the east of the village in a thickly wooded area known as the South Oakley Inclosure. It was just off the road that runs between Burley and Lyndhurst.

A police checkpoint had been set up at the entrance to a visitor car park. There were vehicles parked along the grass verges on both sides of the road, including a TV satellite truck.

Temple lowered his window and held up his ID for one of the uniformed officers to see.

'Just turn left here, sir,' the officer said. 'It's all happening in the woods next to the car park.'

Temple steered the pool car along a gravel track to the parking area, where tall pine trees cast deep shadows across the ground.

The place was packed with uniforms and white-suited forensic technicians. On any other Saturday it would have been busy with tourists and day-trippers.

181

There was an assortment of police vehicles and Scientific Services Department vans. A mobile incident truck was taking up a lot of space at the far end.

Temple parked up and he and Marsh got out. A uniformed sergeant they both recognized approached them, and gestured towards a path that led into the woods.

'You need to follow the path for about fifty yards,' he said. 'It'll take you to where they found the grave.'

Once again, Mason and his partner had chosen a spot close to one of the forest's many car parks. And Temple could see why. They had probably come here at night when it would have been deserted. Their vehicle would have been shielded from traffic passing on the road and together, they would have carried the bodies into the woods where a grave had probably already been dug.

Temple found it a chilling thought that it had been so easy for them to dispose of their victims. And if it hadn't been for Mason's map, the graves would almost certainly have remained undiscovered.

Temple dragged down his shirt collar to loosen it as they walked along the path. When he wiped a hand across his forehead, he felt a thin sheen of sweat there.

The grave was in a small clearing in the

woods, about twenty yards from the path. It was surrounded by scrub and brambles and close to the decaying stump of an old oak tree. SOC officers were going about their work with a calm, concentrated commitment. A couple were preparing to erect a forensic tent over the grave. The air in the clearing was thick with the heavy, rich smell of turned earth.

DC Neil Cornish saw them coming and acknowledged them with a wave of his hand. It was Cornish, a dour Irishman, who had sent the text message to Temple's phone.

He pointed to some plastic stepping plates that had been placed on the ground. Temple and Marsh used them to get up close to the action.

'It took them four hours to locate the grave,' Cornish told them. 'This is the very spot that's marked with a cross on Mason's map so they knew roughly where to look.'

'What exactly have they found?' Temple asked.

'Two corpses that are little more than skeletons. A man and a woman for sure. They were wrapped in bin bags and were lying one on top of the other about three feet down.'

'Is there anything to identify them?'

'Not so far. But the names against this location on Mason's map are Simon and Jane

Cramer, a married couple from London who disappeared while on a touring holiday in this part of the world.'

Temple stepped up to the large hole in the ground. The bodies were still partly covered by remnants of the black plastic bags.

Temple's stomach was strong, but the sight before him made him want to retch. After four months in the ground, the bodies had become badly decomposed and only shreds of blackened tissue remained, along with teeth and strands of hair.

The pair had been buried without clothes or any other belongings and it was going to take a while to confirm their identities.

The hole that had been dug was big enough to accommodate a SOCO who was on his knees examining the bones and the earth beneath them. He was busy taking insect and soil samples that would be examined back at the lab.

When he spotted Temple he stood up and said, 'There's something you need to see, sir. I only just noticed it myself.'

The SOCO leaned forwards and extended his right arm, pointing a finger at the neck of the smallest corpse.

'See that there,' he said. 'It's a short length of electrical cable, which I'm guessing was used to strangle her. The poor woman was buried with it still wrapped around her throat.'

Temple would never have noticed it if it hadn't been pointed out to him. The cable was discoloured and seemed to have melted into the spinal bones at the base of the skull.

'Well, at least we now know how one of the victims was murdered,' he said. 'I wouldn't be surprised if the same method was used on the others too.'

'This is unbelievable,' Marsh said, her voice dropping to little more than a whisper.

Temple turned to look at her standing beside him. The colour had drained from her cheeks and her eyes were stretched wide.

'I think we've both seen enough,' he said.

Marsh followed him back along the path to the car park, which had been invaded by reporters and TV camera operators. When they saw Temple, they immediately surrounded him like a pack of wolves and started throwing questions.

'Is it true you've found another grave?'

'Can you confirm there are two bodies this time?'

'Do the bodies belong to Bob and Rosemary Hamilton?'

Temple stopped walking and fixed his gaze on the reporter who had asked the last question.

'I can tell you that we have found human remains in a shallow grave,' he said. 'But they definitely do not belong to Mr and Mrs Hamilton.'

'So what made you carry out a search in this particular area?' someone asked.

'I'm not in a position to reveal that information at this stage,' Temple said. 'But as you probably know, there's going to be a press conference at police headquarters in Southampton later this afternoon. You can ask that question again.'

'There are rumours that Grant Mason left a map on which he marked the locations of his victims' graves,' the reporter said. 'Is that so? Did you come across the map?'

Temple felt anger stab at him like a knife in the ribs. The media weren't supposed to know about the map.

'Look, as soon as we can release more details we will,' he said. 'But right now I really don't have the time to answer your questions.'

Temple pushed through the scrum and strode over to the mobile incident truck with Marsh in tow. The reporters were ushered away by a couple of uniforms who told them to leave the car park. But that was unlikely to happen. The forest was now a media hotspot and the search for bodies was generating too much interest.

And Temple knew that after this afternoon's press conference, the story was set to get even bigger — after his bosses revealed that Grant Mason had an accomplice.

26

Temple set up a conference call from the mobile incident unit. He wanted to update Chief Superintendent Beresford before the afternoon press conference got underway. Vaughan joined in on behalf of the rest of the team.

They already knew that the decaying bodies of a man and woman had been found, but they were surprised to learn about the electrical cable.

'It tallies with the post-mortem findings on Paul Kellerman,' Vaughan said. 'The pathologist has found markings on what was left of the student's neck. They indicated ligature strangulation.'

'Seems the appropriate MO for a couple of sadomasochists,' Beresford said. 'Plus, it doesn't create a mess, which can be a problem when moving bodies around. What else did the post-mortem turn up?'

'There are a number of other injuries which suggest the lad was subjected to violence before he died,' Vaughan said. 'Three broken ribs, a cracked jawbone and a fractured right arm.'

Temple then described the scene at the South Oakley Inclosure, and said that the grave was only yards from a visitor car park.

'That's something I was going to mention,' Beresford said. 'It's been pointed out to me that all the crosses on Mason's map are close to car parking areas — both official and unofficial.'

'That makes sense from the killers' point of view,' Temple said. 'They didn't have far to carry the bodies.'

'I'll mention it at the presser.'

'Be prepared to answer questions about the map too, guv,' Temple said. 'The media have got wind of it.'

'Now why doesn't that surprise me? So what do you suggest?'

'We don't really have a choice. Might as well confirm that we did find a map in Mason's house and it was what prompted us to start the searches.'

'They'll want the details.'

'Well, I don't think we need to hold anything back since they already know how many graves there are thought to be. We just don't reveal the locations. They'll find out where those are when we start digging.'

'On that point, the Chief Constable is going to make an announcement at the presser,' Beresford said. 'He's arranging for search teams to be sent to all the locations on the map tomorrow, and this will be made possible by drafting in the army to help us.'

'That's a good call,' Temple said. 'There's no point dragging it out unless we have to.'

Beresford then asked if there was any progress in the hunt for Mason's accomplice.

'There's a guy named Tom Fowler who looks a bit sus,' Temple said. 'He was Mason's friend.'

Temple told them what Amanda Cross had said about Fowler being into sado sex, and about his conviction and sentence for manslaughter.

'Sounds promising,' Beresford said. 'What's your gut feeling?'

'I'll let you know after we've spoken to him, which will be in the next hour.'

'So what about the Hamiltons? I don't suppose we've got anything to report there.'

'They're still missing,' Temple said. 'But you need to stress that we're working on the assumption that they're still alive, and that the bodies in the grave are those of an unidentified couple and not Bob and Rosemary Hamilton.'

'Very well. And Paul Kellerman? Can we name him yet?'

'We can,' Vaughan said. 'His parents have been informed, and we've got people standing by to get in touch with the families of Simon and Jane Cramer once we know for sure it's them.'

Temple asked Vaughan if they'd received any word from the other search location near Godshill.

'No news yet, boss. But if there's another grave there I'm sure they'll find it soon enough.'

Temple wished Beresford good luck with the press conference and ended the call. He was glad he didn't have to be there. The event was sure to be beamed around the world. The news channels would probably take it live so the pressure to get it right would be enormous. The fact that it was being fronted by the Chief Constable was a measure of how important the case was. And how big.

In fact, Temple had never felt so over-whelmed by a case in his life. Three bodies had already been found. Two people were missing and possibly dead. And there was a serial sex killer still on the loose.

Was it any wonder that his headache was back and the acid was churning in his stomach?

27

They left the Oakley car park after the conference call and headed back towards East Boldre.

Temple's headache continued to tap away in his skull, so he popped another one of the pills the hospital had prescribed for him. The acid reflux remained a problem, but he was hoping to remedy that by grabbing a bite to eat after their meeting with Tom Fowler.

He lived in a detached house about a mile outside East Boldre. The two-storey property looked run-down. The outside needed a fresh coat of white paint and there were tiles missing from the slate grey roof.

The house was on the edge of a wood and within sight of a small lake. The nearest neighbour was a couple of hundred yards away.

There was a vehicle on the driveway, a spotlessly white and fairly new Ford Focus.

Temple and Marsh got out of the pool car and Temple took a moment to study his surroundings.

The sun shone weakly through the clouds and a current of air stirred the trees behind the house. Out on the moor a couple of ponies were grazing, oblivious to the horrors that were unfolding around them in the forest.

'What are you thinking, guv?' Marsh said.

He managed a grim smile. 'I'm thinking that this would be a good place to carry out systematic torture. There's no one around to hear the screams.'

'That applies to about half the properties in the forest,' she said. 'The solitude, the isolation, the remoteness. It's what makes this place so popular with people who want a quiet life.'

He knew that to be true. He and Erin had actually given serious consideration to moving to the forest just before she was taken ill. Which was why it never happened.

Tom Fowler appeared at his front door as they approached. He was wearing a baggy white shirt, open at the collar, and black jeans.

'Hello again, officers,' he said, his face serious. 'I was beginning to think you weren't coming.'

'We got held up,' Temple said. 'Have we kept you from doing something or going somewhere?'

'Not really. Saturday afternoons I usually chill out in front of the box or go for a long walk.'

They stepped into a spacious entrance hall with stairs and a stand-alone coat rack. The patterned carpet was threadbare in places, and the walls were painted a dull and depressing shade of grey.

They trailed Fowler into an untidy kitchen which had dark, dated units and an old fashioned ceramic sink. The room was big enough to accommodate a large pine table and four chairs.

'Take a seat,' Fowler said. 'I'll put the kettle on.'

The worktops were cluttered with jars, cereal packets, bottles of soft drinks and takeaway food cartons.

There were also several bottles of spirits and a box of canned beers.

He sat down at the table while Marsh remained standing with her back against the wall.

Fowler asked them if they were happy to have coffee because he'd run out of tea bags. They both said they were, and Temple studied him as he filled the mugs.

He was about five foot eight or nine, with broad shoulders and a slim waist. He looked fit and healthy, and Temple reckoned he was about the same size and shape as the man in the balaclava who had attacked him in Mason's house. And he could also have been the guy on the videos wearing the black leather head mask.

Fowler handed Marsh a mug and put Temple's on the table in front of him.

Then he sat down and crossed his arms. 'So how can I be of help to you, Inspector?'

Temple had already worked out in his mind how he was going to approach the interview. He didn't want Fowler to think he was a suspect from the start because that would put him on the defensive.

'It's information we're after, Mr Fowler,' he said. 'We're trying to find out as much as we can about Grant Mason. As you probably know by now, he's being linked to the disappearance and possible murders of a number of people whose bodies were buried in the forest.'

Fowler adopted a solemn expression. 'I've been following it on the news. It's like something out of a horror film. I just can't believe that Grant would have done such a thing.'

'So what exactly was your relationship with him?'

He shrugged. 'We were friends. We drank in the same pub and I went on hikes with him.'

'How and when did you meet?'

'Just over four years ago, he popped into our office in Brockenhurst. He was looking to buy a house in the area. He said he wanted to settle down and write books. I showed him a couple of properties, including the house he eventually bought near here. After that we stayed in touch.'

'I gather you set up a ramblers' group and made him honorary chairman.'

'The group existed before he arrived on the scene, but it was a sensible move because it raised our profile and attracted a few new members.'

'Were you at the book signing last Wednesday when he had his heart attack?'

'Unfortunately, I wasn't. He did invite me, but I had work commitments.'

Temple scribbled a few notes, which gave Marsh the opportunity to ask some questions.

'This is a nice house, Mr Fowler,' she said. 'How many bedrooms are there?'

'Three.'

'And what about a basement? Does it have one?'

He gave her a puzzled look. 'No. Why do you want to know that?'

'Just curious. Do you live here alone?'

His breathing faltered. 'I've been single for over eighteen years since separating from my wife. But it suits me. Life is a lot less complicated than it used to be when I was married. And I don't get nagged.'

'Did Grant Mason often come here?' she asked.

'Not really. He came a few times over the

years but we usually got together at the Court Jester, that's a local pub.'

'And when you were with him, did he ever open up about himself?'

Fowler narrowed his eyes. 'If you mean did he give any indication that he was abducting people and then killing them, then the answer is no. In fact, he very rarely talked about anything other than his books, the forest and politics.'

'So he didn't tell you about his sex life then?' Marsh said.

Fowler's jaw dropped. 'What kind of question is that?'

'It would help if you could just answer it, Mr Fowler.'

Fowler's eyes darted between Temple and Marsh and then settled on the table top.

'Like me, Grant wasn't married and as far as I know, he wasn't in a relationship,' he said.

'Since when do you need to be in a relationship to have sex?' Marsh pointed out.

Fowler shifted in his chair, unfolded his arms and rested them on the table, palms down.

'Are you asking me about Grant's sex life for any particular reason, Detective? Because if you are, then I think it's only fair that you tell me.'

Marsh started to respond, but Temple beat her to it.

'We have reason to believe that Mason was a sexual sadist,' he said. 'He did bad things to his victims before killing them.'

Fowler pulled a face like he'd swallowed something bitter.

'What sort of things?' he said.

Temple leaned forwards and held the man's gaze.

'He inflicted rape and torture on his victims before he murdered them. What's more, we know that he had an accomplice — a man who joined in his depraved acts. That person — who we believe also lives in the forest — is still alive and kicking as far as we know.'

Fowler's features froze and his eyes grew wide in their sockets.

'I . . . I had no idea.'

Temple studied him carefully, noted that small beads of sweat appeared above his top lip.

'The man we're looking for enjoys inflicting pain and humiliation on his victims,' Temple said. 'That's how he gets his kicks. In much the same way as you do, Mr Fowler.'

Fowler's mouth fell open. 'You can't possibly think that I'm that man.'

'It has crossed our minds, given your

criminal record and your love of rough, kinky sex.'

Fowler's features curled in outrage. 'What the fuck is going on here? If you bastards are trying to stitch me up then I want a lawyer.'

'Just look at it from our point of view,' Temple said. 'You were one of Mason's closest friends and you shared a passion for violent sex. Plus, you killed your girlfriend during a violent sex game. So you're bound to be a person of interest to us.'

A sneer rose on Fowler's face. 'What happened to Jessica was an accident. There's not a day goes by when I don't regret it. But it doesn't make me a mass fucking murderer.'

'But it does make you a suspect and the sooner we can eliminate you from our inquiries, the better for all concerned.'

A vein in the side of Fowler's neck started to pulse and his body became ramrod stiff. He ran a hand through his hair and licked dry lips.

'Were you aware that Mason also served time in prison?' Temple asked.

Fowler seemed genuinely surprised. 'No, I wasn't.'

'Is that right? So as a matter of interest, where were you banged up?'

He tipped his head back. 'First the Scrubs and then Winchester. And before you ask, I never came across Grant inside.'

'So did he know that you were into bondage and sadomasochism?'

'Most of my friends do. I've never made a secret of the fact.'

'That's unusual, isn't it?' Temple said. 'Most people who practise BDSM stay in the closet because they feel embarrassed or discriminated against.'

He shrugged. 'That used to be the case. More people than ever are coming out now. I came out a long time ago. I found that once people accept you for what you are, it ceases to be an issue.'

'So are you still active on the S&M scene?' Marsh asked. 'Despite what you did to your girlfriend?'

Fowler lowered his head. 'I am, but not in the same way.'

'Care to explain?'

'I'm a masochist now, Detective. I want to receive pain. After what happened to Jessica, I can't bring myself to hurt anyone. Being punished on a regular basis is my way of dealing with the guilt that's been eating away at me for years.'

'So it's not just about sexual stimulation then?' Marsh said, her tone sarcastic.

'It's always been more than that, Detective. If you're not part of that world then you wouldn't understand.'

Marsh raised her eyebrows. 'So who does the punishing?'

'I use an escort agency that specializes in BDSM,' Fowler said. 'They provide dominatrices.'

'You mean women who are prepared to beat you up and humiliate you?'

His neck tensed. 'There's no need to act like you don't know what I'm talking about.'

'So what's the name of this agency?' Temple asked.

'Extreme Services. It's based in Southampton.'

'And who runs it?'

'A bloke named Ross Cavendish. I've got his number if you want it.'

'We do.'

Fowler took his mobile from his pocket, scrawled through his contacts and read out the number. Temple jotted it down on his pad.

After a long, thoughtful pause, Temple said, 'We appreciate the fact that you've been so candid with us, Mr Fowler. We will want to talk to you again once we've carried out some checks. Now before we go, would you allow us to look around?'

'You mean you want to search my house?'

'Not exactly search it. We'd just — '

'The answer's no, Inspector. Not without a warrant. And not without a lawyer present.'

'You make it sound like you've got something to hide,' Temple said.

Fowler's gaze seemed to intensify as he spoke. 'It's nothing of the kind, Inspector. I'm just exerting my rights and protecting my privacy.'

Temple pushed out his bottom lip. 'Fair enough, but there's one thing I need to ask you before we go. Can you account for your movements on Thursday evening between about seven and ten?'

Fowler didn't even have to think about it. 'I had an early drink at the Court Jester. Left there about seven thirty and came home. I spent the rest of the evening watching television by myself.'

'Why'd you leave so early?'

'It was too depressing. All the talk was of Grant dying.'

'So who can confirm that you were there?'

Fowler heaved a loud sigh. 'The landlord's Mick Russell. He'll tell you. And I shared a table with Noah Cross. He's another regular and was also a friend of Grant.'

Temple frowned. 'Are you sure that Mr Cross was there? We were told he went to London on Thursday afternoon.'

'I'm positive. In fact, he left when I did.'

Temple put his notebook away and stood up.

'Thanks for talking to us, Mr Fowler. We're going to want to see you again, I'm sure. So if you plan on leaving the area during the coming days, you'll need to let me know.'

Temple placed one of his cards on the table, and he and Marsh headed for the front door. He walked slowly to give himself time to look around.

He saw two half-open doors in the hall — one to the living room, the other to a downstairs toilet.

But he saw no other doors that might have provided access to a basement. And that came as a disappointment.

28

The Court Jester was a small, timber-framed pub with a thatched roof and a patio garden at the front. It was picture-postcard pretty, with purple aubrietia spilling from cracks in the walls.

Inside, a fire was blazing away in an open hearth, giving off a warm glow and a sharp, rustic smell.

Heads turned towards Temple and Marsh as they walked in. There was a man in a green waxed jacket at the bar who was sipping beer from a pint glass. At a table to his right sat a middle-aged couple who paused to look up from their ploughman's lunches. In a booth to the left, two young men in suits, who might have been reporters, stared with undisguised curiosity.

At the bar, Temple ordered drinks and sandwiches before identifying himself to the portly server who said he was the landlord, Mick Russell.

'Some other detectives were in here yesterday,' Russell said as he started pouring the drinks. 'I told them everything I know about Grant Mason, which isn't very much.'

'We're aware of that,' Temple said. 'But we've been interviewing some people nearby so we thought we'd pop in for a bite to eat and a chat.'

'And you're most welcome,' he said. 'You've actually come at a good time. We've been packed out with journalists since the news broke. I gave an interview to the BBC not an hour ago.'

'What did they want to know?'

'Anything I could tell them. How often did Mason come here? What did he drink? Who were his friends? What were his favourite bar snacks? If what your lot are saying about him is true, then I wish the bastard had never set foot in here.'

'I gather he was a popular character with your customers,' Temple said.

'Well, he seemed to get on with most of them. He was pretty quiet, though, and shy too.'

'We just spoke to one of his friends, Tom Fowler.'

'Yeah, it was Tom who started the ramblers' group and made Grant chairman.'

'Tom said he was in here early on Thursday evening with some of the other regulars after it was reported that Mason had died.'

Russell finished pouring their drinks. 'That's right. Nobody could believe it.

205

Everyone was really down. But of course we didn't know then what we know now.'

'Can you remember if Noah Cross was also here on Thursday?'

Russell scrunched up his face in thought. 'He was. I remember because he stuck to soft drinks and left earlier than usual.'

'Did he say where he was going?'

'Not to me. Why do you want to know?'

Temple ignored the question and cast his eyes around the pub.

'I don't see any CCTV cameras,' he said.

'That's because we were having too many problems with the system. It was taken out two weeks ago and is due to be replaced next week.'

He pushed their drinks across the bar — half a lager for Temple and a diet coke for Marsh.

'Did Mason mix with everyone or did he have any particular friends?' Temple asked.

'Well, he mostly interacted with other members of the ramblers' group. That's five men and six women. I gave all their names to the other detectives.'

'And they included Mr Cross and Mr Fowler?'

'Of course. Those two were with him mostly because they're regular drinkers here. He usually got together with the others only when a hike was organized, which I suppose was about once a month.'

Temple thanked Russell and gestured for Marsh to follow him to a table.

'I'll bring your sandwiches over as soon as they're ready,' Russell said.

When they were seated, Marsh removed her jacket and pinched her petite nose between forefinger and thumb. She looked exhausted.

'Are you all right?' Temple asked her.

Her voice sounded flat. 'Just tired. And a little shell-shocked as well, I think. This is the strangest and most disturbing case I've ever worked on. When I saw that couple in the grave, it turned my stomach. Mr and Mrs Cramer featured in one of the videos I viewed. Mason and his mate did some terrible things to them.'

It occurred to Temple that Marsh had been unusually quiet throughout the morning. And now he knew why. He hadn't realized that the case was getting under her skin, but he wasn't entirely surprised. And he was sure she wouldn't be the only officer to find it hard going.

He gave her an understanding look, noting that her pewter eyes were dull and opaque, as though someone had turned off the light.

'I'd be lying if I said that things are likely to

get easier,' he told her. 'The truth is we're almost certainly in for a long, rough ride. We could be searching for graves for weeks. And we can't be sure we'll ever find Bob and Rosemary Hamilton — dead or alive.'

Marsh made a face, as if spitting something out.

'That's a scary thought, guv.'

'Then don't think about it. Just concentrate on helping me find Mason's accomplice. That's our priority.'

She picked up a bar mat and folded it down the middle. 'I'm wondering if we've already found him, guv.'

'You mean Tom Fowler?'

'Absolutely. The guy's a real weirdo.'

'I know what you mean, but it won't be easy to disprove what he said. We'll need evidence.'

'We should search his house as soon as we can.'

'I'll try to get a warrant. And in the meantime we'll send someone over to get a DNA swab, although it's not likely there'll be DNA traces on any of the bodies.'

At that moment, the landlord brought their sandwiches and they got stuck in.

Between mouthfuls, Marsh said, 'What about Noah Cross? There's something not right there. His sister lied about him going to

London on Thursday afternoon.'

'Either that or she made a genuine mistake. We'll go and see her again before heading back to town.'

In the end, they had to put off another visit to Amanda Cross's house. Temple took a call from Dave Vaughan, saying that Beresford was holding a three o'clock briefing and he wanted them there.

'There've been a few developments at this end too, boss,' he said. 'The main one being that we might have identified Mason's accomplice.'

29

He was watching through his new binoculars from a distance of about three hundred yards. Behind him was a small coppice and in front, a field of heather and grass that sloped gradually down towards the scene of activity.

Police were gathered in and around the South Oakley Inclosure, most of them in Hi-Vis jackets. The media were also there. Two TV satellite trucks were parked on the side of the road near to the track leading to the car park.

He couldn't see what was going on inside the woods, but he didn't need to. Before leaving the house, he'd watched a televised press conference during which the police revealed that they'd found a grave at this location.

He tried to imagine the state the bodies were in. After four months in the ground they would surely be unrecognizable. He wondered how long it would take the police to establish their identities.

An image of the couple surfaced in his mind. Simon and Jane Cramer. Simon had been tall, muscular, in his thirties. Jane had been blonde and pretty and about the same age.

They had driven into the South Oakley car park on a bleak Friday afternoon, and he and Mason had been waiting. He remembered what a relief it had been after a day of touring the forest looking for victims. The poor weather had kept day-trippers away and most of the parking areas they'd visited had remained deserted.

But just when they were thinking of giving up, the Cramers had appeared. They'd bundled the couple into the back of the hired van and within the hour, they were strapped to the beds in the basement.

For five days and nights, the Cramers had provided a constant source of pleasure. In the basement there'd been nothing that he and Mason couldn't do to them. There'd been no one to stop them, nothing to hold them back.

The couple had been raped, spanked, whipped, pinched, burned and made to perform sex acts on each other. And finally they'd been strangled with electrical cable.

He could well remember how in the dead of night, they had returned here to the woods with the bodies in the back of the van. The grave had already been dug so it had taken just fifty minutes to drop them in and cover them with earth and bracken.

The following day, they'd taken the van back to the hire company before joining a seven-mile hike through the forest organized by the ramblers' group.

The Cramers, like the others before them, were never meant to be found. Their disappearance should have remained a mystery. And it would have if not for Mason.

At the televised press conference, a reporter had asked the Chief Constable if it was true that the police had found a map in Mason's house, a map which was marked with the locations of up to ten graves. The Chief Constable had been forced to admit that there was a map with crosses marked on it at ten different locations.

A map, for God's sake. How stupid was that? How fucking diabolically reckless. Why couldn't the idiot have been satisfied with videos and photos, and the belongings he took from their victims?

And as if that wasn't bad enough, the police had also revealed that Mason had had an accomplice. For that reason they were stepping up the search for Bob and Rosemary Hamilton, whom they believed had been abducted.

It meant that the situation was now more precarious and unpredictable. He would have to make sure he stayed one step ahead of the police. But it wasn't going to be easy. In fact, he wasn't even sure he'd be able to pull it off.

★ ★ ★

He heard the police helicopter before he saw it. It swooped in low over the trees to the north and hovered above the woods like a giant prehistoric bug.

At the same time, more police cars appeared on the scene with their lights flashing.

He decided it was time to go as he didn't want to risk drawing attention to himself. But on the short drive home he saw another helicopter swooping low over the forest and then, to his horror, he was flagged down at a police road check. A uniformed PC asked to see his driving licence and then failed to spot that it was a fake. He then told him to open the boot.

'Thank you, sir,' the PC said when he saw that there was nothing inside but an old blanket and a first-aid kit. 'We appreciate your patience. Now drive carefully and have a good afternoon.'

It made him realize how difficult it was going to be to dispose of the Hamiltons. The police would be maintaining a high-visibility profile throughout the forest with uniforms and marked response vehicles. And if they were randomly stopping cars, then it would be a huge risk to go anywhere with two bodies in the back.

The important thing was to hold his nerve and not to panic. He needed to focus on a way out of this mess. It wasn't as though he could just pack a bag and disappear. He had nowhere to go and very little money left in the bank. His life had taken root here and he'd never felt the need to have a back-up plan if things suddenly went pear-shaped.

The anger swelled inside him and he smacked the palms of his hands against the steering wheel.

'Fuck, fuck, fuck,' he yelled, spraying the inside of the windscreen with spit.

He still couldn't wrap his mind around the fact that everything was falling apart. It was nothing less than tragic. For the first time in his life he was settled. He felt he belonged in the forest. It was his home as well as his hunting ground.

For over two years, he'd been living a glorious lie. Only Mason had known him for what he was and his secret had been safe from everyone else. But now it was all under threat because he, the hunter, had become the hunted.

He aimed another round of expletives at

the windscreen, and decided that he would vent his anger when he got home on the Hamiltons. Might as well make the most of them while they were still imprisoned in the basement. After all, they'd be gone soon and after that, it might be a while before his cravings could be satisfied again.

30

'His name is Ethan Kane,' DS Vaughan said. 'He's a 46-year-old Londoner and he shared a cell in Wandsworth prison with Mason. He was released three years ago. But then he vanished while on probation.'

Temple and Marsh were back in the incident room and Vaughan had taken the floor at the briefing. The Chief Super was there along with the rest of the team, several of whom Temple didn't recognize because they'd been drafted in from other divisions.

'According to the prison governor's office, the pair were as thick as thieves,' Vaughan said. 'But then maybe that's not so surprising since they had a lot in common. Kane was serving an eight-year stretch for a string of sexual offences including the rape of a 30-year-old married woman. And it wasn't his first time inside. He was jailed seventeen years ago for breaking into a house and beating up a young couple who were also sexually molested. The guy sounds like a right nut.'

Kane's mugshot appeared on the big monitor at the front of the room. He had a narrow face with a short dark beard and a shaved head. His nose was badly broken, making him look like a prize fighter.

Temple felt a flicker of recognition, but then after so long on the force, most criminals looked vaguely familiar to him.

'If Kane teamed up with his old cellmate outside prison, then there's a good chance he was Mason's accomplice,' Vaughan said. 'Two violent perverts who may have spent years hatching plans to prey on people when they were both free again. And where better to do that than the New Forest? It's an easy place to acquire victims. Low risk targets. Isolated parking areas. Strike when there's no one around.'

'Plus it was in Mason's back yard and he was already settled there,' Temple said. 'Perhaps he invited his old friend to join him.'

'We've checked the name against electoral registers in the New Forest and neighbouring counties,' Vaughan said. 'But unsurprisingly he hasn't come up. Having jumped probation he's probably using a different name or even obtained a whole new identity. And we all know that's pretty easy these days, especially if you have the contacts.'

'What about his last known address?' Temple said.

Vaughan nodded. 'It was a house in Kent

owned by a woman he was going out with. That's all I know because I'm still waiting for his probation officer to get back to me with the details.'

It was an exciting development and it had the room buzzing. Beresford said he wanted the mugshot circulated to all officers and distributed to the media.

'Let's get his face out there fast,' he said. 'If he's our man, then he'll have been expecting us to make the connection sooner or later, so he might have fled the area already.'

Temple asked Vaughan to collect more information on Kane, including his crime files and any psychiatric reports.

'Did he and Mason serve out all their time in Wandsworth?' he asked.

Vaughan screwed up his face as he consulted his notes.

'No, they didn't. But it's where they both finished up. Before being transferred there, Kane was in Albany on the Isle of Wight and Mason did a stint in Winchester.'

Temple's ears pricked up. 'I want you to check when Mason was in Winchester. Then see if the dates coincide with when Tom Fowler was there.'

'Give me a sec, guv,' Vaughan said as he swivelled in his chair and started tapping at his computer keyboard.

Temple, meanwhile, went on to tell the team what they'd found out about Tom Fowler.

'He has to be another serious suspect,' he said. 'He was probably Mason's closest friend and he's still active on the S&M scene, despite killing his girlfriend some years ago.'

Temple told them about the escort agency through which Fowler apparently met up with female dominants, who were prepared to beat him up for a fee.

'He reckons he's switched from being a sadist to a masochist when it comes to role-playing because it's his way of atoning for his sins. But it could be bullshit so we need to check it out. I want someone to speak to the guy who runs the agency and the women who work there.

'Fowler insists that he didn't meet Mason before he turned up at his office to buy a property in the area. He says they struck up a friendship after Mason bought the house in East Boldre. He claims he had no idea what Mason was up to.

'Fowler refused to let us look around his house without a warrant so I think we should get one.' Temple turned to Beresford. 'Can you swing it, sir? I really think we should go inside.'

Beresford nodded. 'I'll see what I can do.'

DS Vaughan raised his hand so that he could reveal that Tom Fowler had not been in Winchester prison at the same time as Mason.

'Mason was there for two years and Fowler was transferred there for a year,' Vaughan said. 'But there was no overlap. Fowler did his time long before Mason.'

'So they didn't meet up inside then,' Temple said. 'But that doesn't mean they didn't know each other before they moved to the forest. So let's dig deep and see what we can come up with.'

'So we have two prime suspects,' Beresford said. 'Fowler and Kane. That's good. Shows we're making progress. It's a shame I wasn't able to announce it at the press conference.'

'How did that go, sir?' Temple asked.

Beresford cleared his throat. 'As well as could have been expected. They're now aware that we found a map and that Mason had an accomplice. And they know we have evidence which shows that the pair abducted the Hamiltons.'

Temple was glad now that the media were all over the story. They needed to generate as much publicity as possible. It was the only way to draw information from the public, especially those living in and around the New Forest.

Someone might have spotted suspicious activity in woods or on the moors. Or perhaps someone would recognize Ethan Kane when his picture was shown on television. The more people who tuned in to what was going on, the better.

Temple spent a few minutes describing what had been found in the South Oakley Inclosure near Burley. He talked about the electrical cable around the neck of the body believed to be that of Jane Cramer. And he mentioned how the grave was only yards from a path leading from the car park.

'The graves are near to parking areas, which makes sense,' he said. 'And I wouldn't be surprised if that's where the victims were seized. Mason and his pal were probably waiting in a car or van so they could pounce when they saw an opportunity.'

DC Whelan chose then to reveal that van hire receipts had been found during the forensic sweep of Mason's house.

'I've followed it up with the company, which is based here in Southampton,' he said. 'Mason hired transit vans for a couple of days around the times of the disappearances. But the hire company knew him as Jonathan Pearson. He had a fake ID and driving licence and he always paid in cash.'

'Did he always collect and return the vans

by himself?' Temple asked.

Whelan nodded. 'He did. And get this. He was there the Friday before last to pick up a van which he returned on the Sunday. That was no doubt the van used in the abduction of the Hamiltons so we're having it checked over.'

'Does the hire company have CCTV on the premises?'

'It does, but it gets wiped after three days. So I'm checking to see if the van was picked up on any nearby cameras on that Friday and Sunday. If we're lucky we might see who dropped Mason off and picked him up.'

It was an encouraging lead and it made Temple feel more positive about how the investigation was going. He knew that the powers-that-be were monitoring the progress they were making. If it lost momentum, or stalled, then they wouldn't hesitate to bring someone else in or set up a task force.

Beresford, as the senior investigating officer, would take most of the flak, but he and the rest of the team would be hit by the fallout. It was always the same on big, sensitive cases where the force's reputation was on the line and the media were demanding results.

The briefing continued for another half an hour, during which a list of Mason's mobile phone contacts was handed out. It contained only twenty names. There were no surprises and among those he most frequently called were Hilary Dyer, Tom Fowler, Noah Cross and Ross Cavendish, owner of Extreme Services.

Ethan Kane's name did not appear and all the others had been checked out. Which begged the question: *Wouldn't Kane's number be on Mason's phone if the pair had got back together after prison?*

Beresford rounded off the meeting by reading extracts from a report he'd commissioned from a forensic psychologist attached to Hampshire Constabulary.

'These are headline points that were put together in a hurry by Dr Alex Hill and I think they're worth sharing with you,' he said. 'Based on what we know, she believes Mason was a Grade-A sexual sadist. She provides a concise description of what that means. Sexual sadism, she says, is considered a mental disorder and is one of the paraphilias. A paraphilia is characterized by an obsession with unusual sexual activities with non-consensual persons. Paedophilia and voyeurism are other types of paraphilia.

'Sexual sadists frequently have violent fantasies that start in childhood. Once the sadistic behaviour begins, it continues on a chronic course and grows more bizarre and violent over time. The element of fear in the victim, coupled with complete control over them, is the main sexual stimuli.

'She goes on to say that Mason was probably keen to operate with an accomplice because it made him feel more empowered. It also made things easier and less risky. They would have developed a routine for seizing and holding their victims, and they almost certainly thought it was fool-proof.

'Doctor Hill adds that Mason's accomplice will share most, if not all, of his traits. He'll be a sociopath — cold, calculating and completely ruthless. And if he hasn't already murdered Bob and Rosemary Hamilton, then she believes he'll do so very soon unless we get to him first.'

31

After the briefing, Temple retreated to his office with the thoughts of Dr Alex Hill ringing in his ears.

If he hasn't already murdered Bob and Rosemary Hamilton, then he'll do so very soon unless we get to him first.

Temple didn't doubt for a single second that she was right. Mason's accomplice would be aware by now that the net was closing in around him. If he had no links to the community then he might already have fled.

If he was a local man then he'd be desperately trying to cover his tracks and distance himself from Mason. Either way, he wouldn't want the Hamiltons left alive to bear witness to what he had done to them.

Temple sat back in his chair and a shadow of anxiety passed over his face. He suddenly felt less positive about the investigation. True, they already had two suspects in Ethan Kane and Tom Fowler. But they had no idea where Kane was and Fowler might well be guilty of nothing more than being a fan of kinky sex.

Temple knew that it was dangerous to read too much into Fowler's reluctance to have his house searched without a warrant. It wasn't unusual for people — especially those who had form — to adopt that position these days. Television had made the masses more aware of their rights and less trusting of the police and other figures of authority.

And of course there was no guarantee that they'd find anything when they did get to search Fowler's house. It might well prove to be a waste of time.

And time wasn't on their side. The Hamiltons had been missing for a week and Mason had died nearly three full days ago. The odds on finding the couple alive were receding by the minute.

Temple didn't like to dwell on how the couple might have suffered. For four days they were at the mercy of both Mason and his accomplice. But since Wednesday night the other man had had them all to himself. Would he have carried on abusing them for his own sexual gratification? Or would he have taken immediate steps to dispose of them?

The questions just kept on coming, like darts being fired at his brain. Temple rubbed his eyes and sighed. His head was pounding again, and he could feel the tension gripping his body.

He took another painkiller and washed it down with lukewarm coffee. Then he powered up his computer so that he could check his emails before writing up his notes.

Just then his phone buzzed. It was a text from Angel.

I knw u r busy, but any idea when u'll be home? I'll make dinner and we can have tht chat xx

He felt a knot tighten in his throat. Christ, he hadn't thought about Angel — or their unborn baby — since this morning. He'd been so wrapped up in the investigation that he'd pushed them from his mind. But now he was confronted with the issues again. The guilt. The doubts. The fear of being a middle-aged father.

The last thing he wanted to do was go home this evening and talk about it. But he knew he'd have to because Angel was wound up as tight as a ball of twine and eager to get his blessing in respect of the baby, before breaking the news to her friends, including Marsh.

But how would she react if he told her how he truly felt? Would she accuse him of being a selfish bastard for not embracing the idea of them having a child together?

He let go another sigh and tapped out a reply on his phone.

Can't b sure when get home. Best not to cook dinner xx

He pressed the send button and hoped she'd understand. After all, it was the truth. He had no idea when he'd be able to go home. It wasn't as though he was deliberately trying to delay the inevitable. This wasn't a run-of-the-mill case he was working on.

Still, perhaps responding by text wasn't very sensitive. He should call her, explain that he was up to his neck with work but was thinking about her the whole time.

He pulled up the pre-programmed number on his phone, but just as he was about to press it, Vaughan came rushing into his office.

'We just had word from the team at Godshill, guv,' he said. 'They've found another body.'

Temple didn't make the call. Instead, he grabbed his coat and said, 'I'll go straight there. No point anyone coming with me.'

32

The tiny village of Godshill is nestled on the western escarpment of the New Forest. The third grave had been discovered at a nearby beauty spot known as Deadman Hill, which apparently got its name from the fact that it was used as a mass grave during the second world war.

The large visitor car park was surrounded by woods and open heathland, with views across the forest in every direction.

Just as with the South Oakley Inclosure, the parking area was packed with police vehicles, while the media traffic was spread along the road in both directions.

The grave site was just inside some woods about seventy yards from the car park. A tent had already been erected over it, and uniformed officers were positioned around it to keep reporters and press photographers away.

For Temple it was a depressingly familiar scene. SOCOs in white suits and boot covers. Flashing cameras. High-powered spotlights. Skeletal remains on a rough bed of soil and stones and shredded black plastic.

'There's one body,' the senior SOCO told him. 'Been here seven or eight months is my guess.'

'Male or female?' Temple asked.

The SOCO hitched his glasses higher on the bridge of his nose.

'The supraorbital ridge on the skull is not pronounced which indicates a female. As does the size of the pelvic cavity. I reckon these are the remains of a young Caucasian woman about five-foot-two. It's too soon to know the cause of death.'

Temple felt the rush and tingle of adrenaline. The name against the location on Mason's map was Angeline Bedel, a 22-year-old foreign exchange student from France. The date next to the name was 1st August — only days after she went missing.

Temple stepped out of the forensic tent and took a couple of deep breaths. His skin felt clammy despite a sudden drop in temperature as the night started to close in over the forest.

There was a bitter taste in his mouth and he felt the acid rise in his throat again. He stood outside the tent for a while, wondering how many more horrors would unfold in the days ahead.

The body count had already reached four and there were eleven more names on the map. Plus, at least two more people were missing, possibly dead.

The smiling face of the monster responsible leapt unbidden into Temple's mind. He wondered how Mason had managed to get away with it for so long. How had he deceived everyone who had known him into believing that he was a decent, normal guy?

It was a question they'd be asking themselves for the rest of their lives.

And so will I, Temple thought. I'll forever wonder if I should have seen the madness in his eyes on the few occasions I met him.

Because it must have been there all along, hidden behind a fake façade of respectability.

★   ★   ★

Temple didn't bother to hang around. It wasn't as if there were any witnesses to interview or statements to take.

He left Deadman Hill to the SOCOs and headed back towards Southampton. But on the way he decided to swing by Mason's house.

He hadn't been back there since Thursday night and he'd been meaning to. An inventory of objects taken away for examination and analysis had been sent to him. In addition to the stuff from the loft, the list included clothes, a diary, a half-finished manuscript and a box full of utility bills and correspondence. But conspicuous by their absence were photographs of Mason or any references to his life before he set up home in the forest.

The house was still a crime scene and a police officer stood at the entrance to the lane. Inside, two SOCOs were still at work, checking every square inch of the place.

Fingerprint dust coated much of the furniture, and Temple could see where Luminol had been spread on the floors and walls in the search for traces of blood that might have been washed away.

Temple told the SOCOs he just wanted to look around and he was given paper shoe covers. But after a few minutes he wondered why he'd bothered to come. The house had been tidied up and he was able to walk around without having to step over anything.

But if he'd been hoping it would give him an insight into the sick world of Mason the monster, then he realized he was going to be sourly disappointed.

The place was cold and impersonal, with muted colours and few creature comforts. It gave no clue as to what had made Mason tick. What had made him become a sadistic killer? The house was totally devoid of personality.

'Is there much more work to be done here?' he asked one of the SOCOs.

'We'll probably be here another few days, sir. Tomorrow we're taking up some of the floorboards and digging up parts of the garden.'

'So why are there only two of you?'

'The others have finished for the day. They went to the local pub. I'll be joining them in a bit.'

'You mean the Court Jester?'

'That's the one. It's just down the road.'

Temple looked at his watch. Eight o'clock. Too late to go back to the incident room and too early to go home if he wanted to avoid having a heavy conversation with Angel.

So he sent her a text message saying he'd be late and headed for the pub.

33

'Your ears must have been burning, Inspector,' landlord Mick Russell said when Temple stepped up to the bar in the Court Jester and ordered a drink.

'What do you mean?'

Russell grinned. 'Well, earlier tonight, you were the subject of a conversation at this very bar.'

'Is that so? Who was talking about me?'

'Tom Fowler and Noah Cross. Tom was ranting on about how you and your female partner gave him a hard time today. Noah was saying you'd spoken to his sister, Amanda.'

'That's right,' Temple said. 'She told us her brother wasn't coming back from London until tomorrow.'

'Well he got back earlier this evening and dropped in here for a couple of pints. He's only just left.'

Temple looked around. The bar was busy and in one of the booths, he saw a couple of SOCOs he recognized. One of them gave him a wave and he waved back.

'So where is Mr Fowler now?'

Russell angled his head to the left. 'In the loo. He's had a few too many as usual. Wouldn't surprise me if he's throwing up.'

As if on cue, Tom Fowler emerged from the toilets, looking like he was struggling to stay upright. His eyes scoured the floor as he stumbled towards the bar. When he reached it, he announced for the benefit of anyone within earshot that he'd lost his keys.

'How the fuck am I supposed to get home?' he said.

Then he spotted Temple and stared at him through eyes that struggled to focus.

'What the hell are you doing here?'

'Having a drink,' Temple said.

Fowler wiped at his mouth with the back of his hand. The front of his beige polo sweater was streaked with vomit.

'Well, since you're here, you can find out who's pinched my frigging keys,' he said, slurring his words. 'They were on the bar. A whole fucking bunch of 'em.'

When Temple failed to respond, Fowler turned and pointed an accusing finger at the landlord.

'Have you got them, Mick? Are you trying to wind me up?'

Russell rolled his eyes. 'I swear I haven't seen them. Are you sure you didn't leave them in the car like you did before?'

235

'Of course I'm fucking sure.'

'Well, it's not as if you'll be able to drive home anyway, Tom. You're too drunk.'

'Yeah, but I've still got to get into the bloody house. How am I supposed to do that?'

Fowler leaned up against the bar and grabbed a pint glass with only a small amount of beer left in it. He swallowed that in one go and held the glass out towards Russell.

'I'll have the same again.'

Russell shook his head. 'You've had enough, Tom. If you have any more you won't be able to stand up.'

'Oh, come off it. You're only saying that because the filth are here.' Fowler turned to Temple. 'Will you tell him it's all right and he won't get into trouble? It's your bloody fault I'm pissed anyway.'

Temple's brow knitted up. 'How do you work that one out then?'

Fowler's tone rose even higher, filled with aggression.

'You came into my house and virtually accused me of being in cahoots with Mason. You're trying to tar me with the same brush just because I've got form. And now you've turned up here to harass me. You're out of fucking order.'

'I suggest you calm down, Mr Fowler,'

Temple said. 'You were one of several people we interviewed today and we're not accusing you of anything.'

Fowler slammed his glass down on the bar and raised his voice another notch.

'That's bollocks. You think I've lied to you. Well, I bloody well haven't. Everything I told you is true.' Fowler turned back to Russell. 'Is this a pub or a fucking police station? Are you just gonna stand there like a gawping idiot while this bastard harasses a paying customer?'

'He's not harassing you, mate,' Russell said. 'He's just asking you a question. So keep cool.'

Fowler's eyes filled with a dark fury. 'Don't call me mate. And don't be stupid. He's trying to get me to put my foot in it because he knows I'm drunk. That's how these bastards operate.'

'Why don't you go and sit down, Mr Fowler?' Temple said in an attempt to diffuse the situation. 'Or better still, I could drive you home and help you get into your house.'

Fowler turned slowly towards Temple, his lips pulling back in a wide, sardonic grin.

'I don't need your advice, copper. So why don't you fuck off and leave me alone before I decide to make an official complaint.'

His voice was now so loud that he had the

attention of everyone in the bar. Temple felt his muscles tense because he knew from experience that the actions of an angry drunk were entirely unpredictable.

Fowler turned back to face the bar, picked up the empty glass again and told Russell to fill it up.

'Leave it out, Tom,' Russell said. 'I've already told you that I'm not letting you have any more.'

That was when Fowler snapped. He blurted out a word that was unintelligible and hurled the glass at the shelves behind the bar. There was an almighty explosion of shattering glass, and Russell had to jump back to avoid being struck by flying fragments.

Fowler tried to execute a repeat performance by grabbing someone else's glass from on top of the bar, but Temple managed to seize his wrist before he could throw it.

'Get off of me, copper,' Fowler yelled.

But Temple twisted his arm up behind his back and forced him face down on the floor. He always carried a pair of plastic cuffs, so he pulled them from the inside pocket of his jacket and slipped them over Fowler's wrists.

Fowler's rage quickly subsided and he stopped struggling after about twenty seconds.

'That was really stupid of you,' Temple

said. 'I'm now going to have to arrest you and you'll be spending the night in a cell.'

'And he's barred from this place for life,' Russell shouted. 'I can't believe he did that.'

Temple got one of the SOCOs who rushed over to call for a patrol car. Then he dragged Fowler to his feet and marched him outside, where the cold air hit him like a slap to the face. He dropped to his knees and was violently sick on the gravel. Then he rolled onto his side and passed out.

Temple made sure he was breathing OK and wasn't about to choke on his own vomit. Then he called 999 himself and asked for an ambulance to be sent to the pub to be on the safe side.

Mick Russell came out to see what was going on. 'I'll be making sure he pays for the damage,' he said. 'He smashed two bottles of vodka and a bottle of my finest brandy. Not to mention three glass shelves.'

'Does he always get this drunk?' Temple asked.

'He gets drunk a lot and when he does, he's loud and aggressive. But I've never seen him this bad. I reckon you must have really upset him today, Inspector.'

Temple saw an upside to what had happened. It meant he could get Fowler into custody overnight and then question him first thing in the morning when he'd sobered up.

This time he'd be interviewed under caution — and not just about causing damage to property in a pub.

34

A paramedic turned up before the patrol car. She brought Fowler round and checked him over to make sure that he was all right.

'He's just drunk,' she concluded. 'Nothing that a good night's sleep won't sort out.'

After Fowler was carted off to the nick to be charged and held overnight, Temple went back into the bar to finish his drink.

Russell and his staff were still clearing up the mess, but all the customers were back to drinking and chatting as though nothing had happened.

'Is Tom being paranoid or do you really think he was involved in those killings with Mason?' Russell said.

Temple drained his glass and gave a wry smile, which Russell reciprocated.

'You know him better than I do, Mr Russell. Do you think it's something he'd be capable of doing?'

Russell sucked in air through a gap in his front teeth. 'I'm not really in a position to answer that, Inspector. I knew Grant Mason pretty well and I never thought he would ever harm a fly.'

As Temple left the pub he noted the time. Nine fifteen. He decided it wasn't too late to drop in on Noah Cross and his sister, Amanda. He wanted to find out why she'd told them that her brother got a train to London on Thursday afternoon when he'd been drinking with Tom Fowler until around seven in the evening. There was probably a straightforward explanation, but given that Cross was another of Mason's friends, it needed to be checked out.

The downstairs lights were on in the house so he assumed they were up, and Amanda Cross's Vauxhall Corsa was still parked on the driveway.

Her brother was the one who answered the door, and Temple was taken aback to see that he bore a striking resemblance to his sister. Then he remembered they were twins.

Their features were almost identical, but *his* hair was much darker and cut in a smart, fashionable style.

'You must be Noah Cross,' Temple said, holding out his ID. 'I'm DCI Temple of Hampshire police. I came here yesterday and spoke to your sister.'

Cross nodded. 'She gave me your card. I was going to get in touch tomorrow.'

'Well, I thought I'd save you the trouble. May I come in?'

'My sister's been in bed for about half an hour. She'll be asleep by now.'

'There's no need to wake her. It's you I'd like to have a chat with.'

In the living room, Temple was invited to sit on the armchair and Cross sat on the sofa, from where he turned down the volume on the television with a remote.

He was wearing jeans and a T-shirt, and it didn't seem like he was fazed by having an unexpected visit from the police.

'I gather you want to ask me about that vile scumbag who's been turning our forest into a cemetery,' Cross said.

Temple nodded. 'Did you ever suspect that he wasn't quite what he seemed to be?'

'I wish I had. He conned us all, Inspector. I considered him a mate. We drank in the same pub and I used to go on hikes with him. As far as I was concerned, he was a normal bloke who spent his life walking around the forest and writing about it.'

'You sound angry.'

'Too bloody right I am. Wouldn't you be? The creep has been in this house. I've bought his books. And he's been alone with my sister. I feel like a fool because I didn't spot that he was a murdering perv.'

'It seems that no one did, including me. I met him a few times.'

'Is that right? Then you'll know what I mean.'

Temple could tell that the guy was steaming. He was clenching his fists, the knuckles whitening with the pressure.

'I understand you were in the Court Jester this evening with Tom Fowler,' Temple said.

His eyes went up in a quick question mark. 'How did you know that?'

'I just came from there and the landlord mentioned it. In fact, you missed all the drama by leaving early.'

'Oh?'

Temple told him how Fowler had kicked off after discovering he'd lost his keys.

'It doesn't surprise me,' he said. 'Tom can't handle the booze. And he's lost his keys more times than I've had hot dinners. He probably dropped them outside.'

'Your sister told me that you're not very fond of him.'

'Well, it's not that I don't like him. It's that he can be so obnoxious. And when he's been drinking, he talks about his sexual fetish. It makes me cringe. Don't get me wrong. I'm not saying I disapprove. I mean, whatever floats your boat and all that. I know it's the drink talking, but it makes me uncomfortable when he goes on about it.'

'What does he say?'

Cross stared off into the middle distance as he struggled to find the right words. 'He tells me about those weird parties he goes to. But I don't get it and I wish he'd keep it to himself.'

Temple then asked him where he was on Thursday evening and he said he was at a stag party in London.

'I thought Amanda told you. I got back late this afternoon.'

'She did. But she also said you travelled to London by train on Thursday afternoon. And I've since discovered that you were in the pub that evening.'

He shrugged. 'There's no mystery. I was halfway to Southampton when I heard on the radio that Mason had died. So I turned around and came back. I went straight to the pub and then caught a later train in the evening.'

'And you didn't tell your sister?'

'There was no need. Look, what's Thursday got to do with anything anyway? Did something happen?'

'Grant Mason's house was broken into on Thursday evening by a man wearing a balaclava,' Temple said. 'We're anxious to rule out all Mason's friends and acquaintances.'

'Jesus. Well I was in London by ten and you can check if you don't believe me.'

'Your sister said you were staying with a friend.'

'That's right. Jack Wise. He picked me up from Waterloo station.'

'Would you mind giving me his contact details? It's just routine.'

Cross went through his phone and read out his friend's mobile number and address in London.

'I don't suppose you have a key to Mason's house, Mr Cross?'

'Of course not. We weren't that close. Besides, I've only been to his home twice. He rarely invited anyone back there.'

'Do you know who might have a key?'

'You could ask Hilary Dyer, his PA. Or maybe Tom.'

Temple made a few notes. 'Have you been following developments on the news?'

'Of course. It's awful. The New Forest is supposed to be a rural haven. Not a place where people are kidnapped, murdered and then buried.'

'Then you'll have heard that Mason had an accomplice. A man who carried out the crimes with him.'

Cross's expression froze, as though all the muscles in his face had ceased to work.

'You've got to be kidding,' he said in a shaky voice. 'Are you saying you suspect me of being that person?'

'No, I'm not,' Temple assured him. 'I'm just wondering if you might know who it could be. We think the guy's local and he must have known Mason for over two years.'

Cross went silent for several seconds as he gave it some thought, but then he said he didn't believe it could be anyone he knew.

Temple took from his pocket a photo of Ethan Kane that he'd printed before leaving the office. He showed it to Cross.

'Have you seen this man around here or in Mason's company? Bear in mind he might well have shaved off his beard since that picture was taken.'

Cross studied the photo and shook his head. 'Who is he?'

'He was a friend of Mason's in prison.'

'I didn't even know Mason had been to prison until I heard it on the news. Is that guy a suspect?'

'One of several,' Temple said.

'Well, if I see him I'll call you straightaway. He looks like a boxer so it won't be hard to spot him around here.'

35

Angel was asleep on the sofa when he got home, the light from the muted television flickering on her face. She was wearing her white towelling robe and fluffy indoor slippers. On the floor next to the sofa was a book entitled *Expecting Your First Baby*.

Temple stood there for a while, watching her sleep. Her breathing was heavy and audible, and he smiled at the way her bottom lip trembled with every breath.

Suddenly, all the horrors of the past couple of days were pushed to the back of his mind. The graves, the bodies, the gruesome video clips.

Instead, he focused with an almost physical intensity on the woman who had brought meaning back into his life. After Erin died, he had fallen into a pit of despair from which he thought he'd never emerge. But then Angel moved to Southampton from London after breaking up with her boyfriend. At first, it was just a mutual attraction. But to his surprise, it led to something deeper and he broke one of his own rules and started an affair with a member of his team.

It turned out to be one of the best moves he had ever made. She was pretty, warm, intelligent and self-deprecating. And she'd told him that she didn't want children, which had been music to his ears.

They'd talked about it a few times in the early days, of course, and she'd been adamant that she was among the growing number of young women who had chosen a path other than motherhood.

He was pretty sure that she would have stayed on that path if she hadn't fallen pregnant accidentally. And he didn't doubt that it *was* an accident. If Angel had decided that she wanted to try for a baby then she would have told him. She wouldn't have deceived him and then lied about it afterwards.

But whatever she had said in the past, the fact remained that there was a baby in her belly. His baby. And yet he still couldn't bring himself to be pleased about it. In fact, his brain felt somehow disengaged from what was happening. Even now, as he thought about it, the anxiety flooded in.

He knelt down next to the sofa and kissed her gently on the forehead. He noticed then that she'd been crying. The tears had dried to salty tracks on her cheeks.

The cold weight of guilt settled in his

stomach, and he told himself he had to accept the situation instead of being resistant to it. There was, after all, only one other option and that was for Angel to have an abortion. But if she did that he knew they would never be able to forgive themselves.

She'd regret throwing away what was possibly her only chance to have a child. And he would never get over the fact that he had allowed a life to be extinguished simply because he feared the chaos and emotion of parenthood.

The voice in his head told him it was time to man up and put Angel's needs before his own. He could begin by showing support and being more positive. And if that meant putting on an act and suppressing his true feelings then so be it. He had to be there for her. He had to find it within himself to embrace an uncertain future, no matter how daunting the prospect.

'You're home,' Angel said as her eyes fluttered open. 'What time is it?'

'Just after ten.'

'I must have fallen asleep. I feel so tired.'

'Then let's go to bed.'

'Are you all right?'

'I'm fine. And I'm sorry I got back late. I know you wanted to talk.'

'What happened today?'

'I'll tell you in the morning. Come on. Let's get you up.'

He helped her to her feet and when she was standing, he gave her a hug.

'I love you, sweetheart,' he said. 'And I want you to know that I *am* pleased about the baby.'

She stepped back and looked at him, a sleepy grin on her face.

'Tell me you mean it, Jeff.'

'I mean it.'

She started to laugh. 'I knew you'd be OK once the shock had worn off. And I'm so glad because I now want this child more than I've wanted anything in my entire life. We'll be a family, Jeff. And we'll have more to live for than just our work.'

She sounded so happy that he knew there was no going back. He was going to be a father again, whether he liked it or not.

36

He'd had the dream before and as always, it was frighteningly vivid. He was in his bedroom and a storm was raging outside. Windblown sheets of rain were rattling against the window.

He was ten at the time but in the dream he looked much younger.

His father was drunk as usual and so were the men he had invited over. There were two of them that night. The one named Dan had been to the house at least three times before. The other man was called Raymond and it was his first time.

They'd arrived earlier in their cars and his parents had begun the evening by entertaining them downstairs. He had lain on his bed, listening to their voices and their laughter, dreading what was to come.

He knew how much they paid his parents because he'd heard his father on the phone.

'A hundred quid buys you half an hour with the boy,' his father had said once. 'If you want longer it's negotiable.'

He saw himself waiting for the door to open. They'd made him put on a girl's dress again. It was the pink one with the frilly neckline. Underneath he had to wear the yellow pants from Primark.

He'd been subjected to pain and humiliation from the age of eight and he knew there was nothing he could do to stop it. His parents had warned him that if he told anyone he'd be taken away and put into a children's prison. And he'd believed them because he was too young to know the truth.

And he was too young to understand that all the suffering and abuse would cause him to grow up to be just like them. If only he'd had someone to talk to other than his parents. Like a brother or sister. Or even a friend.

In the dream the door opened suddenly. He closed his eyes and mouthed a silent prayer. Not that it ever did any good. God never once came to his rescue.

The men entered the room together. He heard them whispering to each other so he opened his eyes and turned to face them.

They were both smiling as they started to undress themselves. That's when he realized that for the first time two of his father's friends — or clients as they were sometimes called — were going to share him.

From this point on, the dream started to turn into an unbearable nightmare and he woke up screaming. His face was covered in sweat and fierce tremors were running through his body.

It was several seconds before his heart dropped to an even rhythm. He felt physically weak, drained of energy and emotion. He suddenly remembered what Grant Mason had once told him when they were sharing the secrets of their troubled childhoods.

'In the end I got my own back on my dad,' he said. 'I burned the house down with him in it.'

He wished he'd done the same to both his parents instead of running away from home. He never saw them again, and he never had the satisfaction of watching them suffer for what they'd done to him.

37

Sunday was not going to be a day of rest for Temple. He awoke at the crack of dawn after a fitful night. Too many thoughts were tumbling through his mind and even before he got out of bed, his stomach was knotted with tension.

He crept out of the bedroom without waking Angel, and went downstairs to make himself some coffee and toast. He switched on the TV in the kitchen and Sky News immediately drew his attention.

A reporter was voicing over shots of police activity at Deadman Hill.

'Today the army will be searching for more graves,' he was saying. 'So far, three have been found and there could be up to seven more. Last night it was confirmed that the latest grave had been discovered in woods near the village of Godshill. It contained the remains of a woman.

'In another development to this shocking story, police have named a man they want to question. He's Ethan Kane, a convicted sex offender who apparently served time in prison with Grant Mason before he was released several years ago.'

Kane's mugshot appeared on the screen for several seconds before they cut to the reporter who was standing next to a sign that read *Deadman Hill*.

'Meanwhile, there's growing concern that what has happened in the New Forest will impact on visitor numbers. Millions of sightseers and holidaymakers come here every year, but there are reports that people are already cancelling hotel bookings.'

It was something Temple hadn't yet considered, but he could see now why the discovery of so many clandestine graves might have a serious impact on tourism in the short-term. And in the longer-term, it would undoubtedly sour the reputation of the forest as a place of peace and beauty.

The reporter was explaining that the forest covered over 200 square miles of Southern England.

'There are 30,000 acres of woodlands and about a further 90,000 acres of heaths, grasslands and bogs,' he said. 'The forest was originally established as a royal hunting reserve by William the Conqueror in 1079. It's hard to believe that nearly a thousand years later, it's become the scene of such horrific events.'

Temple was still watching the blanket news

coverage of the story when Angel appeared in her dressing gown. She sat at the breakfast bar while he made her a cup of tea.

'I saw you on the news last night,' she said. 'You were out near Burley with Fiona.'

He joined her at the breakfast bar, and told her where they were with the case and why he was so late getting home.

'It's going to be another long day,' he said. 'Are you going to be OK on your own?'

'I was hoping to see Fiona this afternoon but I suppose that's out of the question with so much going on.'

'I'm afraid so,' Temple said. 'Were you planning to tell her about the baby?'

She gave him a sheepish look. 'I was hoping to. She is my best friend after all, and I don't want to break the news over the phone.'

He thought it prudent not to object. After all, the cat would soon be out of the bag now that he had declared his full support for the pregnancy.

'Maybe she'll have time to pop over later,' he said. 'It all depends on what happens.'

'Meanwhile, I intend to ring my parents and let *them* know. Is that all right with you, Jeff?'

She flashed him a hundred-watt smile and there was no way he was going to burst her bubble. For weeks she'd wallowed in self-pity and mild depression as she recovered from the crash. But the pregnancy had put the colour back into her cheeks and the glint back into her eyes.

'Of course I don't mind,' he said. 'Whatever makes you happy.'

38

When he got to the central police station Temple went straight to the custody suites to check on Tom Fowler. He was still sleeping through what must have been a whopping hangover.

The duty officer told Temple that Fowler hadn't yet been charged because when he was brought in, he'd been too drunk to understand what was going on.

'Has he been out cold all night?' Temple asked.

'He woke up once, screaming and yelling, but he didn't cause any trouble.'

'Let me know when he's awake then. Might as well interview him before we press charges.'

Upstairs, the incident room was already filling up. Both DC Marsh and DS Vaughan had arrived and Beresford had let it be known that he was in his office.

Temple spent the first fifteen minutes bringing himself up to speed, and writing up his notes on what had happened the previous evening at the Court Jester.

The briefing got underway at eight sharp

and Beresford came along to find out how things were progressing, and to announce that another press conference would be taking place that afternoon.

'The pressure is really on us to find the Hamiltons and Mason's accomplice,' he said. 'The brass are even talking about setting up a task force because they think it's getting too big for MIT. But I'm resisting because I'm convinced they're wrong. This is our patch and our case and I want us to be the ones who solve it.'

He then opened up the floor so the detectives could provide updates. Vaughan was the first to raise his hand.

'I had a call back last night from Ethan Kane's probation officer,' he said. 'His name's Frank Meade and according to him, Kane is a really nasty piece of work.'

'What did he tell you?' Temple asked.

'Quite a lot, including some useful background stuff. Kane's parents lost control of him when he was a teenager and he was expelled from secondary school because of his violent behaviour towards other pupils. Several girls and a boy claimed he sexually abused them. Early psychiatric reports described him as seriously disturbed. One labelled him a sexual sadist. Another wrote that he was a cross-dresser. He apparently carried out two sex attacks on young men while wearing women's clothes.'

'Did you ask Meade if he thinks Kane could have been Mason's accomplice?' Temple asked.

'I did and he said it's quite possible. He believes that any man who enjoys torturing people is more than capable of committing murder.'

'Does he know where Kane is?'

'No, he doesn't, but there's an interesting story around his disappearance. Soon after being released from prison, he started frequenting dating sites on the internet. He met a woman named Theresa Bellamy and they hit it off. Five months into their relationship, he moved out of his rented flat in London and into her detached house in the Kent countryside. He was open about it and registered the address with the probation service. But then a few months later, he suddenly disappeared. Miss Bellamy was questioned by police and she told them that he just walked out without an explanation. She went to the shops one day and when she got back, he was gone with all his belongings.'

'And I take it she didn't know where he went.'

'That's what she told police, but the strange thing is that just weeks after she was questioned, she sold her house and vanished herself.'

'How do we know? Was she under surveillance or something?'

Vaughan shook his head. 'Her daughter went to the police because she thought that something bad might have happened to her mother. Her married name is Ruth Kogan and she was living in Australia at the time. She received an email in which her mother told her she was selling up and moving abroad. When she tried to contact her mother she got no response. So she asked a friend to go to the house, and that's when she discovered her mum had gone and the property had been sold.'

'So what happened next?'

'Kent police made inquiries and discovered that in the weeks leading up to the house sale, Miss Bellamy's bank account was emptied of all her savings and she sold all her jewellery. They came to the conclusion that she'd either upped sticks and moved away by herself or had run off with Kane.'

'So did they try to trace her?'

'Of course, but they got nowhere.'

'What about the money from the sale of the house? That must have been paid into a bank account.'

'It was paid into her own account. But then

she withdrew all £300,000 straightaway in order to buy gold ingots. She then closed the account and that's where the money trail ended. We can only assume that she then sold the ingots so she could use the cash to start a new life.'

'So the case must still be open,' Temple said.

Vaughan nodded. 'It is, but Kent police aren't pursuing it with any vigour. They say Miss Bellamy hasn't done anything wrong and Kane's not a priority.'

'Well, he is now,' Temple said. 'So we need to follow it up ourselves. Let's contact the daughter. Find out what she knows.'

'I'm already on it, guv. She lives in Aldershot now with her husband. I actually spoke to her briefly last night and she's agreed to come in later this morning to talk to us.'

'That's good work, Dave. Stick with it and see what else you can come up with.'

'Well, there's one other thing I need to mention,' Vaughan said. 'The probation officer told me that soon after leaving prison, Kane had an operation to straighten his broken nose. So he looks very different now to how he looks in the mugshot.'

39

As the briefing continued, Temple became aware of a growing level of excitement in the room. His detectives could see that in Ethan Kane they had a viable suspect. There was also a sense of collective purpose that instilled him with confidence in his team.

They all looked tired, though. He spotted a few red eyes and stifled yawns. But it was clear from the various updates that they were working flat out and doing a good job.

He was told that the bodies found in the grave near Burley had been positively identified as those of Simon and Jane Cramer. The post-mortems were to be held today. However, there was still no confirmation on the identity of the corpse at Deadman Hill, although they were pretty certain it would turn out to be the foreign exchange student, Angeline Bedel.

The team had had some luck with traffic camera footage near the van hire company in Southampton. The van taken out by Mason the week before had been caught on several cameras, but none had captured him being dropped off or picked up there. The van in question was now with forensics, who were examining it for fingerprints and for any evidence that the Hamiltons had been inside.

Ross Cavendish, the guy who ran the agency which supplied Fowler with S&M prostitutes, had been questioned by DC Whelan.

'He's a right spiv and at first, he denied having met Fowler,' Whelan said. 'But he changed his tune when I threatened to arrest him for obstruction and pimping. Then he confirmed what Fowler said about using the agency. They've supplied him with whiplash whores for a couple of years. He goes to them about once a month and he's always the submissive.'

'So where do the sessions take place?'

'There's a house here in town that's fully equipped with all the S&M paraphernalia. It's a glorified brothel and three so-called mistresses work from there, offering a specialized service. We checked it out late last night but it's obviously not the room featured in the videos found in Mason's loft.'

Temple then told the team that Tom Fowler was in a cell and described what had happened in the pub the night before.

'It's given us an opportunity to interview him here under caution,' he said. 'Hopefully we'll be able to search his house at the same time.'

'I'll chase up the warrant,' Beresford said. 'Is he still in the frame then?'

Temple nodded. 'For the time being he is.'

He then reported on his chat with Noah Cross and asked Marsh to check out Cross's alibi.

'He's given me the number of a friend he's been staying with in London. He claims he got a late train up on Thursday and his friend met him at Waterloo. If it's true, then he couldn't have been the man who broke into Mason's house and attacked me.'

Temple went through task assignments, and then Beresford brought the meeting to a close by reminding everyone that the army was joining the search teams at the other seven locations marked on Mason's map.

'This is an unprecedented deployment of police and service personnel,' he said, his voice solemn. 'By the end of today, it's possible that we'll have discovered the bodies of more murder victims.'

40

Tom Fowler looked like death warmed up. His stubble was a charcoal shadow on his jaw and there were dark smudges beneath his bloodshot eyes. He also reeked of alcohol and vomit, which made it uncomfortable in the interview room.

Temple handed him a coffee from the machine and sat down to face him across the table. Fowler's hand shook as he picked up the cup and slurped from it.

'So, what can you remember about last night, Mr Fowler?'

Fowler held the cup in both hands and lifted his head to look at Temple.

His voice was thin and wheezy. 'I remember I got angry and broke a few glasses. You made a big deal out of it and I was arrested. You treated me like a fucking armed robber.'

'You broke more than a few glasses,' Temple said. 'And I'm sure that if I hadn't stepped in, things would have turned even uglier.'

'That's total rubbish. I'd had a couple of drinks so I was a bit tipsy. And I was pissed off because I'd lost my keys. Then you started harassing me. So is it any wonder that I lost my temper?'

'You were acting like someone who's really stressed out, Mr Fowler,' Temple said. 'Was it because we gave you a fright when we came to see you?'

His jaw stiffened. 'Don't be ridiculous.'

'Well, if I was in your shoes I'd be shit scared too. After all, given your relationship with Mason and the fact that you're a sado masochist yourself . . . '

Fowler slammed his fist down on the table and stared daggers at Temple.

'You're trying to fit me up because I'm an obvious target. Well, I'm not going to make it easy for you. There's no evidence linking me to what Mason did and there's no way you'll get me to incriminate myself. So don't bother trying.'

Temple sat back, crossed his arms. 'OK, let's play it your way. Tell me again about your first encounter with Grant Mason.'

Fowler shook his head. 'No way. I've been arrested for what happened in the pub. Charge me in relation to that or let me go.'

'You'll be charged in due course, Mr Fowler, but your legal rights don't extend to telling me what questions I can ask you.'

Fowler uncrossed his arms and leaned forwards, resting on his elbows. He released a breath and Temple caught a blast of alcohol.

'In that case, I'm not saying another word until I've talked to a lawyer.'

Temple tutted and looked at his watch. 'I can arrange for you to see a duty solicitor or you can call in your own brief? What's it to be?'

'The duty solicitor's fine.'

'In that case I'll get right onto it. Meanwhile, you'll remain in custody.'

'Then I want some breakfast. I'm starving.'

'I'll sort it.' Temple got to his feet. 'You should also know that I've just obtained a warrant to search your house. A forensic team will be going there shortly.'

Fowler sprang up, knocking over the cup and spilling hot coffee across the table. He stabbed a rigid finger at Temple.

'You bastards have no right to invade my privacy. I haven't done anything wrong. This is a stitch up.'

'Don't be absurd, Mr Fowler. We're just doing our job. Yours won't be the only property we search during the course of our investigation into Grant Mason and the murders he committed. And if you have nothing to hide, then you should have nothing to worry about.'

41

Ruth Kogan arrived at ten after driving down from Aldershot. DS Vaughan went to meet her in reception and brought her up to Temple's office.

She was in her late twenties with a broad, homely face and small button nose. Her short brown hair was shiny and neat, and she wore a dark tank top over jeans that were tight around the hips.

Vaughan had already explained to her over the phone that they wanted to ask her about her mother's former live-in boyfriend, Ethan Kane. And she'd gleaned from the TV that he was being sought in connection with the New Forest murders.

'I knew nothing about Kane's past until I returned from Australia three years ago and spoke to the police about my mother's disappearance,' she said. 'And of course I never met the man so I don't know what he was like.'

She went on to say that she was still desperately worried about her mother because she hadn't heard from her in all that time.

'I'm convinced that Kane must have had

something to do with it,' she said. 'That's why I decided to come straight down here today. If you're going to start looking for him again, then I want to do all that I can to help.'

Tears filled her eyes and she blinked them back.

'Were you and your mother close?' Temple asked.

'We were at one time. My father died when I was ten and my mother brought me up by herself. We got on well until I was twenty-four and went to Australia on holiday. While there, I met a man and fell in love so I decided to stay. My mother was devastated and even refused to come to the wedding a year later. Eventually, she flew down to meet my husband and we stayed in touch after that by phone and email.'

'I gather Kane moved in with her soon after he was released from prison.'

She nodded. 'He didn't tell her he'd been to jail. She met him through an online dating agency, and he said he was divorced and had been living in Spain where he'd owned a bar. She wrote, telling me that he was moving in and she was really smitten. I was happy for her and he sounded like a nice man so I saw no need to worry. But all that changed when I got this email.'

She picked her handbag up off the floor

and took from it a sheet of folded A4 paper.

'I've kept it all these years,' she said. 'I'm sure it's the reason Kent police didn't put much effort into finding her.'

She handed the sheet to Temple. It was a print-out of the email from her mother.

Dear Ruth

I want you to know that Ethan has left me and I feel terribly depressed. There's no one here to help me through it so I've decided to start my life all over again. I'm selling the house and all my jewellery, so I'll have enough cash to go anywhere in the world. I won't tell you where I'm going because I need to be completely by myself for a while. Perhaps if you were here for me things would be bearable, but you're not and I wouldn't dream of dragging you away from your perfect life in Australia. So don't worry about me. I'll get back in touch in the not too distant future to let you know how and where I am.

Your loving mother xx

'It's a strange note,' Temple said, handing the sheet to Vaughan.

'It came from my mother's email account but I can't be a hundred per cent sure that she wrote it.'

'So do you think she went off with Kane and that's why she doesn't want anyone to know?'

'I think it's quite likely,' she said. 'My mother's never been one for grand gestures and she doesn't like taking risks. In fact, she hates change, which partly accounts for why she was so upset when I moved away.'

'What about her friends? Couldn't they have shed light on what happened?'

'She didn't have any friends in Kent. She suffered from severe bouts of depression, so she didn't work and hardly ever went out. And the house was in the country and quite remote so she had no close neighbours. It was after I left that she decided to try to meet someone through the dating sites.'

'So what did you do after receiving this email?'

'I tried to contact her but she didn't respond to phone calls or emails. After a week or so, I asked a friend of mine in Kent to go to the house and that's when I heard back that it had been sold. I came back to England a week later and went to the police. It was then I discovered that they were looking for Kane because he hadn't reported to his probation officer. But they insisted there was no evidence to suggest that my mother had run away with him.'

'So what happened next?'

She heaved her shoulders. 'Before I went back to Australia I made my own enquiries. I talked to her bank and the estate agent who sold her house. The estate agent only met her once but he said she seemed fine and she told him she was going abroad to live. She lowered the price substantially to secure a quick sale.'

'What about the bank?'

'Well, all they could tell me was that my mother withdrew all her savings in cash — about £10,000 — in the weeks leading up to when she sold the house. Then when the money from the sale came through, she used it almost immediately to buy gold from a dealer in London. Days later she disappeared and got a house clearing firm to take away all the furniture.'

'Did the bank not think it odd that your mother was withdrawing so much cash?'

'Not until I raised it with them. Then they looked back at all the withdrawals to make sure they were in order. And they were.'

'What about her credit cards?'

'She only had one and she used it right up to the day she disappeared. According to Kent police, she paid off the entire balance and closed the account.'

Temple pondered for a few moments what he'd been told. He could see why Ruth

Kogan was worried about her mother, but at the same time he wasn't convinced that finding her would lead them to Kane.

It was obviously the same conclusion that Kent police had come to. But to them Kane would have been a low-priority perp, and they would have been reluctant to commit too many man-hours and resources to finding him.

But now things were different. Kane was a suspect in a series of kidnappings and murders, and it was necessary to explore every lead — no matter how tenuous — in the hope of tracking him down.

'What you've told us is really useful, Mrs Kogan,' he said. 'I agree that it's possible your mother went off somewhere with Ethan Kane, and I hope that when we find him it will solve that mystery for you, one way or the other.'

'I hope so too, Inspector. I just want to know that she's all right.'

'Of course you do. And I promise to contact you if we come up with anything. You're living in Aldershot now, I take it.'

'Yes, we are. We left Australia nine months ago after my husband was offered a job in London. We're renting at the moment because we can't decide whether or not to stay permanently.'

Temple asked her if she had contact information for the bank and estate agent her mother had dealt with. She said she did and pulled out her mobile phone.

Temple then turned to Vaughan and asked him to get in touch with them.

'It's a long shot, I know,' he said. 'But there might be something that was missed at the time by Kent police. And check to see if Miss Bellamy used a firm of solicitors to sell the house. She may well have given them some indication where she was going.'

After providing the details, Ruth Kogan asked Temple if he wanted to see a photo of her mother.

'Of course,' he said.

She held up her phone and he saw an attractive, middle-aged woman with an oval face framed by long, dark hair.

'I can't help feeling responsible,' she said, choking back tears. 'If I hadn't gone away, then she would probably never have met Ethan Kane and would still be at home.'

'You weren't to know what would happen,' Temple said.

'But I do know one thing,' she said. 'I know my mother wouldn't just go away and not stay in contact. So either someone is stopping her from getting in touch or else she's dead.'

42

They found the fourth grave at 11 a.m. that morning. The search team had been at it for five hours when an object showed up on the radar equipment three feet below ground.

The news spread like wildfire. TV reporters did their live links directly from the scene and Temple and his detectives watched it on the screens in the incident room.

The location was a forest glade north of the village of Minstead. There were two names against the spot on Mason's map — Joseph Pearson and Heidi Frobisher. They were an engaged couple in their twenties who had disappeared fifteen months ago. It was believed they had gone out for a drive one Thursday afternoon when they both had a day off work. Their abandoned car was found near their home in Poole, just west of the New Forest.

Temple felt compelled to go and check it out on the way to Tom Fowler's house, where he planned to join in the execution of the search warrant.

He told the duty solicitor that he wouldn't be interviewing Fowler formally until the afternoon. By then, they would hopefully have finished the search of the house and decided whether he should remain in the frame.

He told the rest of the team to focus their efforts on finding Ethan Kane, which meant chasing down all his relatives and known acquaintances.

'He's the prime suspect,' he said. 'From the sound of it he's as crazy and sadistic as Mason was. They would have made a formidable pairing. He hasn't been seen for almost three years since he walked out on his girlfriend and jumped probation. The dates on Mason's map go back about two years so we have to consider the possibility that Kane came down here to live near his former cellmate and together they embarked on a killing spree.'

Temple drove to the forest on autopilot as his brain struggled to assimilate the thoughts that were crashing through it. He found it difficult to focus because there were too many distractions. Helicopters flew overhead, police cars were everywhere and army trucks thundered along the country roads.

It was dry outside and the sky was a steely grey. Yet for a Sunday, the forest was not at all busy. There were few cyclists and hikers and the parking areas were virtually empty

It made Temple feel distinctly uneasy. To him, the forest had always been a place of natural beauty and tranquillity, where locals and visitors alike felt safe and secure.

But from now on many people would probably find it hostile and threatening. The landscape had been blighted by the blood of Mason's victims.

And it would be hard for them not to wonder just how many other gruesome secrets were buried beneath the woods and heathlands.

★ ★ ★

The grave near Minstead contained the remains of two more people.

Temple felt his heart give a single heavy thump as he stared down at the dirt-smothered skeletons. There was no doubt in his mind that he was looking at Joseph Pearson and Heidi Frobisher.

He couldn't remember what they had looked like even though he'd seen their photographs along with all the other missing persons. And that made him feel bad.

Around him the scene was one of semi-organized chaos. There was the usual band of white-suited SOCOs, plus officers in uniform and a group of soldiers armed with shovels instead of weapons.

It was almost surreal.

Once again, the grave was close to a visitor car park that was now packed with vehicles and hordes of reporters. Temple reflected on how strange it was that the scene was being repeated at six other locations throughout the forest. So many graves and so many bodies, the cruel legacy of two sadistic killers who had used the area as their own personal hunting ground.

Temple made a visual assessment of the scene and spoke to those in charge. He was introduced to a forensic anthropologist, who'd been called in to examine the bones and who confirmed that the remains were those of a man and a woman.

As Temple walked back to the car park, a dozen reporters closed in around him, microphones out.

He pushed past them without answering any of their questions and was relieved when he got to his car. Once behind the wheel, he closed his eyes and felt his body grow rigid. A coldness gnawed at his gut and his breath came out in shudders.

He knew that it was a reaction to what he'd seen over the past couple of days. He had witnessed the exhumation of no less than six corpses. And it was all the more distressing because he'd seen most of them on video being abused and tortured before they'd been put to death.

* * *

Temple headed south from Minstead towards East Boldre, a distance of about five miles.

On the way, he passed the scene of another search operation, this one near a beauty spot called Honey Hill. There was police presence on the road and off to the left, he saw soldiers gathered in the car park. But he didn't stop because he assumed they hadn't yet come across a grave.

As he drove, the events of the past few days ran through his head on fast-forward. It had started out as a straightforward missing person case and was now something that would be talked about and analyzed by criminologists for years to come.

But despite all the resources they had been throwing at the investigation, Bob and Rosemary Hamilton were still unaccounted for.

It was hard for Temple not to fear the worst, but harder still for him to accept defeat. He was clinging to the hope that if they found Mason's accomplice, then they would find the Hamiltons.

43

The sun was threatening to break through the clouds as Temple arrived at Fowler's house. Two police vehicles and a SOC van were parked on the road out front.

Temple pulled onto the grass verge opposite the driveway entrance. He got out and held back from crossing the road to let a car approaching from the right drive by.

But the car slowed down and pulled onto the verge behind his car. He frowned when he realized that it was the blue Vauxhall Corsa he'd seen on Amanda Cross's driveway. Her brother Noah was sitting behind the wheel.

Temple stepped up to the car on the driver's side and Cross lowered his window.

'Hello, Inspector,' he said. 'I didn't expect to see you here.'

'I could say the same about you, Mr Cross.'

'I tried phoning Tom this morning to find out what happened to him last night. When he didn't answer or return my calls, I thought I'd drive over and see if he was in.' He pointed his chin at the house. 'So what's going on? Is Tom inside?'

'Mr Fowler is still in custody,' Temple

replied. 'We've obtained a warrant to search his house and that's now in progress.'

'Why are you doing that? All he did was throw a tantrum in a pub.'

'I'm afraid I can't say anymore, Mr Cross. So I suggest you get on with your business and I'm sure you'll learn in due course what's going on.'

Temple moved away before Cross could ask another question. He hurried across the road and up Fowler's driveway. He entered the house after he was kitted out with a forensic suit complete with hood and boot covers.

Inside, the SOCOs and detectives were painstakingly searching every room. The senior crime scene officer was a DC named Rory MacBride. Clean-shaven, fair-haired, bad complexion. He responded to Temple's questions in a rich, West Highland accent.

'The loft is hardly big enough to swing a cat in,' he said. 'And there doesn't appear to be a basement. So I think it's safe to say that this isn't where the victims were held while they were being tortured and abused.'

'Are you sure about the basement?' Temple said. 'I've been in a few houses where the entrance to the basement was concealed.'

MacBride shrugged. 'Well, if there is a door we haven't found it yet and we've looked bloody hard enough.'

'What about the garden and the woods in the immediate area?'

'It doesn't look as though any of the earth in the back garden has been disturbed recently. We haven't yet checked out the woods and fields around the house.'

Temple went from room to room and was struck by how bland the place was. The walls throughout were the same dull shade of grey and there were very few pictures to brighten them up. There were no carpets upstairs, just untreated floorboards that creaked when anyone walked on them.

Temple was surprised that a man who made his living as an estate agent hadn't put more effort into making his own home more comfortable.

One of the bedrooms was being used as an office with an old teak desk and a couple of Ikea filing cabinets against the wall. On the desk sat two laptop computers and a SOCO was checking both of them.

'Why has he got two of those?' Temple said.

The SOCO looked up and shrugged.

'That's what I'm about to find out, sir. One's a Mac and quite new. The other's a top-of-the-range Dell, so he might like to switch between the two. Are we sure that Tom Fowler lived here alone?'

'As far as we know he did.'

'Well the Mac definitely belongs to him,' the SOCO said as he tapped at the keyboard. 'His name's on documents and email accounts.'

The SOCO turned his attention to the Dell which had also been fired up.

Temple decided to leave him to it and stepped towards the door. But just as he was leaving the room, the SOCO said, 'Holy shit.'

Temple stopped in the doorway and snapped to attention.

'What is it?' he said.

The SOCO swivelled in his chair to face Temple and gestured towards the laptop.

'This one doesn't belong to Fowler.'

'How do you know?'

'Because it's crowded with documents created by Grant Mason, including book manuscripts and correspondence between him and his publisher. I reckon this could have been stolen from Mason's house the night you were attacked there.'

Temple felt the blood stop pumping through his veins. But before he could react, he heard MacBride yelling for him to come downstairs.

He hurried down and was summoned outside where a group of SOCOs were gathered around a wheelie bin. On the ground next to the bin were spread the contents of a black plastic bag.

'The bin had been left at the bottom of the driveway so the rubbish could be collected,' MacBride said. 'When we checked it, we found those blood-soaked clothes.'

There was a small pile of clothes amongst the rubbish. Temple's eyes were drawn to a purple sweater with black stripes on it.

He was pretty sure it was the one Rosemary Hamilton had been wearing on the day she disappeared.

44

Temple placed two transparent evidence bags on the table in the interview room. One contained the blood-soaked sweater from the wheelie bin on Fowler's driveway. The other contained Grant Mason's laptop.

'We found these during the search of your property, Mr Fowler,' Temple said. 'Can you explain how they got there?'

Fowler stared at the bags for a few seconds through narrowed eyes. Then he switched his gaze fearfully between Temple and Vaughan.

'What the fuck is this?' he said.

His lawyer, who was sitting next to him, put a reassuring hand on his shoulder. His name was Ralph Lister. He was bald, with sharp features and a sharp mind.

'It's best if you just answer the question,' he told his client.

Fowler's eyes shifted back to the table. He leaned forwards, his squint becoming more pronounced.

'The laptop isn't mine,' he said. 'I'm not even sure what that other thing is.'

'It's a woman's sweater,' Temple said. 'And it has quite a lot of blood on it.'

Fowler raised his eyes and shook his head. 'I've never seen it before. In fact, I've never seen either of them. They couldn't have been in my house.'

Fowler's hangover had worn off but if anything he looked even worse than he had that morning. His clothes had been taken away for forensic examination and he was wearing an ill-fitting jumpsuit.

He and his lawyer had been told that he was now being questioned in connection with the murders of at least four people, plus the abduction of Bob and Rosemary Hamilton. The lawyer had been given time to brief his client before the interview started, but they hadn't been told until now what the search had turned up.

'The sweater was among a number of clothes that were put in a black plastic bag and left in a wheelie bin on your driveway,' Temple said. 'The other garments are also stained with blood. Our forensic technicians have established that the blood is only about twenty-four hours old. Which means it was shed yesterday afternoon.'

Lister clucked his tongue. 'If the wheelie bin was on the driveway then anyone could have put it there, Inspector. You know that as well as I do.'

Temple tapped a finger on the laptop. 'But

this was found inside the house. In the office, to be precise. And it belonged to Grant Mason.'

'That's not possible,' Fowler said. 'Why would I have it?'

'Because you took it from his home on Thursday evening. That was after you ransacked the place and attacked me.'

'That's bullshit. I didn't go to his house on Thursday. And I'm not the one who did all that stuff with Mason. I've already told you that.'

Temple reached into a briefcase on the floor next to his chair and brought out yet another evidence bag.

He placed it on the table between them. 'Can you see what that is, Mr Fowler?'

Fowler swallowed hard. 'It looks like a flogger whip.'

'That's right. As you well know, it's a sexual contraption used by a dominant to inflict pain on a submissive in an S&M encounter. I'm sure you've used them before.'

'That one doesn't belong to me.'

'Really? Then why did we find it in a suitcase under your bed along with various other S&M gizmos, including wrist restraints, canes and gags?'

Fowler's tongue flicked briefly across his lips. 'The other stuff's mine, but not that. I don't own a flogger whip.'

Temple lifted the bag above the table. The flogger whip inside was black with a studded handle and thirty or so leather tails about a foot long.

'Look at that, Mr Fowler. There's blood on the tails. We've already carried out a quick check and determined that it matches the blood on the sweater. The blood group is B negative, which is quite rare. But we know that Rosemary Hamilton, who was abducted by Grant Mason a week ago, is B negative. So it seems certain that it's her blood on both objects. She was wearing the sweater when she disappeared.'

Fowler shot Temple a cold, hard stare. 'This is insane. You must have planted those things in my house.'

Temple blew out a frustrated breath. 'Don't be daft. Why the hell would we want to entrap an innocent man?'

'You tell me.'

Temple felt his face tighten. 'Why don't you just come clean and save everyone a lot of time and trouble?'

Fowler turned on his lawyer. 'Are you just going to sit there and let them get away with this?'

'Just stay calm, Mr Fowler.'

Lister tried to put his hand on Fowler's

shoulder, but this time it was pushed away.

'No, I won't stay fucking calm. Why should I? These things don't belong to me. I swear to God. I'm being set up.'

'What have you done with Rosemary Hamilton and her husband?' Temple asked him.

Fowler stared at Temple, his eyes bulging out of their sockets.

'I haven't done anything. You've got it wrong. All I know is what you told me and what I heard on the news.'

'We've got you banged to rights,' Temple said. 'Bob and Rosemary Hamilton's clothes were found on your property, along with the flogger whip that has traces of blood on it. In addition, you had Grant Mason's laptop. They're damning pieces of evidence that tell us you're the man we've been looking for. You were Mason's accomplice.'

Fowler flared his nostrils. 'It's not true.'

'Then explain what you were doing with these objects,' Temple said. 'And it won't wash just to say that you don't know how they got there.'

'But I don't. You have to believe that.'

Temple's lips twisted into a thin smile. 'The case we have against you is watertight already. You have a criminal record for killing your girlfriend during a kinky sex session. You were one of Mason's best friends. And then there's this lot. So stop lying and get it off your chest.'

Fowler's eyes turned small and fierce. 'I'm not fucking lying. How many more times have I got to say it? I'm not the bloke you're after.'

'And no matter how many times you say it I won't believe you,' Temple said. 'So I suggest you accept that the game is up and confess.'

'I'm not confessing to something I didn't do and you can't make me.'

Temple's gaze hardened as he leaned across the table.

'Where can we find the Hamiltons? Are they still alive?'

'My client has already told you that he doesn't know where they are,' Lister said. 'And I object to your aggressive tone, Inspector. Mr Fowler has answered your questions and has made it clear that he knows nothing about those objects and he did not commit those crimes alongside Grant Mason.'

'But he's lying,' Temple said. 'Anyone can see that.'

At that moment, Fowler broke down and started sobbing. He tried to speak between sobs but what he said made no sense.

Temple wanted to continue pushing him in

the hope of extracting a confession, but Lister kicked up a fuss and demanded that the interview be stopped until his client had composed himself.

Temple had no choice but to agree, so he said aloud for the benefit of the tape recorder that the interview was being suspended.

He and Vaughan then got up. As they left the room, Temple said, 'We'll come back in half an hour.'

45

The mood in the incident room was upbeat. The team were of the firm belief that they had got their man. As far as they were concerned, the evidence against Tom Fowler was overwhelming.

But Temple was anxious to curb their excitement. He knew only too well that cases often fall apart even when you think you have them sewn up tighter than a hangman's noose.

He called everyone together to brief them on how the interview had gone, and to find out if any more incriminating evidence had been found at Fowler's house.

But so far nothing more had been discovered, and there were no clues on the property as to the whereabouts of Bob and Rosemary Hamilton. But Fowler's home computer had been seized and the experts were wading through the contents.

More officers had been sent to the house and they'd started digging up the garden and searching the woods and heaths around the property.

'It's too early to start celebrating,' Temple

said. 'Fowler hasn't yet confessed and he hasn't been charged. So the pressure is still on us. It means we have to keep chasing all the other leads. So let's start with Ethan Kane. Where are we on that?'

Dave Vaughan had been working on it before joining Temple in the interview room. He said he had spoken to the estate agent who had arranged the sale of Theresa Bellamy's house.

'They told me they had no idea where she intended to move to,' he said. 'I also managed to get in touch with the solicitor who represented Miss Bellamy on the sale. It was a straightforward arrangement apparently, and the buyers were a retired couple from London who paid in cash. Miss Bellamy went to the lawyer twice so she could sign the various documents and provide forms of identification. He said she was by herself both times and she didn't mention the name Ethan Kane or tell him where she was going to live. But he's going to dig out the file with his notes just in case he's missed something and email it to me when he's back in his office tomorrow.'

Temple turned to DC Marsh and asked her if she'd managed to check out Noah Cross's alibi for Thursday evening.

'The number he gave you checks out,' she

replied. 'It's registered to a man named Jack Wise who lives in Bermondsey. But I've called him three times and he hasn't answered his phone or responded to my messages.'

'Then get the local station to check out his address. According to Cross, he arrived in London by train on Thursday evening and stayed with his pals for a stag do until yesterday.'

'Do you think he could be lying, guv?'

Temple shrugged. 'Probably not, but I'm keen to tie up the loose ends as quickly as possible.'

One of the other detectives drew Temple's attention to the TV screen. The BBC was carrying a news flash claiming that Hampshire police had arrested a man in connection with the New Forest murders.

'The man is believed to live in the village of East Boldre, less than a mile from the house owned by Grant Mason,' the newsreader intoned. 'We understand he was a close friend of Mason and works as an estate agent in the New Forest.'

The newsreader then went on to talk about the latest grave to be discovered near Minstead.

'The remains of six people have now been unearthed,' he said. 'But the search for more bodies is continuing at six other sites across the forest.'

Chief Superintendent Beresford had been watching the same news broadcast. When Temple went to his office to update him, his boss could barely contain his excitement.

'I've called a press conference for six o'clock,' he said. 'Any chance I can announce that we've charged the bastard?'

'I think that would be premature, sir. He's denying all knowledge of the stuff we found at his house, so it's all circumstantial evidence.'

'Maybe so, but it's plenty strong enough to get us a conviction.'

'That's probably true, but we still have no idea what's happened to the Hamiltons and if we charge Fowler, we can't press him on that.'

Beresford chewed the corner of his lower lip as he thought about it.

'That's a good point, Jeff. So what time was he brought in last night?'

'Around eleven.'

'Well that means we can keep him in custody without charge for another six hours.'

'We might need more time, especially if the lawyer takes the view that we're putting him under too much pressure and demands that he has a break.'

Beresford nodded. 'Very well. I'll get a magistrate's order so that we can hold him for up to ninety-six hours without charge.'

'That's great, sir. While you're at it, it'd be a good idea to get another warrant to search his office and have a look at his work computer.'

'Consider it done. In the meantime, I'll just confirm what the press already knows — that we're questioning a suspect. But be warned, Jeff. The media blitz is going to get even more intense.'

46

The stench of Tom Fowler's body odour filled the interview room. It didn't help that he was sweating profusely and the alcohol he'd consumed the night before was still seeping through his pores.

But at least he'd regained his composure, and for two hours he sat next to his solicitor and continued to deny that he knew what had happened to Bob and Rosemary Hamilton. He insisted he had no idea why their blood-stained clothes were in his wheelie bin or why Mason's laptop was in his office.

They were forced to suspend the interview again so that he could have something to eat and drink. Temple took the opportunity to see what else had come in, but the news was disappointing. Fowler's computer contained a collection of S&M porn videos, but all of them had been downloaded from legitimate sites on the internet.

There were no homemade movies of the kind found in Mason's loft. And no incriminating emails and text messages between him and Mason. Plus, none of the prints found on the van that Mason had hired the week before belonged to Fowler.

His prints did turn up in Mason's house, but he explained those away by saying he'd been there a number of times.

A magistrate signed an order allowing them to hold him for up to ninety-six hours without charge, so to some extent the pressure was eased. But it didn't feel that way to Temple. He was desperate to know about the fate of Bob and Rosemary Hamilton.

He found it hard not to conclude that they were already dead. Why else would their clothing have been dumped in the bin? And that in itself raised several questions. All the clothes — which included Mr Hamilton's shirt and trousers and Mrs Hamilton's jeans — were intact apparently. Forensics were saying that there were no holes in the fabrics to indicate puncture wounds of any kind.

Of course, that didn't mean they hadn't suffered fatal injuries to their heads or exposed flesh. The fact that the blood had been shed as recently as twenty-four hours ago suggested that the couple had been kept alive for a week.

Did that mean Fowler had murdered them in a panic? Had he gone to the pub afterwards to get drunk?

Temple put these questions and more to Fowler but he didn't falter in his denials.

'Look, I'm no angel,' he said. 'I made a terrible mistake some years ago and I'm still paying for it. I'm also guilty of enjoying a form of sexual behaviour that most people find abhorrent. But I was not Mason's accomplice and I had nothing to do with that couple's disappearance. On the Saturday they went missing, I was at work. So someone is setting me up and if it isn't you lot, then you need to find out who it is.'

'So you're saying that someone broke into your house and planted the laptop and flogger whip?' Temple said.

'Of course I am. How else would they have got there?'

'But there are no signs of a break-in.'

'Then whoever did it had a key.'

'You've already told us that you didn't give your key to anybody.'

'What about the one that was stolen from the pub last night? Have you thought about that?'

'Actually we have,' Temple said. 'The landlord of the Court Jester called us this morning to say that he'd found your bunch of keys on the ground next to your car. That was presumably where you dropped them.'

Temple called a halt to the interview at eight o'clock because Lister insisted that his client had faced enough questions for one day

301

and was in no fit state to answer any more.

'I suggest you give careful thought overnight to your position, Mr Fowler,' Temple said. 'The interview will resume tomorrow morning and I urge you to see sense and start telling us the truth.'

Fowler was too tired to react as he was led back to the cells with his brief in tow.

Temple walked into the incident room feeling hugely frustrated. He'd tried desperately to get Fowler to confess and had failed. He felt like he had let the Hamiltons down.

He was given the grim news that three more graves had been uncovered in the forest by the search teams. They were located close to the villages of Sway, Ashurst and Bransgore.

The media were now in even more of a frenzy. TV news crews were reporting live from the crime scenes and from the pavement outside the central police station.

Detectives had been dispatched to each location and would be reporting back with the details.

Since most of the team was still in, Temple decided to hold a final briefing before going home to Angel. But DC Marsh got to him before he could get everyone's attention.

'There's been a surprise development, guv,' she said. 'We just had a call from a man who claims he saw Ethan Kane two weeks ago.'

Temple felt his heart lurch. 'How does he know it was Kane?'

'He says he's a former prison officer and was at Albany prison where Kane spent two years before being transferred to Wandsworth. He now runs an outdoor leisure shop in Lyndhurst, selling camping equipment and fishing tackle. He reckons Kane came into the shop to buy something and he recognized him.'

'So why is he calling us now?'

'He saw the photo of Kane we put out on the news. And I'm convinced he's genuine because he says Kane doesn't look anything like he looks in the picture.'

'What's that supposed to mean?'

'Well his actual words were: *the bastard no longer looks like a boxer. He's had his nose straightened and his hair dyed.*'

47

Temple hadn't counted on making another trip into the forest, but he decided to go with Marsh to meet the former prison officer who had called in.

His name was Seth Peters and he lived in a flat above his shop in the centre of Lyndhurst. The town was always quiet on a Sunday evening. Only a few pubs remained open.

The shop was on the High Street and Temple parked the pool car right outside on double yellow lines.

Peters was waiting inside. He was in his late fifties, with lean, angular features and grey hair that rested on his shirt collar.

The shop was closed for business but all the lights were on. Temple saw that it was well-stocked with camping equipment, fishing tackle, hiking accessories and lots of outdoor clobber.

Peters invited them into the back office where he explained that he'd taken over the shop a year ago after retiring from the prison service.

'I spent most of my time at Albany,' he said. 'And that's where I came across Ethan

Kane. He made quite an impression on me, which is why I recognized him when he came in, even though he's gone to great lengths to change his appearance.'

'And this was two weeks ago?' Temple said.

Peters nodded. 'It was on a midweek afternoon and there were no other customers. As soon as he walked in, I thought he looked familiar, but I wasn't sure so I didn't say anything.'

'What did he want?'

'He was looking to buy a pair of binoculars. We only had a few in stock so I showed him those and he bought a pair. As he was paying, I caught him giving me a strange look and realized that he'd tumbled who I was.'

'So what did you do?'

'I said, 'long time no see, Ethan.' But he gave me a blank stare and said that wasn't his name. I told him that I knew who he was, but that it wasn't a problem. He clearly wasn't happy, though. He threw a twenty-pound note on the counter, picked up the binoculars and stormed out without waiting for his change.'

'And you're sure it was him?' Marsh asked.

'Absolutely sure. He looked different, of course, but not enough to fool me.'

'Did you get to know him well in prison then?' Temple said.

'He was one of those I'll never forget because he was a sick bastard then and no doubt still is now.'

'Did he get up to much on the inside?'

'I know he raped at least two young guys but they wouldn't ID him so we could never prove it.'

'We've seen his criminal files. He carried out some pretty nasty assaults. Some while he was wearing women's clothes.'

'That's right. I seem to remember being told that he was badly abused as a boy. His father used to farm him out to blokes for money and he was made to wear dresses. I once caught him giving his cellmate a blowjob while wearing make-up and a skirt made from an old T-shirt.'

Temple asked Peters if he would come to the station in the morning to help a police artist to work up an impression of Kane. Peters said he'd be happy to come in but it would have to wait until the afternoon when there was someone to look after the shop.

On the way out, Marsh spotted two pairs of binoculars in a display case. She asked Peters if Kane had handled these as well as the pair he bought.

'Indeed he did,' Peters said. 'In fact I let him go out onto the pavement to try them all.'

'Has anyone except you touched them since then?' she asked.

'Not to my knowledge.'

'And was he wearing gloves when he came in?'

Peters paused for a lengthy moment before shaking his head.

'Definitely not.'

Marsh looked at Temple. 'In that case, his prints will be on them.'

An hour later, the two pairs of binoculars were in the forensic lab back in Southampton. The prints lifted from them were compared with those on Kane's file.

They were a perfect match.

48

Angel was still up when Temple finally got home. He was pleased because he felt bad for not having called her during the day.

But she wasn't cross with him this time. Quite the opposite. She poured him a cold beer and told him she'd been following events on the news during the day.

'Now you can give me a first-hand account,' she said. 'I've been dying to hear what's really been going on.'

Temple relished the lift the beer gave him and when Angel produced a chicken sandwich from the fridge, he felt made up.

He was also pleased to see that her mood had improved and she was more like her old self. That was no doubt down to what he'd told her the night before about looking forward to being a father again. It had taken an enormous weight off her shoulders and allowed her to avoid having to make a difficult decision.

His own reservations hadn't gone away, though. Being so busy had merely spared him the agony of having to dwell on them.

She listened intently as he told her about

the investigation and where they'd got to.

'So tonight we have Tom Fowler in custody,' he said. 'He's a man who admits to being a masochist and he killed his girlfriend some years ago during a kinky sex session. He said it was an accident but was convicted of manslaughter. But he's denying he was Mason's accomplice, despite the strong circumstantial evidence that suggests otherwise. In addition, we've just found out that Mason's depraved former cellmate, Ethan Kane, has been seen in the forest, which ratchets up the case against him.'

And that was a problem they were now faced with. The pressure to bring charges against Fowler based on the evidence found in his home would grow. But where would that leave them with Kane? Would the brass be tempted to ignore his presence in the area? Or would the search for him continue in earnest, thus undermining, to some extent, the case against Fowler?

'So what does your gut tell you about Fowler?' Angel said. 'Is it possible that he's telling the truth and is being fitted up?'

Temple shrugged. 'I honestly don't know. Part of me thinks that if he *was* Mason's accomplice, then he wouldn't have been so stupid as to leave that stuff in his house and on his driveway. But the other part of me thinks he probably didn't expect us to turn up out of the blue to carry out an official search.'

Those thoughts continued to churn over in Temple's mind after they got in bed. They kept him awake into the early hours as Angel snored lightly beside him.

When he did finally drop off to sleep, there was still no escape from the horrors of this particular case. He dreamt of skeletons in shallow graves and men and women being raped and tortured in a dingy dungeon.

And he saw Bob and Rosemary Hamilton running for their lives through dense woods, their naked bodies smeared with their own blood and tears.

Twice his eyes snapped open in the darkness and he woke up.

And twice Angel had to wipe the sweat from his brow and hug him for a while before he could get back to sleep.

49

Monday morning arrived with heavy storm clouds and more unpleasant news.

Overnight, two more graves had been dug up in the forest, taking the total number found to nine. The two latest locations were in woods near the villages of Beaulieu and Fritham. It took the body count to thirteen. All three had been buried over a year ago, according to Mason's map.

The one consolation was that friends and relatives of the victims would at last have closure. They wouldn't have to wonder for the rest of their lives what had happened to their loved ones.

But Temple knew it would do nothing to lessen the pain of grief. Or stop them from imagining the terrible suffering their sons, daughters, brothers and sisters had endured at the hands of Grant Mason and his accomplice.

There was more blanket coverage on the news channels. Temple watched some of it before leaving home.

The arrest of Tom Fowler was given equal prominence alongside the discovery of the graves. There was slightly less airtime devoted to the couple who were still missing, although photos of the Hamiltons were being screened about every thirty minutes.

All the channels were also naming Fowler as the man in custody, but a police spokesman was refusing to confirm that. As a consequence, local residents in and around East Boldre were laying siege to his house in order to vent their anger and disgust. In one shot on Sky News, it looked as though about thirty people had gathered along the roadside outside the house.

A number of talking heads gave their reaction to what was happening, including one of the local MPs, a middle-aged woman named Trudie Nelms.

'This is a shocking episode in the history of our beloved New Forest,' she said. 'I feel for the families of those poor people who fell victim to the depravity of Grant Mason. And I pray that he and the monster who committed those heinous crimes with him will get their just reward.'

Next up was an official with the National Park Authority who wanted to make it known that the forest was still open for business. He urged people not to stop coming.

'Despite what has happened, the New Forest remains a beautiful, vibrant and very special place. The livelihoods of thousands of people will depend on the continued support of holiday-makers and day-trippers.'

The BBC carried an exclusive interview with the parents of Paul Kellerman, the student whose body had been the first to be found. His mother, a thin, hollow-cheeked woman, described her son in glowing terms before breaking down on air.

Her husband, a thick-set man with a shiny comb-over, said, 'Paul was our only son and we loved him. I can't describe how much we miss him. I hope the two men who took him from us will rot in hell.'

It was a sentiment shared by many others, from local councillors to the friends of the victims.

Angel came downstairs just in time to see the Prime Minister condemn what he described as a series of crimes that were beyond wicked. And he promised an inquiry into why the police hadn't spotted a connection between so many disappearances over a two-year period.

'It was because Mason was shrewd enough to make sure the cars belonging to the victims were dumped well away from the forest,' Temple said for Angel's benefit. 'There was no obvious pattern. They were therefore treated as separate missing person cases by various forces, including ours.'

Angel didn't respond so he turned to look at her. She was sitting at the kitchen table with her face in her hands.

'Are you feeling OK?' he asked.

She lifted her head and tried to smile. 'I've just been sick in the loo upstairs and I feel bloody awful.'

'Isn't that what happens to women in the early stages of pregnancy?'

She puffed out her cheeks. 'I didn't imagine it would be this bad.'

'Well, you'd better get used to it, sweetheart. It'll get worse before it gets better.'

He walked over and gave her a kiss.

'I take it you don't want me to make you a full English breakfast with eggs, bacon, sausages, beans and toast,' he said.

She pulled a face. 'Piss off to work, you cruel man.'

And so he did, after pouring her a glass of cold water and giving her a long, affectionate hug.

50

'OK, listen up everyone,' Temple said. 'We've got a big day ahead of us so we all need to focus.'

It was 9 a.m. and most of the team were in for the briefing, including two guys from media relations and a strong uniform contingent. Beresford was in a meeting with the Chief Constable and had phoned to say that he'd be along soon.

'The first thing to report is that nine out of the ten graves marked on Mason's map have now been uncovered,' Temple said. 'The search for the tenth at Honey Hill is still going on. It was held up during the night because of heavy rain.'

He reminded everyone that thirteen bodies had so far been discovered and there were two names on the map against the Honey Hill site, which would take the total to fifteen. The team listened in silence, awed and repelled by the grim statistics.

Temple talked about his meeting with Seth Peters and the need to find Ethan Kane.

'Peters is coming in later to help us work up an artist's impression,' he said. 'Kane looks very different to his photograph apparently so we should circulate the new description as soon as possible. This guy's presence in the area concerns me. We need to know if he's been in contact with Mason and Fowler.'

Temple told the team what Peters had said about Kane's antics while in Albany prison.

'That was before he moved to Winchester and shared a cell with Mason,' he said. 'I can't believe that those two sick bastards didn't collude in some way. And if they did then where does Fowler fit into it? Are we wrong to assume that Mason had just one accomplice? Is it possible he had two?'

They were still discussing this startling possibility when the Chief Super joined them. He was sceptical at first and tried to pick holes in the theory.

'So how come Mason's videos and photographs show just one other man?' he said. 'The man in the mask.'

'We can't be a hundred per cent certain that it's the same man in all the sequences,' Temple pointed out. 'And we don't know if there are more videos and photos featuring a third person. Maybe the others also have their own collections.'

The conversation switched to Tom Fowler and it was confirmed that a warrant had been obtained to search his office and work computer.

The latest from the forensic team at his house was that no other incriminating evidence had been found there. This morning, the search of the garden and the woods around the property would continue.

'I want us to talk to all his friends and colleagues,' Temple said. 'And we should go back to East Boldre and talk to his neighbours in the village.'

The Chief Super made it known that he was anxious for Fowler to be charged, regardless of whether Ethan Kane might also be implicated in the killings.

'The guy's guilty as sin,' he said. 'I've spoken to the CPS and they believe we already have more than enough to get him convicted of abducting and killing the Hamiltons. They've made it clear that they'll press ahead with a prosecution without a confession and without any bodies.'

51

As soon as Temple started interviewing Fowler again, he knew that he wasn't going to get a confession. The man continued to maintain his innocence, and having had a night's sleep he was more coherent and much calmer.

He repeated that he did not know where Bob and Rosemary Hamilton were. Temple pushed him hard on this but he was insistent that he had never met them.

Temple said that the evidence spoke for itself, but Fowler's lawyer challenged this assumption. He asked if his client's prints or DNA were on the flogger whip and laptop found in the house and on the clothes left in the wheelie bin.

'Those objects are still undergoing forensic analysis,' Temple said, though in truth he'd been told that the only prints found on the laptop and flogger belonged to Mason.

During the first break, Temple held a quick meeting and was given updates. Marsh told him that police in London had interviewed Noah Cross's friend, who confirmed that he had picked Cross up from Waterloo Station on Thursday evening about ten and that Cross had then stayed with him until the weekend.

'Meanwhile, I've asked to see the CCTV footage from Southampton Central Station for Thursday evening just to double check his alibi,' Marsh said.

DC Whelan had been talking to Fowler's work colleagues at the estate agents.

'They say he's a good agent who gets on well with everyone,' he said. 'None of them knew that he had a criminal record for manslaughter and they didn't know he was into S&M. But they did provide a piece of information that came as a surprise. They said that Fowler did not go into work on the Saturday before last.'

'He told us he did,' Temple said.

'Well, he was either lying or he forgot. He apparently called in sick.'

Temple decided to try to catch Fowler out. Back in the interview room, he asked him a series of questions he had already asked him and then said, 'So remind us where you were on Saturday of last week, the day that Bob and Rosemary Hamilton went missing.'

Fowler pinched his cheeks, exhaled a heavy breath. 'I've told you already. I was at work until the middle of the afternoon.'

'But you're lying,' Temple said. 'According

to your colleagues, you didn't go in at all that day.'

Fowler creased his brow and made as if to think about it.

'Oh, that's right. I wasn't feeling too good so I decided not to go in.'

'So how come you didn't say that before?' Temple asked him. 'Why lie about it?'

'I forgot. It's as simple as that. I can't be expected to remember everything.'

'So what did you do on that day?'

'I stayed at home. I might have gone to the pub in the evening, but I don't remember.'

'And what about on the Sunday?'

Fowler moved his shoulders. 'I think I went for a walk. It's what I usually do on Sundays when I'm not being harassed by you lot.'

Temple kept up the pressure for another two hours, firing questions until he was convinced that Fowler wasn't going to change any of his answers.

It was 3 p.m. when he decided to charge him with abducting Bob and Rosemary Hamilton. He read Fowler his rights and told him he'd be held in custody until he appeared before a magistrate.

'If you have a change of heart and want to tell us what you've done with the Hamiltons, then inform your lawyer right away,' Temple said.

As he left the interview room, hot and exhausted, he was approached by an anxious-looking Fiona Marsh.

'I've just had a call from Angel, guv,' she said. 'She's been trying desperately to contact you.'

'My phone's been switched off,' he said. 'What's up?'

'An ambulance is about to pick her up and take her to the hospital.'

'My God — what for?'

Marsh moistened her lips. 'I'm afraid she thinks she's having a miscarriage.'

52

Rosemary Hamilton was still nursing her wound when he went back down to the basement.

She was sitting up on the bed while wrapping a clean bandage around her left leg. He had cut her on the inside of her thigh, but only deep enough to produce a decent amount of blood that could be applied to her sweater and jeans. He'd then given her a couple of butterfly strips to stem the bleeding, along with the bandage.

Her husband was watching from the other side of the bed, his eyes glazed, his breathing faint.

Getting blood from him had been more difficult because he'd tried to resist. But he'd been too weak to put up much of a fight and a couple of blows to the head had rendered him unconscious. So he hadn't felt the knife slice across his left buttock and the blood spill onto the mattress.

Now Bob was lying on his side and the huge plaster he'd been given covered the shallow wound. It looked as though the life as well as the blood had been drained out of him.

'When are you going to let us out of here?'

It was Rosemary again. Her voice was a scratchy whisper. She was the one who did all the talking, asked all the same questions over and over.

He didn't answer her. He rarely did because he didn't like to engage in conversation with his playthings unless he had to.

He had planned to kill them last night, but had changed his mind when he realized that the pressure was off. Fowler was under arrest and it came as a big relief because it meant he didn't have to rush things. He could have one more night of fun with Rosemary and Bob.

According to the news, Fowler had now been charged with abducting the Hamiltons. He'd become the focus of the police's attention. They were convinced he'd been Grant Mason's accomplice, and that he had broken into Mason's house and stolen his laptop.

And that was just great. His little plan to incriminate Fowler had worked like a dream. Now he could relax and give careful thought to where he should go from here.

'We want to see our son again,' Rosemary said. 'Why are you keeping us here?'

He offered her a smile instead of an answer. She didn't have to know that she was going to die tonight along with her husband. He'd already dug the grave. It was in the woods just a few yards from the house and he was confident it would never be found.

He would have preferred to bury them somewhere else, but with the forest crawling with police, it was too risky to move them.

He walked over to Rosemary's bed and placed a bottle of water on the mattress next to her. She stank of urine and sweat, a smell that evoked bitter memories from his childhood.

A lot of the men who came to his bedroom were fat and sweaty and he could remember two of them actually pissing on his body after they'd sodomized him. One of them had even got him to take off the soaking wet dress he'd been made to wear so that the creep could keep it as a memento.

It was the same man who had once described him as their plaything. And for a long time that was how he saw himself. A young, helpless boy who was there to be used and abused by anyone who was prepared to pay a fee to his father.

A prison psychiatrist had told him once that his father was ultimately responsible for what he'd turned into. But he'd already known that; just like he'd known as a young teenager that he was never going to be a normal person. That had been obvious since he'd started to feel the overpowering urges to hurt and humiliate his fellow human beings.

By the time he was eighteen or nineteen, he'd come to believe that some people existed merely to satisfy his own relentless cravings.

And that's when he also started referring to his own victims as his playthings.

★   ★   ★

'You're a wicked, perverted madman who should never have been born.'

Rosemary's sharp words brought him out of his reverie with a start. She was staring straight at him, her eyes boring into his.

'You have no right to treat us like animals. We're people. Parents. We don't deserve this.'

It was the first time in days that she'd flared up and it surprised him. He thought she'd given up the ghost like her husband had. But not so.

Despite all she'd been through, she was still able to strike a note of defiance. It was more than he ever did when the men came into the bedroom. But then he'd been just a boy, and his father's beatings had made him docile and submissive.

'I beg you to let us go,' Rosemary whined. 'Please show us some compassion.'

He wanted to laugh because he had never felt compassion for anyone or anything. The concept was completely alien to him, as were the ideas of love and empathy. For him, life was about pain and pleasure. Nothing more. He wasn't religious and he'd never wanted to be burdened with a family of his own.

Grant Mason was the only person who had ever come near to understanding how he felt. And that was probably because they were so much alike.

He stared down at Rosemary Hamilton and felt something stir inside him. Her lean, blood-smeared flesh made his heart beat a little faster and flooded his throat with saliva.

She must have seen something in his expression because she started to shake her head and back away from him.

'Not again,' she begged. 'Please. No.'

But he was in the zone now and she knew it. And so did her husband. He started shaking the chains that bound him to the bed and pleading for mercy.

But it fell on deaf ears. Instead of showing them mercy, he was going to spend the next few hours overdosing on pain and pleasure.

It would be a good way to celebrate the fact that he no longer had to worry about being exposed by the police.

Another man was now going to pay for all the crimes that he and Grant Mason had committed.

53

Temple got to the hospital before the ambulance arrived with Angel. He waited anxiously at the entrance to the accident and emergency department. His heart was pounding, and he felt a terrible panic rising inside him.

When the ambulance pulled up and she emerged from the back in a wheelchair, he was shocked to see how pale she looked. He rushed over, grabbed her hand as a paramedic wheeled her inside.

'Are you OK, sweetheart?' he said. 'What's happened?'

'I started bleeding heavily,' she murmured, her voice strained. 'And it hurts. Like a cramp in my stomach.'

Inside, under the fluorescent lighting, he saw that her eyes were swollen with bright, shiny tears.

'I'm losing the baby, Jeff,' she said. 'I know it.'

He squeezed her hand. 'You can't be sure of that. Just try to relax.'

But it didn't look good. He knew that. Bleeding heavily during the early stages of a pregnancy was serious and often signified a miscarriage.

Oh God.

The medical staff responded to Angel's arrival with alacrity. The paramedic spoke to a nurse as she was wheeled in to a cubicle.

Temple suddenly felt dizzy and unfocused. He couldn't believe this was happening, not after Angel had been through so much. Just months ago, she'd been brought to this same emergency department after the crash on the M27. And she still hadn't fully recovered physically and emotionally from her injuries.

Now she was back and it made him angry that fate had been so unkind to her.

She was helped onto a bed and as the curtains were pulled around her he was asked to wait outside. He didn't want to leave her but Angel told him to go.

'I'll be all right,' she said. 'I just want them to find out what's going on.'

He stood beyond the curtains, feeling helpless and confused. A cold shiver convulsed his entire body and tears pressed at his eyes.

He heard them asking her questions and telling her that she would need to have a scan. But then his mind turned inwards and he was hit by the first wave of guilt.

He hadn't wanted this baby even though

he'd told Angel that he had. And he probably wouldn't have stopped her having an abortion. So was this God's punishment for being so callous and selfish?

He closed his eyes and his lips moved in silent prayer. He asked a God he had never really believed in to save their child, hoping the hypocrisy in his words would be overlooked.

Around him the emergency department was hectic. Doctors and nurses were attending to patients, talking on phones, staring into computers. Temple felt strangely detached from it all, as though he was watching from behind a window.

After about ten minutes, he was told they were taking Angel down for a scan. When the curtains were pulled back he saw that she was now wearing a hospital gown. Her face was hollow, eyes sunken into the back of her head.

'Can I go with her?' he asked the doctor and was told that he could.

He held onto Angel's hand as the bed was wheeled to the X-ray department. It seemed to take an eternity and along the way, he could feel his heart twisting in his chest.

When they got there, the ultrasound scan was quick and simple. A lubricating gel was spread over Angel's stomach and the doctor moved a sensor across it. They both watched as the inside of Angel's uterus appeared on the monitor.

Temple experienced a jolt of alarm when the doctor frowned and leaned forward to have a closer look.

'Is the baby OK?' Angel asked him, her voice filled with desperation.

He didn't respond for almost a minute as he concentrated on the screen. Then he clenched his jaw and turned to Angel.

'I'm afraid there's no heartbeat, Miss Metcalf,' he said. 'I'm sorry to say that you have indeed suffered a miscarriage.'

54

Silent tears trailed down Angel's face as she was wheeled up to a ward. They wanted to keep her in overnight for observation and because she was suffering severe abdominal pain.

For Temple, the shock had been joined by a feeling of intense loss. He hadn't wanted a baby and had dreaded the impact it was going to have on his life. Yet now he wished he could turn back time. It was a cruel irony.

On the ward, the curtains were pulled around the bed and Angel was given tablets for the pain. She was clearly devastated, and Temple struggled for the right words to say to her. He didn't think that platitudes and empty phrases would make her feel any better.

'I'm so sorry, Jeff,' she said through the tears. 'I can't help feeling responsible.'

'It's not your fault, sweetheart,' he told her. 'These things happen. You heard what the doctor said. It's not uncommon between eight and ten weeks into a pregnancy. No one is to blame.'

He felt a strong urge to say sorry to *her* for

not being more enthusiastic about the baby when she first told him. He was going to find it hard to forgive himself for that.

The pair of them sat without speaking for a while, wrestling with their own troubled thoughts. For Temple, the investigation was briefly forgotten as the drama in his own life took centre stage.

He was oblivious to the sounds around him; the voices of the other patients, the squeaking wheels of medication trolleys, the beeping of bedside monitors.

Time passed quickly and before they knew it the evening was drawing in and Angel was finding it hard to keep her eyes open.

'You should go home now,' she told him. 'There's nothing you can do here. I'll be fine.'

He sensed she wanted to be alone, to grieve for the baby she'd lost before it was even born.

'I'll come back in the morning,' he said. 'Try to get some sleep.'

'I will.'

'I love you, sweetheart.'

'I love you too, Jeff.'

55

It was 7 p.m. when Temple left the hospital. But he couldn't face the prospect of going home to an empty house. He wanted to stay busy for fear of sinking into a well of despair.

The guilt now hung like a lead weight around his neck and he couldn't help wondering how Angel was going to cope with another major set-back. The last couple of months had been difficult for her. She'd struggled with depression and had developed an irrational fear of the future. The pregnancy had lifted her spirits and given her something to look forward to. But now that glimmer of hope had been extinguished.

Would she want to try for another baby? Or would she take the view that the miscarriage was a sign that she was destined not to be a mother? He resolved not to try to second-guess her or attempt to discourage her from trying again.

He got so lost in his thoughts that he didn't realize he'd been driving aimlessly around the city. By the time he did, he was somewhere in the Bitterne area of Southampton. He did a swift U-turn at the first opportunity and headed back towards the central police station.

Most of the detectives had left for the day and the incident room was quiet. There were only four people in, including Fiona Marsh and Dave Vaughan. They both acknowledged him as he walked straight to his office. As soon as he was seated behind his desk, they appeared in the doorway.

'How's Angel, guv?' Marsh said.

He felt his voice drop low in his chest.

'She had a miscarriage. They're keeping her in overnight but she should be OK.'

They both stepped into the room and he felt self-conscious suddenly.

'How far gone was she?' Marsh asked.

'About nine weeks. She only broke the news to me a couple of days ago. She'd been planning to tell you at the weekend.'

'I didn't have time to go and see her,' Marsh said.

'She knows that and so do I. This case has taken over our lives.'

'I'm really sorry, boss,' Vaughan said. 'I didn't realize that you two were trying for a baby.'

'We weren't. Angel always said she didn't want one. It was an accident.'

They fell silent and there were a few awkward moments before Temple said, 'I didn't want to go home by myself so I thought I'd come in and do some work. I need something to keep me occupied.'

'We could go for a drink,' Vaughan said.

Temple stuck a finger in his collar, stretched his tie loose. 'I'd rather not. If I do I'll probably end up drunk. So come on, guys. What's been happening since I left here this afternoon?'

They sat down across the desk from him and Vaughan began by saying that the search team still hadn't located a tenth grave at Honey Hill. They were going to work through the night because the forecast for tomorrow was heavy rain.

'I've also just received an email from the lawyer who handled the sale of Miss Bellamy's house,' Vaughan said. 'There's an attachment which I haven't yet opened, but I can't imagine it will tell us anything useful about Ethan Kane.'

'Did Seth Peters come in to work with the artist?'

'He didn't, but he's on his way now. Whoever was supposed to man his shop earlier failed to turn up so he couldn't get away. I checked with the artist and he's happy to hang around.'

'We need to get that picture out there.'

'I know and I'm on it.'

Marsh then said that she was still checking out Noah Cross's alibi for Thursday night.

'As you know, the Met spoke to his friend in London who said he arrived there about ten,' she said. 'But I thought I'd check CCTV at the central station anyway. I looked at tapes that were running between six and eight, but he's not on them.'

'So what about his car?'

'That's the thing, guv. I checked with the DVLA and according to them, he doesn't have a driving licence and there's no car registered in his name.'

'Well, he's probably driving around without a licence then, like thousands of other people. As for the CCTV, well we've all missed someone on those tapes, especially when there are a lot of people around.'

Marsh looked at her watch. 'I'd better go and see him. Check that there's nothing more to it.'

'It can wait,' Temple said. 'Go tomorrow. Right now I want you to bugger off home to that boyfriend of yours. If he sees any less of you he might call off the wedding.'

She grinned. 'Thanks, guv. I'll pop over and see Angel tomorrow night if that's all right. Hopefully she'll feel like a chat.'

Marsh and Vaughan then left the office and Temple sat back and inhaled a shallow breath. He realized he wasn't going to be able to concentrate. His mind was in tortuous turmoil and it felt like a pneumatic drill was going off in his head.

Perhaps I should have gone for that drink, he thought. Or perhaps I should go straight home and get plastered.

He switched on his PC and brought up the live feed of the BBC News Channel. And there was the Chief Super fronting the latest press conference, and telling the world that Tom Fowler had been charged in connection with the disappearance of Bob and Rosemary Hamilton.

'We anticipate that more charges will follow,' he said. 'In the meantime, every effort is being made to identify the bodies that have been recovered so far from the graves in the New Forest.'

He was making it sound pretty straightforward, but Temple was no longer convinced that it was. Something gnawed at him about this case. Something he couldn't quite reach. But it related to Ethan Kane. Of that he was sure.

He just couldn't accept that Kane hadn't got involved again with his former cellmate. Why else would he have turned up in this part of the world? And if he and Mason had been in touch, then surely Tom Fowler would have known about it. Which came back to the possibility that all three had been acting together. Three ex-cons with a taste for violent, unconventional sex living out their sadistic fantasies.

Temple was beginning to wonder if he should have delayed bringing a charge against Tom Fowler. Maybe they could have eventually worn him down before the ninety-six hour deadline and got him to open up.

It was a mystery to Temple why he hadn't already since the evidence against him was stacked higher than an Egyptian pyramid. The blood-soaked clothes, the flogger whip, the fact that he'd lied about being in work on the day the Hamiltons had been abducted.

Surely he could see that there was no way he'd be able to wriggle out of it. His lawyer must have advised him that he could probably make it slightly easier on himself by confessing.

And yet he'd refused to and in so doing, had left a bunch of crucial questions un-answered. Such as where they'd held their victims while they abused them. Were the Hamiltons still alive? How did Kane fit into the picture? Were there more bodies buried out there in the forest?

Temple felt the pressure building behind his eyes. He was struggling to focus. It was as though his mind was crammed with too many thoughts.

He needed to get out of the office, perhaps go for that drink after all.

But as he was slipping on his jacket, Vaughan appeared in the doorway with some news.

'I just received word from our man at Honey Hill,' he said. 'They've found the tenth grave. Do you want me to go out there and check it, boss?'

'No, leave it to me,' Temple said. 'It'll give me something to do.'

56

Temple forced himself to think about the case as he drove into the forest. He owed it to the fifteen people whose graves had been uncovered and to Bob and Rosemary Hamilton.

But it wasn't easy to switch away from the tragedy in his own life, from Angel's suffering and his own burden of guilt.

The thing was, he felt that he was missing something. Something important. It was lurking somewhere in his subconscious and he needed to flush it out.

He trawled back in his head over the events of the past week. The various crime scenes. The people he had interviewed. The shocking information about the past lives of Grant Mason, Ethan Kane and Tom Fowler.

If he *had* missed something then it wouldn't be the first time. All detectives at times struggle with those elusive clues that get buried in the pockets of their minds. Most times, the clues eventually surface and prove instrumental in the success of an investigation. But occasionally they stay beyond reach and cause immense frustration.

Temple usually got there in the end. He had a good record when it came to solving cases. But there were a few he hadn't solved and most of those he'd worked on when he wasn't firing on all cylinders.

Was that why he was having problems with this case? he asked himself. Had his personal life been too much of a distraction? Should he have let someone else take the lead? The questions swirled around inside his head, and by the time he pulled into the visitor car park at Honey Hill, he was feeling even more miserable and frustrated.

He switched off the engine and told himself to get a grip. Now was not the time to start questioning his own performance.

He closed his eyes and blinked the thoughts away, then got out into the cold night air.

He was in what was known as the Culverley car park that bordered the heavily wooded area of Honey Hill. Normally at this time of year it would have been pitch black, but it now resembled a dazzlingly bright town centre. Police vehicles and media trucks were giving off enough light to be seen for miles around.

About thirty yards into the woods, several arc lamps had been set up around a forensic tent which had been put up over the grave.

Temple made his presence known and was told the search team had been on the verge of giving up, when an object had shown up on the ground penetrating radar machine.

'There are lots of trees and bushes here,' the crime scene manager told him. 'We had to use chain saws and mowers to clear parts of the area. Plus, it's been very wet which makes it more difficult for the radar equipment to detect anomalies under the ground.'

According to Mason's map, the two people whose remains were in the grave were a married couple from Luton who had vanished ten months ago while on holiday in the south. They'd been staying in London and no one had even known that they'd hired a car in order to visit the New Forest.

This was the last grave marked on Mason's map and Temple hoped to God that there weren't any more that they didn't know about. He felt it necessary to look at the remains, but under the harsh light from the arc lamps they seemed unreal. He stared at them until his eyes glazed over and then walked slowly back to his car.

Honey Hill was on the main B-road between Lyndhurst and Beaulieu. Temple realized that it was the closest of the ten graves to East Boldre, which was only about three miles south.

He decided to drive to the Court Jester pub and have another chat with Mick Russell, the landlord. At the same time he could get something to eat and have a pint.

On the way to the pub, he drove past Amanda Cross's house and saw that the lights were on inside. He also noticed that her Vauxhall Corsa was on the driveway. He'd last seen the vehicle yesterday when her brother had pulled up in it outside Tom Fowler's house.

It brought to mind what Marsh had told him about Cross not being on the DVLA database. Did that mean he drove everywhere in his sister's car?

But as Temple thought about this, he remembered that when Cross was in London, the car had been parked on the driveway. So he couldn't have used it to get to the station. And there was another oddity. When he'd dropped in on Cross that second time the Corsa was there again. But no other car.

So did it mean something? He wasn't sure, but it made him curious and he could see why Marsh felt inclined to pursue it.

Temple eyed the digital clock on the dashboard. Nine thirty. On impulse, he decided it wasn't too late to call in on Noah Cross and his sister. If there was one thing he hated it was a loose end. So there was no time like the present to tie this one up.

He pulled over to the side of the road and executed a U-turn.

57

He decided it was time to put them out of their misery. He'd had his fun and now he was completely exhausted.

Killing Bob and Rosemary Hamilton would be a fitting finale to one of the most intensely pleasurable evenings of his life.

He had subjected them to three glorious hours of torture and sexual molestation. Their screams and their tears had aroused every cell in his body.

He'd used whips, clamps, dildos, surgical blades, leg spreader bars and his own sharp teeth.

Rosemary's breasts and buttocks were covered in bite marks and there was blood dripping from every orifice, including her mouth.

Her husband was sporting two black eyes and his bruised scrotum was the size of a grapefruit.

He felt a lot better for having indulged himself. He'd needed to release the tension that had been building up inside him since Grant Mason's death. He wasn't used to feeling threatened or vulnerable and he didn't like it. It reminded him too much of when he was a boy and the men came to have their way with him. He'd been forced to bottle up his feelings then because he'd been too scared to vent them.

On the few occasions when he did make a fuss, his father gave him a severe beating. The blows were always to the body, never the face. That was because the punters obsessed over his angelic looks. They liked the fact that he looked like a girl, especially when he wore the dresses. It was what set him apart from the other boys the men abused and made him so valuable to his parents.

But the tables had turned since then. Now *he* was the one with the power. The one who instilled fear in others.

The pleasure that gave him was incalculable. And it was thanks to an addiction that could never be cured. He was lucky in that respect because it meant he would never have to stop what he enjoyed doing. And he could look forward to bringing many more playthings to his lair.

Bob and Rosemary had been pretty special because he hadn't had to share them with Grant. For that reason he was really going to miss them. But all good things come to an end.

Getting them up the stairs was going to be

the most difficult part. They'd strangled the others down here in the basement and he and Grant had carried them up to the van. But he couldn't lift the Hamiltons by himself. His plan, therefore, was to tell them that he was going to take them to another part of the forest and let them go. Then one by one, he would lead them up the stairs and outside where he would do the deed and drag their bodies the short distance to the hole in the ground.

After that, he would lie low until things settled down and the forest returned to normal. Then for him, it would be business as usual — while Tom Fowler languished in prison for a series of crimes he didn't commit.

'You'll be pleased to know that I'm going to release you both,' he said as he approached Bob's bed. 'So be sensible and don't make it difficult for me.'

He wasn't sure they believed him but he didn't care. He knew that for them anything was going to be better than staying down here.

He reached out with the key to unlock the shackle around Rosemary's wrist. But at that moment, the wireless adaptor in the wall picked up the signal from the doorbell, filling the basement with a loud, shrill tune.

His stomach clenched and a flame of unease flared inside him.

He couldn't believe it.

Who the hell could it be at this time of night?

58

Temple rang the bell and stepped back, wondering if he was wasting his time coming here.

He could just as easily have left it to Marsh to talk to Noah Cross in the morning. After all, the business with the car and his trip to London no longer seemed relevant to the case.

But suddenly the thought he'd been desperate to retrieve from his sub-conscious popped into his head. It was like a light being turned on in a dark room.

Fowler's keys. Of course.

They went missing the other night in the pub and Fowler claimed he'd left them on the bar. Yet the following day, the landlord found them in the pub car park, which led to the assumption that Fowler had dropped them there.

But supposing he hadn't? Supposing he did take them into the pub with him and placed them on the bar? Was it possible that someone picked them up, then used them to enter Fowler's house and plant the laptop and flogger whip, before dropping them in the car park?

Temple cursed himself for not having grasped the significance of the keys before now. He should have paid more attention to their disappearance — and reappearance. Fowler's lawyers were bound to make a big thing of it when they started preparing a defence.

He made a mental note to find out who was in the pub that evening. It had been fairly busy and among the customers were several SOCOs who'd been searching Mason's house.

Noah Cross hadn't been there when Temple arrived, but according to the landlord he'd been drinking with Fowler and had only just left.

Did that mean . . .

His train of thought was interrupted when the door opened and Amanda Cross appeared. She was wearing a blue towelling dressing gown and her long hair was a riot of curls. She peered at Temple quizzically through her thick-framed glasses.

'You woke me up,' she said, sounding drowsy. 'What's going on?'

He forced a smile. 'I'm sorry to bother you so late, Miss Cross, but I was wondering if I might have a word with your brother.'

'He's not in. He went out.'

'Do you know where he is?'

'He didn't say. And I don't know when he'll be back. Is it something I can help you with?'

'Possibly. Do you mind if I come in?'

He could tell from the look on her face that she did, so he told her that it was important and couldn't wait until tomorrow.

With obvious reluctance, she opened the door wider so he could step inside and gestured for him to go into the kitchen.

He sat at the table while she put the kettle on, but she didn't ask him if he wanted a drink.

'Hopefully this won't take long and you can go back to bed,' he said.

She turned to face him, a strange expression on her face that was difficult to read.

'So what is it you want to know, Inspector?'

'First of all, can you tell me what kind of car your brother drives?'

Confusion flickered across her face. 'Why do you want to know that?'

'Well, we carried out some routine inquiries after you and your brother told us he went to London on Thursday evening. And we discovered by chance that he doesn't have a driving licence even though he drove himself to the station. Plus, the DVLA confirmed that there isn't a vehicle registered in his name.'

Something passed over her eyes, too quick

for Temple to read it.

'I think that's the kind of question you need to ask him,' she said.

'But you must know about the licence.'

She shrugged. 'I'm sure he has one, Inspector. Someone at the DVLA has probably made a mistake.'

'What about the car?'

'He has a dark blue one. An Audi, I think.'

'And he's driving that now, is he?'

She nodded and ignored the kettle as it started to boil.

'I assume the car outside belongs to you then,' Temple said.

'That's right.'

'Then may I ask why your brother was driving it yesterday when he went to Tom Fowler's house?'

'He often takes my car,' she said. 'He prefers it to his own.'

'I see.' Temple paused, then added, 'Coming back to Thursday, Noah told us he got the train from Southampton to London. But he doesn't appear on any of the CCTV footage that was recorded that evening at the central railway station.'

Irritation flashed in her eyes. 'That's probably because he would have driven to Southampton Parkway and gone from there.'

Temple hadn't thought of that. Parkway

was the first stop after leaving the central station and a lot of rail commuters preferred it.

'Look, I really do need to speak to your brother about these and other matters,' he said. 'Perhaps if you called him for me now on his mobile, he might be prepared to come straight home.'

She blinked warily, clearly nervous. 'What else do you want to ask him?'

'Well, I know he had a drink with Tom Fowler on Saturday night in the Court Jester, but he left before Fowler realized he'd lost his keys. I just wondered if your brother might be able to shed light on what happened to them.'

'Why would he know that?'

'It's a question I'll be putting to everyone who was in the pub that evening, Miss Cross. Not just your brother.'

'But why are the keys so important?'

'Because we believe that someone might have used them to enter Fowler's house without permission.'

She sucked on her lower lip as she considered a response. At the same time, she dropped her arms to her sides and straightened her spine. The tension oozed out of her body like an aura.

'So how about calling Noah?' Temple said. 'At least if you speak to him I'll know if it's worth hanging around.'

'There's no point,' she replied too quickly. 'He usually switches his phone off when he goes out.'

Temple cocked his head on one side and frowned at her.

'It sounds to me like you're trying to cover up for your brother, Miss Cross. Is it perhaps because he hasn't gone out? That he's actually in the house?'

Her face hardened and she drew a quick breath before speaking.

'Of course he's not in the house. I'd tell you if he was. I've got no reason to lie.'

'Then you won't mind if I have a look around.'

She gave an unconvincing shrug. 'If you must, but when you see I'm telling the truth I want an apology.'

Temple stood up. 'In that case I'll start downstairs.'

Just then his phone buzzed with an incoming text message. His first instinct was to ignore it, but it occurred to him that it might be from Angel.

'Do you mind if I check this?' he said, taking out his phone. 'It might be urgent.'

She didn't respond, just stood there staring at him as her ample chest rose and fell with every breath.

Temple opened up his messages and saw that the text was actually from Dave Vaughan, and there was a media file attached.

The message read: *You need to see this, boss. It was in the file from Miss Bellamy's lawyer. It's the passport photo she gave them as proof of identity when selling the house. Only it's a different woman to the one in the photo that her daughter showed us. Any thoughts?*

Confused, Temple opened up the attachment and when he saw the photo, a shudder crawled up his spine.

Oh, sweet Jesus.

Amanda Cross must have sensed from his reaction that something was very wrong — because she was on him before he had even lifted his eyes to look at her.

59

She rammed into him shoulder first, throwing him back against the wall. He lost his balance and fell sideways, knocking over the chair he'd been sitting on.

He hit the floor with a heavy thud and rolled onto his back as Amanda's full weight came crashing down on him.

She let out an animal howl and shoved her knee into his groin. The pain exploded through his body, driving the air from his lungs.

He started twisting and bucking, desperate to get her off him, but she was much stronger than she looked and he couldn't shift her.

Her face was above him, her eyes flashing with anger, her mouth foaming. She was snarling and spitting as she pressed her hands into his shoulders, pinning him to the floor. Then she drove her forehead into his face and his nose erupted with a crack of bone and a blast of pain.

He cried out and grabbed her arms, then bunched up his muscles and gave a mighty shove with all the strength he could muster. He managed to push her off him and roll away from her. He clambered to his knees, but as he tried to stand up he was assailed by an intense dizziness.

He struggled to get his vision back, his senses, but the room was spinning and everything became a blur.

Which was why he didn't see the next blow coming.

Amanda pounded a fist into his mouth and it drove him up against one of the kitchen cabinets. He gave a yelp of pain and felt blood and saliva gushing out of his mouth.

'This is your own fault, copper,' Amanda yelled. 'You asked too many fucking questions.'

Temple sat there, stunned, as he gulped down oxygen and braced himself for another attack.

He opened his eyes, tried to focus, saw Amanda moving quickly towards him.

Instinctively, he kicked out with every bit of force he had left inside him and managed to sweep her legs from under her. She screamed out in surprise and anger as she toppled over.

Temple heaved himself to his feet and his limbs trembled with the effort. Thankfully his vision cleared enough for him to get his bearings. He saw that Amanda was also pulling herself up.

He staggered towards her and let fly with a

punch that was aimed at her face. But she turned and his fist glanced off the side of her head.

She responded by lunging forwards and grabbing his neck, then digging her thumbs into his throat. Her breath was hot on his face and there was madness in her eyes.

Temple seized her hair with his left hand and used his right to deliver a blow to her stomach. She let out a manly grunt and loosened her grip on his neck.

He pummelled her shoulder with the heel of his right hand and she stumbled backwards. But to his shock and amazement, her hair came away from her head and he found himself holding onto a wig.

Confused and disoriented, he just stared, his eyes bulging in disbelief.

Then suddenly it dawned on him that he was no longer looking at Amanda Cross.

She had turned into her brother!

'That's right, copper,' she yelled. 'We're one and the same.'

Temple was too distracted to see that his attacker had regained her — or rather *his* — balance and was reaching for an object on the worktop.

And he didn't see that it was the kettle until it was flying through the air towards him.

He tried to duck but it smashed into his left shoulder and sent steaming water across the back of his neck. The pain was excruciating and it took his breath away.

He felt himself falling and placed a hand against the wall to stay upright.

Then he heard his attacker's ragged breath behind him. He spun round, raising his arms to protect his face. But the blow that came struck him on top of the head and shattered his senses.

A second later, waves of darkness crashed over him.

60

When Temple came round he had no idea how much time had passed. He felt woozy and light-headed. Pain was beating a tattoo against his brain and each time he inhaled, it felt like daggers piercing his lungs. His neck was throbbing where the hot water had scorched the flesh. His mouth tasted of blood and he was pretty sure that his nose was broken.

It took several moments for him to fully emerge from the stupor and realize that he was sitting on a chair next to the kitchen table. The room swam in and out of focus. His hands were bound behind his back with what felt like a plastic flex-cuff.

Noah Cross was standing directly in front of him — minus the female wig and glasses — and he had a demented grin on his face. He had also shed the dressing gown and was now wearing jeans and a white T-shirt.

Temple felt his heart start to bounce in his chest.

'Don't worry, I'm not going to hurt you again,' Cross said, holding up a ceramic pestle, which Temple assumed had been used to knock him out. 'There's no need.'

'I called for back-up before I got here,' Temple said quickly. 'A team of officers will be here at any minute.'

'That's a lie,' Cross said. 'I checked your phone. I also responded to the text you received from Detective Vaughan. I told him you were busy and would call him later. And I told him not to show the passport picture to anyone else.'

It came back to Temple then. The photo Vaughan had sent him of the woman purporting to be Theresa Bellamy.

The 'woman' was Amanda Cross.

Temple tried to make sense of it. He understood that like most other people, he'd been duped into thinking that Noah and Amanda Cross were twins, when in fact they were the same person. A wig, fake breasts, big glasses and heavy make-up had turned Noah Cross into a convincing woman. That explained why there was only one car — the Corsa — and why they never seemed to be at home at the same time. But it didn't explain why Amanda Cross's photo appeared on Theresa Bellamy's passport.

'I can see you're confused,' Cross said. 'You still haven't put it together, have you?'

Temple squinted at him. 'Well, it's obvious to me now that you were Mason's accomplice. But how did Tom Fowler fit into it?'

'He didn't,' Cross said. 'I needed a scapegoat so I took his keys from the bar in the pub and planted the evidence that I hoped would convict him.'

'And I take it you also broke into Mason's house the night after he died.'

'That's right.'

'But what about your alibi? The stag party in London.'

'If you'll remember, you first phoned me on the number Hilary Dyer gave you. So I had to answer as Amanda. And when you said you wanted to speak to Noah, I made up a story on the spot to explain his absence. I feared that if *I* gave him an alibi you might at some point want to speak to us both together. So I called a pal in London and got him to lie for me. I told him I'd been involved in a fight and needed the police to think I was in London. He had no idea it had anything to do with Mason.'

'So why go to Mason's house?'

'I had to find out if he had left anything around that would give the game away. If you hadn't turned up I would have had time to check the loft. I'd have found all his stuff — including that frigging map — and stopped everything from getting out of hand.'

'But why invent a sister? And why pose as Theresa Bellamy?'

But as he was asking these questions the answers jumped out at him. Suddenly everything came together in his head with a clarity that made him gasp.

'My God, you're Ethan Kane,' he blurted.

When there was no response, Temple continued. 'You posed as Miss Bellamy so you could sell her house and get her money. Then you came down here to link up with your old cellmate.'

The man he now knew to be Kane merely nodded.

'Theresa was a means to an end,' he said. 'I didn't have a penny to my name. She was the third woman I met after leaving prison and the one I knew I'd be able to impersonate. She was my height, lived alone with hardly any friends and her daughter was in Australia. I had to kill her, of course, but not until I'd extracted all her financial details. When the police came calling, I pretended to be her and told them that Ethan Kane had left. Since they didn't know Theresa and weren't particularly interested in her they simply accepted that. I then sold the house and took all her money.'

He said it like it was something to be proud of.

'So what did you do with Theresa's body?'

'It's buried in a wood in Kent.'

Temple took a breath that caught in his throat. 'So you sent the email to her daughter.'

Kane nodded. 'I wanted her and the cops to think that Theresa had done a Shirley Valentine.'

'So you came to the forest and created a whole new identity for yourself.'

'That's right. A friend from prison sorted out all the false paperwork. It enabled me to buy this place with Theresa's money.'

'Why bother creating a twin sister then?'

'I didn't. My father did that years ago when he started dressing me in girl's clothes. She's been with me ever since. Now I wouldn't be without her. Switching genders is something I enjoy doing. It's who I am.'

'Did Mason know?'

'Of course, but he's the only person who did know. He liked having Amanda around because as a male-female couple it made it easier for us to get close to our victims. None of them felt threatened when we approached them in the parking areas.'

'So that's how the abductions started?'

'Well, Grant was active long before I came on the scene. He told me so. But working with me made it more fun and less risky. It was something we'd talked about in prison and it's why he suggested I move to the

Forest. He said we could make hay together and we did. We were a good team.'

A wave of fierce anger whipped through Temple. He strained to extract his hands from the cuff, but it didn't give an inch.

'You insane bastard,' he seethed. 'You talk about it as though it's no big deal.'

With a lopsided sneer, Kane said, 'To me it isn't. I don't see the world as you do, Inspector. And I don't expect you to understand.'

Temple started to speak but his throat turned to sand and he felt sick. He closed his eyes, steadied his breathing, swallowed back the sour taste of vomit that rose up from his stomach.

Kane looked at his watch. 'I've got to pack up and get going. I want you to get to your feet.'

'What are you going to do?'

Kane pulled out a drawer and took out a large carving knife.

'I'm going to slit your throat if you don't do as I say. Now stand up.'

Temple did as he was told.

'That's sensible,' Kane said. 'Now this is what's going to happen. I'm taking you down to the basement so I can get sorted and make myself scarce. Lucky for you I don't blame you for all the shit that's happened. If I did you'd be dead by now. Grant was responsible and you're only doing your job. So I'm going to let you live. Eventually your colleagues will turn up and let you out.'

'That might not be for days.'

'Well, don't fret about that. You'll have company down there and I'm sure the three of you will have a lot to talk about.'

61

He would never have known the door was there. It was set in a wood-panelled wall below the stairs and there was no frame or handle.

Kane removed a hanging mirror to reveal a keyhole. Into this he inserted a key and pushed the door open. Then he reached in and switched on the light.

He told Temple to step inside first, holding the carving knife up to his throat to make sure he didn't resist.

It was a short flight of stairs into the large, low-ceilinged basement. As he walked down them, Temple was struck by the strong smell of sweat and fear.

And blood.

When he reached the bottom, he was ill-prepared for the sight that greeted him. It was so horrific that he was suddenly oblivious to the pain that racked his own body.

He stood there staring into a vision of hell.

There were two beds and two people were chained to them. They were sitting up with their backs to the wall. He knew instinctively that they were Bob and Rosemary Hamilton even though they were almost unrecognizable from their photographs.

A sob rose in his throat and his gut clenched with revulsion.

The couple were naked and their bodies were covered in blood, cuts and bruises. They gazed back at him but their eyes were devoid of any meaningful expression.

'Meet Bob and Rosemary,' Kane said. 'I believe you've been looking for them.'

They didn't say anything and Temple wasn't even sure they were able to. They looked traumatized. Or maybe they'd been sedated. He couldn't tell.

A bolt of genuine horror shot through him and his eyes flicked wildly around the room. He'd seen it all before in the videos and photographs. The sex toys and instruments of torture hanging from the walls. The table on which the victims had been raped and abused and perhaps murdered.

The images exploded in his mind and he started to form his own grisly picture of what the Hamiltons must have gone through.

'They should be thanking you,' Kane said. 'I was about to kill them when you showed up. I even dug the grave. But now that I'm forced to leave here and make a new life for myself, there's no longer any need to.'

Temple released a breath he wasn't aware

he'd been holding. He turned to Kane, his pulse roaring in his ears.

'What kind of monster are you?' he yelled.

Kane smiled. 'I'm the kind that gets pleasure out of other people's pain and suffering, Inspector. I'm not proud of it, but I'm not ashamed of it either. Some people are born to be good and to conform. Others, like me, are born to be bad. As I see it, we're the ones who have the most fun.'

Temple felt the blood rush to his head. He'd come across some psychos in his time but none of them shone a torch to this maniac. He was the devil incarnate. The very epitome of evil.

Temple knew that if Kane walked away from here tonight, he would go on to claim more victims. It was clear that he was shrewd and calculating and would have no trouble establishing a new identity for himself in another part of the country or even abroad.

And Temple couldn't let that happen.

'Go and sit on the floor between the beds,' Kane said.

Temple moved his body as though to comply, but then spun round suddenly and lashed out with his right foot, catching Kane's arm and knocking the knife to the floor.

His aim was perfect and he followed it through by hurling himself at Kane. The impact sent them both sprawling across the floor.

But Kane wasn't encumbered by having his hands tied behind his back, so he recovered more quickly. He managed to retrieve the knife before Temple could drag himself to his feet.

And then with a guttural cry, Kane rushed forward.

Temple backed away, but immediately came up against one of the beds. He looked on helplessly as Kane charged at him with the knife and plunged it into his side, just below the ribcage.

62

Temple choked back a scream as fire lanced through his belly. He slumped to the floor next to the bed and a juddering breath racked his chest.

Kane stood astride him and pulled his lips back in an angry snarl.

'For that, you're going to die, you pathetic, fucking moron,' he raged. 'But because you've really pissed me off, I'm going to make you watch while I kill these two other lovebirds.'

Temple felt his heart slump when he saw the determination in Kane's wild eyes.

But then something unexpected happened.

A chain was thrown over Kane's head and wrenched up tight against his windpipe.

Kane's eyes ballooned in size and he slumped back over the bed that was directly behind him. As he tried to struggle free he dropped the knife, which clattered on the floor.

Temple hauled himself up and watched as Kane flailed about like a fish on a hook.

Rosemary Hamilton had managed to tighten the chain around his neck and she was holding onto to as she attempted to squeeze the life out of him.

His face went red, then purple, and saliva foamed at the corners of his mouth. He tried desperately to pull the chain away from his throat, but when he couldn't get a hold with his fingers he started to twist his body in the hope of working himself free.

That's when Temple threw himself against him over the edge of the bed so that his movements were restricted. He pressed his weight into Kane's body, ignoring the pain that passed through every fibre of his being.

The sound of Kane choking to death rang in his ears and gave him a strange, perverted pleasure.

★   ★   ★

When Kane's body was at last still, Rosemary Hamilton started sobbing uncontrollably.

She removed the chain from around his neck and rolled away from him across the bed.

Temple noticed that one end of the chain was attached to a bedpost and the other to her wrist.

As he pulled himself upright, a dizzy sensation washed over him and he became acutely aware of the pain in his side. He looked down and saw blood seeping out of the knife wound.

'You've got to get help while you still can,' a voice said behind him.

He turned. Bob Hamilton was on the edge of his bed, and no doubt conscious of the fact that the loss of blood would soon sap Temple's strength and cause him to faint.

'The knife,' he said, pointing. 'Kick it this way and I'll be able to reach it. Then I can cut the cuff and free up your hands.'

Temple looked down. His vision was blurred but he could just make out the knife on the floor. He managed to shift it closer to the bed, and Hamilton stretched down and picked it up. Hamilton then severed the flex-cuff and Temple had his hands back.

'Now go straight upstairs,' Hamilton said, raising his voice above his wife's deep, wrenching sobs. 'You have to get help.'

Temple had the presence of mind to check in Kane's pockets first to see if he had a phone on him. But he didn't.

Shit.

He felt so weak and dizzy he wasn't sure he would make it up the stairs. But he knew he had to try.

He moved across the room like a drunk, pain and adrenaline keeping him from losing consciousness.

He crawled up the stairs on all fours and at the top stumbled through the door and into the hallway.

He had no idea if there was a landline in the house or where Kane would have left his mobile phone. There were none in the hallway so he went into the kitchen. And that's where he saw his own phone resting on the worktop.

It was only a little way across the kitchen, but to Temple it seemed like miles. His head was swimming and he was losing the strength to stay on his feet.

One step, two steps, three . . .

His knees buckled just as he was reaching for the phone and he collapsed in a heap on the lino.

As the darkness reared up to claim him, he thought he heard the distant wail of a police siren.

63

He woke up in an ambulance, but only briefly. Dave Vaughan was sitting next to him, his face taut with concern.

'You're on your way to hospital, boss, and you're going to be OK,' he said. 'We got to you just in time. You've lost quite a lot of blood, but the paramedics say the wound isn't fatal.'

Temple had an oxygen mask over his face and his arm was attached to a drip.

'The Hamiltons are safe and they told us what happened,' Vaughan said.

It was a moment before the brain fog cleared and Temple remembered how he had climbed the stairs out of the basement, but hadn't reached the phone in the kitchen before passing out. He also remembered hearing a siren.

He raised his arm and lifted the mask away from his face.

'How did you know?' he muttered, his voice low and hoarse.

'It was the passport photo I sent you,' Vaughan said. 'I got your text telling me not to show it to anyone, but by then I'd already circulated it and Fiona came back to me. She went with you to speak to Amanda Cross so she recognized her immediately. We tried to call you but your phone was switched off, so we took it upon ourselves to come out here and arrest her — or rather, him.'

Temple could not believe his good fortune. He would surely have bled to death if the cavalry hadn't turned up when they did.

64

He woke up late the following morning in the hospital. He was in a private room. His head ached and he was hurting all over. For a moment everything was blank. Then he remembered why he was there and the memory brought nausea bubbling to the surface.

'Hi there, sweetheart.'

It was Angel. She was standing over him, wearing the kind of smile that lit up her face.

'Thank God you're all right,' she said. 'You had me really worried there for a while.'

'How bad am I?' His voice was a hoarse whisper.

'You were lucky that the knife didn't penetrate any vital organs. You've been stitched up and will be as good as new in a few weeks. You've got a large lump on your head, but the blow didn't cause any internal damage. I'm afraid your nose is broken, but that'll be put right. As for the roasted skin, well that'll be very sore for a couple of days.'

Temple tried to smile, but it hurt his mouth. 'What about you? Are you OK?'

She rolled her eyes. 'I'm fine, you idiot.

You're the one who's been stabbed and burned and beaten. I know you like to pretend you're Robocop, but this is taking things to extremes.'

He could tell from her eyes that the smile and the banter were purely for his benefit, and he loved her all the more for it.

'It's not been our week, has it?' he said. 'What with all this and the miscarriage.'

She shrugged. 'But at least we're both still alive. And when all is said and done, you can't ask for more than that.'

But of course they both knew that it wasn't exactly a happy ending. He thought of Bob and Rosemary Hamilton and although they'd survived, he knew they would never really come to terms with what had happened to them. Their terrible ordeal would blight the rest of their lives and it remained to be seen if they could be happy despite that.

'You're the hero of the hour according to the news,' Angel said. 'The Hamiltons have issued a statement saying that you saved them.'

'Well, I'm glad they're alive,' he said. 'But what they went through doesn't bear thinking about. They're going to need a lot of counselling.'

'They're actually in this hospital, Jeff. They've apparently said that they'd like to see you at some point because they didn't get a chance to thank you.'

'I'd like to see them too. If Mrs Hamilton hadn't done what she did, I wouldn't be here now.'

Angel told him that a bunch of other people were also keen to see him, including Fiona Marsh, Dave Vaughan and Mike Beresford.

'The Chief Super said he'd like to get a formal statement from you later today if you're up to it. Mrs Hamilton has told him how Kane died and it's being treated as a clear case of self-defence.'

'What about Tom Fowler?'

'The charge against him has been dropped and he's being released as we speak.'

'I should never have charged him,' Temple said. 'I should have realized he was being set up. If it had gone to trial there's a good chance he would have been convicted. The so-called evidence was stacked against him.'

'Well, thank God that didn't happen, Jeff. So you shouldn't let it play on your mind.'

Temple winced from a sudden pain in his gut and Angel took his hand and squeezed it.

'I can't believe I let Kane fool me like he did,' he said. 'How the hell did I not spot that Amanda Cross was really a bloke?'

'You weren't the only one, Jeff. I spoke to

Fiona. She was taken in too. She showed me a copy of the artist's impression that was worked up and he's got an effeminate face.'

'Even so.'

'Don't beat yourself up about it. If you'd spotted it early on, you'd have probably thought that he was just another weirdo and not made the connection to Kane.'

Temple knew that she was right, but it bothered him just the same.

'Be grateful that you got there in the end, Jeff,' she said. 'Neither Grant Mason nor Ethan Kane can hurt any more people. It's all over, thank God.'

Epilogue

But it wasn't all over. Two days later, another grim discovery was made by the forensic team searching Mason's house.

They found a cardboard folder that had been concealed behind the exposed insulation on the underside of the loft roof.

Inside was another map of the New Forest. It was older than the one that had been pinned to Mason's wall.

On this map there were names and dates next to nine religious crosses and they were spread all over the forest.

The most recent date was just over two years ago, not long before Mason had joined forces with Ethan Kane.

The earliest date was eighteen months before that — shortly after Mason had moved to East Boldre.

The day after this second map was found, the search for more graves began.

We do hope that you have enjoyed reading this large print book.

Did you know that all of our titles are available for purchase?

We publish a wide range of high quality large print books including:
Romances, Mysteries, Classics
General Fiction
Non Fiction and Westerns

Special interest titles available in large print are:
The Little Oxford Dictionary
Music Book
Song Book
Hymn Book
Service Book

Also available from us courtesy of Oxford University Press:
Young Readers' Dictionary
(large print edition)
Young Readers' Thesaurus
(large print edition)

For further information or a free brochure, please contact us at:
Ulverscroft Large Print Books Ltd.,
The Green, Bradgate Road, Anstey,
Leicester, LE7 7FU, England.
Tel: (00 44) 0116 236 4325
Fax: (00 44) 0116 234 0205